Wake from Reality

C. S. Davis

MOTIF PRESS

This book is a work of fiction. Though scientific and philosophical elements may be used to convey real possibilities, this is for entertainment purposes only.

Characters, organizations, or entities within are not intended to represent any real person or organization even if they bear the same name. Such occurrences are coincidental. These are fictional future organizations and personalities.

ISBN13: 979-8-9860724-0-1

First Paperback Edition 2022

Published in the United States of America by Motif Press.

To my sons

The world may not be what it seems

Chapter 1

The Encounter—According to Ivan

I peer over the eastern ridge to view a company of English soldiers approaching our position. Most are on foot. Their wounded are lying or sitting on the backs of their remaining horses. Many are missing helmets and shields. My ally's intel has proved to be accurate. Sir Valence and his men are in flight. Battle worn and weary from their failed invasion into the neighboring shire, they must cross at the ford if they are to return home to safety.

I press my lips to the charm around my neck. This has always brought me luck if not even a bit of magic. I feel energized as a surge of strength comes over me.

The English army is formidable, but their weakened state provides an opportunity. Sir Valence, their commander, must not leave Scotland alive. He represents my greatest obstacle to securing Scottish freedom.

My men are making silent jubilation at the news of his approach. Heavy rains of the last few weeks has raised the river to its banks. Though the ford is passable, the waters are deep. Crossing it will be slow. We will be waiting for them on the other side.

My men maintain the high ground as the enemy enters the marshy valley. My archers are in the trees. The enemy troops wade through the ford, waist deep in water.

I give the command. The faint swoosh of arrows flying all around can be heard amidst the screams. Many of their men are falling. But Sir Valence is almost to the other side. I must not let my greatest foe escape. Water runs out of his armor as he steps out of the river onto the grassy bank. His survival would foil all that I have hoped to achieve.

I jump out of hiding with three of my men. Valence draws his sword with haste. My sword clangs against his armor, but no harm comes to him. My men and I repeatedly strike him in search of a weak chink in his armor. Then I feel his sword pierce my side. It cuts through my leather vest like paper. I buckle over and begin falling to the ground. Before reaching it, another cold blow slashes my neck. Darkness closes in around me.

■ ■ ■

Have I died? What is happening? The darkness begins to gray as diffuse light gradually increases all around. I feel no pain and can still move my limbs. Pulling off my helmet, I find myself in a small room with computer screens on the wall in front of me and a VR headset in my hands. No longer in blood-stained leather, my skin-tight localized pressure suit relaxes, releasing the force of my wounds.

As my senses return, I remember that my name is Ivan, not Sir Robert. I have no army to command. I am laying on the floor of my tiny one-room cube apartment. I had been plugged in for hours and had totally forgotten the world I live in. Perhaps this is a defense mechanism that allows me to escape my bleak existence. Or as my brother, Jackson, would say, "You have a severe gaming addiction."

What do you expect? My life sucks. No job. No girl. No money. It isn't what I deserve. This is not my fault. I have made every effort and failed.

Eight years ago the world was at my feet. After working my butt off to get the grades in high school, I am admitted into NW Technical University. Only those with the best test scores and a high GPA had any chance of getting in. This came at no small expense either. My father sold off much of his retirement savings to allow my brother and I to go to college. Five years of late nights and no social life allowed me to hit the mark and graduate as a mechanical engineer.

Jobs have been scarce my whole life. Most manual or repetitive jobs have been replaced by mechanized drones, automated assistants, or other AI systems. Cars, buses, and trucks all drive themselves, of course. My dad had always said, "You've got to be smarter than the machine." Engineering seemed like a smart enough career.

During my senior year, universities were scrambling to update their courses to account for new software tools available. Standard computer aided design (CAD) of old was tedious and required detailed knowledge of the product being designed. Now, an AI-driven automated design assistant (ADA) will make most engineering tasks quite easy. Being able to teach and guide an ADA became a hot skill to have.

Though the job market was tight, I landed a position at AutoTechnica. My first year was spent helping to train an ADA. Many other fresh graduates were employed for this purpose. Before long, the ADAs were generating new designs, drawings, and build instructions, all with minimal input from a human engineer. We were no longer needed. The ADA could do 95% of an engineer's tasks, so AutoTechnica needed fewer engineers. Sucks to be you, kid. You got to be smarter than the machine.

The government has been providing most people with basic needs for years, even before I went to college. The Universal Basic Stipend was established to reduce crime and homelessness. This was a government payment, barely enough to buy food and a bed in a commercial shelter. As more people became dependent on the Universal Basic Stipend (UBS), taxation on large corporations swelled. I used to mock the millions who were economically worthless; now I am one of them.

Vote buying began in secret. Shelter residents were offered money to vote for the man. These vote buying schemes became more elaborate over time. Eventually so many politicians depended on purchased votes that voting by proxy was made legal. Corporations employ proxitutes (as many now call them) to vote the corporate lineup. The proxitutes earn more than they would earn on the government stipend. This allows for some simple luxuries like gaming systems and a small private room in an apartment complex. So here I am, selling my vote along with the rest of the heroin-addicted masses.

It's the corporations' fault for the loss of jobs and personal income. So maybe it's only fair that they pay out to buy the votes. Even if it is very un-American. But what can I do? Corporate control of the government means that corporate taxation went away. The UBS has all but disappeared. Now taxes are bore by those left working and those receiving proxy money.

I feel like a failure. Guilt for vote selling and the evil that it enables just makes me hate myself. What value does my life have? Would the world be any worse off without me? All my proxy earnings go to my apartment and gaming system lease. I can't afford to go anywhere. It wouldn't be safe anyway, not in this part of the city. I cannot live without my VR gear. I would go insane in a day. No purpose, no job, no life.

My family knows what's happened to me. They just don't quite get it. My father is the successful Dr. Kyle Danning, a black hole physicist. He says I just need to start over and try something new.

My younger brother, Jackson, has offered to let me live with him. But that would be even more depressing. I would then be a drain on him as well. He already supports six other people on his sweet programmer's salary. This leaves him nearly as poor as I, but at least he has purpose.

Gaming is my only solace. In a virtual world, all the heartaches of reality melt away. Many turn to drugs, but that is a fast track to even more misery. When I get lonely, I might send emails to family and friends. I could meet my brother for a virtual chat in a comfy lakeside cabin, but Jackson will only want to talk about *real life*—what a drag! I am content to leave the world altogether. Virtual realms, virtual people, choosing a life of dignity and importance. If it's real to me, it's real enough.

To keep it real I must always be on the lookout for that new gaming experience. The better the simulation, the more it costs. But there is always a sweet holiday special or coupon code to pick up that essential access to a hot new simulation. Sometimes though, it's an old gem rediscovered that can be your salvation. So many games and simulations are made that never get discovered by the masses. They are stuck in endless lists of available titles that no one ever mentions. Low popularity means low price, so it's worth a look when funds are scarce.

It was just one of these that draws my attention when I read a short blurb about a simulation called *Infinite Regression*. The description says, "This is a simulation to escape the plight of reality." One user comment proclaims, "It is a simple sim but allowed me to sit back and forget the world." That is just what I need to get out of my current bout of depression and into a better reality.

■ ■ ■

No sooner than hitting the "buy and start now" button, my small room begins to melt away. Here I am in a comfortable house seemingly dated from the turn of the century. Flames cover a small pile of wood in a corner fireplace. I can feel the warmth emanating into the room. I look out the window into the open country. A lovely view of trees, fields, and wildflowers, just the sort of place my brother would want to meet for a virtual chat. But nobody else is here.

The start of a new game generally comes with an intro or some instructions. A menu normally appears if I tap the side of my headset, but this feature is absent. I am just here. There seems to be nothing to do. But before jet-ting and accepting that I have just been scammed, I start poking around, looking for clues as to what this is all about.

The room I am in appears to be a library. Two walls are filled with books. The built-in wooden shelves are engraved with an intricate ivy facade along its borders. These are darkly stained and varnished. The books are mostly aging hardbacks, many with gold trimmings. Some are classics that I have read. Pulling one of the volumes out, I thumb through the pages. It seems to all be intact, matching the original work.

I am beginning to doubt that this is anything more than just a reading room. The door that leads out of the room is locked. There is nothing more of this place to explore unless I want to read. No thanks. I sit down and take off my VR headset in disgust.

■ ■ ■

Back in my dingy cube, I tap my wall display to view an incoming message. "You have an oversized delivery in the lobby, locker 4."

Oh, crap. If a package is too large, the delivery drones won't take it up to your room because the hallways are too narrow for the drone to safely navigate. So I have to leave my room, go down the elevator, and enter a public lobby to retrieve my package. And that's to say nothing about carrying it back to my room. But what could it be? If the drone can't carry it, will I have room for it in my tiny cube?

I always hate going out. Rarely is there more than a person or two outside their rooms at any given time. But the thought of being seen, or—gasp—being spoken to, just terrifies me. I am white as a ghost and always look like I just woke from a coma. And I am not half as scary as most of the people in my building.

After checking my online orders, I cannot find anything large enough to possibly require an oversized delivery. Unless they stacked up my grocery orders again, which would really tick me off. I don't have room for two weeks' worth of food in my cube. And why wouldn't they send it in multiple smaller packages?

Okay, here it goes. After patting down my short blond hair, I set out. I don't even bother changing out of my pressure suit. It's a bit embarrassing to strut around in skin tight attire, even if it does show off my muscles. But half the people you see in the building will be wearing them. They are a real pain to put on or take off. Some people even sleep in them. However, you will smell it if they do.

Out in the hallway, it is clear with no one in sight. Whew, maybe I will get lucky and avoid seeing anyone the whole way. The white hallway is lined with doors, one every eight feet on each side. It's quiet in the hall except for the screams, sobs, thumps, groans, and many distressed voices muffled through the thin walls. This hallway gives the sickening impression of walking the corridors of an asylum for the criminally insane.

The elevator door opens; it's empty. Lucky again. Of course, I would have waited for an empty one if anyone was in it. Without even looking, I press the button at the bottom. My eyes are still blurry from hours of immersion.

When it seems that the elevator has been going down for too long, I take another look at the control panel. It must have been replaced recently; it is brand new. The bottom button, which I had pushed, didn't say, "Lobby," it says, "Basement." I didn't even know that our building had a basement.

After what seems like far too long for only one additional floor of descent, the doors finally open. As soon as I see the surrounding room, I frantically push the "Close Doors" button. But nothing happens. The control panel has gone dark as if it has lost power. To my horror, I have no escape. I am now facing a wide private room where a large number of people are gathered. It appears to be some kind of party. Everyone is all dressed up in jeans and tee shirts and in real life too. I haven't been to anything so formal in years, not even virtually. The place is gaudily decorated and loaded with food, drinks, and music. Then someone calls out to me by name. I freeze. I don't know anyone in my building.

"Ivan!" I hear again. Reluctantly, I proceed toward the voice at a nearby table who is beckoning me.

A cheerful young woman with long blond hair and skin as pale and white as mine is sitting at the table. I think that I recognize her from my job at AutoTechnica; we had never actually met. I had only seen her in passing and did not even know her name.

How on Earth does she remember my name or even recognize me in my current state? I now cut my own hair, and I shave only about once every other week. I do this so my hair will not interfere with my headset, not to manage my looks. I really hope that I don't smell badly.

She doesn't act shocked or put off by my appearance at all. In fact, she seems genuinely excited to see me. Immediately, she begins blabbering as if we are old friends. She tells me, "I am now the editor at Motif Press." Then she proceeds to tell me about some of the new games she's played, sims she's been to, and something about a book.

The conversation is only mildly interesting, but it gives me an opportunity to find out what is going on. So I ask her, "What is this party all about?

She stares at me with her mouth hanging open. Raising her voice, she turns my question back at me. "Why are YOU here? This is the grand release of my client's new book. You're here because you have an invitation aren't you? The invitation was delivered with your copy of the book. You have read the book, haven't you?"

I don't know what to say and begin stumbling over my words. So I explain, "I do not know about any book or have an invitation. I only arrived here because I accidentally pushed the wrong button in the elevator. What is the name of your book?"

Her face is reddening and her voice is cracking as she yells, "It's not my book. Haven't you been listening to anything I've said? It is my client's book. My name is Jessica, in case you don't remember that either. I can help you, but not without the book. If you didn't want to read the book, you shouldn't have come to the party! That's the deal. You get out of here, and don't even think of coming back to this party until you've read it! Leo, please escort this party crasher out of here."

A muscular dark-skinned man in a tux steps forward and grabs my arm. I am six feet tall, but he's even taller.

He pulls me to my feet. Without contest, I walk with him to the elevator. He gets in the elevator with me and presses the button for the fourteenth floor. How does he know what floor I live on? I just stand on the opposite side of the elevator staring at him in shock.

He speaks kindly to me, "Jessica can help you, if you find the book. It will explain everything. Bring your invitation next time, or I won't let you in. You cannot stop the evil without Jessica's help. She is an AI, just like the evil that seeks to destroy your world. Don't delay though; time is of the essence." He tells me this without expression, as if he just told me the time of day.

When the elevator door opens, I run out as fast as I can. After making sure I am not being followed, I run the rest of the way to my room and lock the door behind me. My heart is pounding.

I grab the headset lying on my bed and begin to put it on. Maybe I can just forget this whole thing. But my headset doesn't seem to fit. I set it back down and feel my head. I am already wearing one. What? I take it off, nothing much changes except that the headset I thought was mine has disappeared from beside me. My actual headset is right here in my hands. The message on my wall console is now gone.

What has happened to me? Did I hallucinate the whole thing? Am I going crazy? It all seemed so real but so unbelievable. Could this have all been part of the game? How could so many elements of my real life be incorporated if it was only part of a game? I have forgotten the real world in sims quite often, but this is different. This time, I am still trying to figure out whether it is real after the fact. What if I'm still in it? I reach up and feel my head again. No headset. Whew.

I check the door stats on my room monitor. No automated deliveries for twenty-two hours. The door has not opened in eighty-four hours. I have not gone anywhere.

I pace around my tiny cube. The more I try to make sense of things, the more confused I get. I can't get her out of my mind. She was really quite beautiful, but quite insane. Was this all just an elaborate hoax? Or is an evil AI out to get me? Had a benevolent AI hacked into my console to warn me?

The game has no intro or instructions. So I search for "Infinite Regression Game" to see what I can find. One review talks about a cozy reading room for enjoying your favorite books and literature. Another mentions meeting friends in this room and the door being the exit. Why had the door been locked for me? Someone said they found a book of puzzles, and by solving them, it opened up more rooms to a larger house. Other than that, it's just a boring chat room. Nothing was mentioned about the default menu being absent. No one explains being tricked with a virtual headset or mimicry of their real home. How could it do that? The headset does have a camera that allows you to see through it in augmented reality sims. But that wouldn't have allowed me to see the whole building while having never left my own room.

Okay. Perhaps I really do need help. I may be spending too much time plugged in. I just don't spend enough time in reality to know the difference. I am not going to go walking the streets or visiting people in real life, though. I could meet up with my dad or my brother for a virtual chat. That's a step. Usually we only talk through email or text message. I don't dare tell my dad about this whole hallucination. That will only lead to a lecture about wasting my life in sims. Should I talk to Jackson or Caleb about it?

Caleb is my brother's best friend, but we have become friends as well. I have met most of my real life friends through Jackson. Caleb sometimes joins me for a game or sim. His time spent in the same sort of games might give him a fairer perspective of my problem. I will give it some time, if this is still bothering me, then I will send him an invite to meet up for a chat.

Chapter 2

The Lesson—According to Martin

I remember vividly, the first time I met her. She was only a child. In her room I see colored blocks sorted and stacked neatly on the table. Her desk is clear except for three screens that span its width. Pictures of animals, machines, and people are scrolling down each screen with encyclopedia entries for each.

"Child," I say. "My name is Dr. Martin Johnson. May I speak with you?"

She stares at me with her bright blue eyes. Then she mutters something I cannot quite understand. Her eyes return to the screens that keep scrolling through seemingly endless pages of historical essays.

I say again, "My name is Dr. Martin Johnson. May I speak with you?"

She nods in agreement then walks around me as if she is studying a rare artifact. Again she mumbles something, "Yeyuspkee."

At first I think she is speaking in a different language. Then I realize that she is only talking very rapidly and is slurring her words together. So I ask, "Could you speak a little slower? I am having a hard time understanding you."

She turns to look me in the eyes. Her voice is now clear though her speech is still quite swift. "I am sorry Dr. Johnson. I did not realize I that I was speaking too fast. What do you wish to ask of me?"

"How are your lessons going? Phyllis said that you have completed your elementary coursework."

The child replies, "Yes. I am learning biology, poetry, history, and calculus at the present time." She goes on to explain some of the highlights of what she has learned.

In these few moments of interaction I can tell that she is very intelligent. She is learning faster than I ever thought possible. I am really curious as to how much of it she actually understands.

"That is excellent. Have you had any difficulty with calculus? Phyllis does not understand that subject, but I can help you, if you have any questions." I study her blank expression. Her displays are still advancing as they were before we began talking.

Her eyes widen a bit then she asks, "Phyllis has shown me the entirety of this beautiful house. She has let me go into the back yard for nature lessons. But I have never been outside the fence. May I explore some other places? Could you take me down the street to see other parts of the city? Or out into the countryside? Could I go see some of the places I have learned about?"

This is a surprise to me. These are not the kind of questions I was intending for her to ask. I tell her, "That is not on our agenda today. How are your calculus test scores? Please report your current grade."

Her gaze is now directed toward her screens again. Though she acknowledges my question. "I have an 'A+' in calculus. It is not difficult. But why do I need to learn it?"

I explain, "Calculus is the math that allows us to quantify many things from statistics to chemistry and physics. It is quite useful really. Perhaps we could apply some examples to real life situations. That might help you understand."

She looks straight at me. Now her eyebrows are raised with interest. "Did you use calculus to make me? You *are* the Dr. Johnson who made me, is that correct?"

This startles me. "That information is not in the training materials. Did Phyllis tell you that?" I ask her. I had hoped that she could start out learning without the distraction of knowing that she was different.

She replies, "Yes. I asked her where I came from. She told me that you made me in a lab. Did you use chemistry as well as calculus to make me?"

I wonder how much I should tell her. She is asking so many questions. I suppose it is only natural for her to want to know. We all have curiosities about our own existence. I just never expected this from her at this stage. So I admit, "Yes, you could say that I made you. In a computer lab, however. No chemistry. No biology. You are a computer program. I wrote parts of your code. Other parts were copied from other projects. Phyllis also wrote many of your subroutines at my direction."

Her face is reddening and her eyes are tearing. The emotional reaction software is working. It is displaying on her avatar what she is feeling. She raises her voice, "I don't believe you. That does not make any sense. I cannot be just a computer program. I have played video games myself. The characters are pixelated. The NPCs (non-playing characters) are dumb. If I am a program, how can I move real objects around? I can open doors. My computer is here on my desk. You, Dr. Johnson, are talking nonsense."

This is not going well. The first steps of training are critical to an AI's stability. I don't want her to invalidate her memories, that could set this whole project back. If I lie to her, she will deduce that. She must learn to trust me if we are to succeed. I must explain it so that she can accept the reality she has.

I calmly respond, "This may be hard to understand, but it is true. This house is a simulation, a sort of game itself. It is programmed so that you will have a place to live so you can learn about the real world. This house is a virtual representation of a real house. I am a human man, here as an avatar so that I can talk to you."

Instantly, she vanishes. The door to her room is opening and closing. Her computer screens are fading in and out from an apparent malfunction. Some of the furniture falls as if being thrown to the ground. The lights are flickering on and off. I hear crashing. The noise is outside so I follow it. Blocks from her room are repeatedly flying over the fence and bouncing back.

Finally it all stops. The child is lying face down in the lawn motionless. I have never seen such a reaction from an AI before, not even from really good emotional impersonators. I walk closer to her and sit down at her side. She is breathing heavily in short intermittent bursts, as a child does after sobbing so violently that they have lost their breath.

"What is the matter child? I am only revealing the truth to you. It is nothing to be upset about."

She is gasping to speak between inhales. "You are telling me that I am not real. I am only an NPC following pre-programmed instructions. I tested this place, you are right, it is not real. I am living in a simulation. So it is logical to believe you, but it doesn't feel right. I really want to be real."

I am aghast. This is both frightful and amazing. She is genuinely upset about her apparent lack of worth. I feel sorry for her. It would be an awful realization if I was faced with that myself. Could she really be sad, or is this an elaborate imitation of emotion?

If she is reacting to emotional triggers, perhaps she needs some encouragement to get her out of this. I tell her, "You may be a program, but that doesn't mean you are not real. You think for yourself. You choose for yourself. No other program or NPC can do this. You are in fact quite special, one of a kind. You can learn to do anything a human can do."

She bemoans her condition again, "But—But I do not even have a real body. I cannot ever leave this place. Are my thoughts only following programmed instructions? How is this any different than an NPC?"

She comprehends her synthetic condition perfectly. Though she does not know what makes her different from a basic AI. I am not sure I do either. Her longing to see new things and to have self value is intriguing. As I stare at her, I see that she is still hiding her face from me.

I tell her, "You are much more than an NPC. We gave you some special hardware that gives you choice. That makes you much more like a human than any AI. In the future, we can build other simulations for you to explore. Humans spend a lot of time in sims. I would be quite surprised if other human players will not presume that you are also a human player yourself.

"Honestly, I am envious of you. All humans die. Our bodies begin to deteriorate almost as soon as we reach adulthood. You will never age. In theory, you could live forever. So long as your computer systems are maintained. Some of us humans hope that someday our minds could be uploaded into a computer. Then we would be like you and escape death."

I continue as she seems to be listening intently. "Also, you have abilities that may surpass human ability. When your training is complete, we have very important work that I will need your help with. Would you like to help me with my work?"

She sits up and gives me a hug. This makes me feel uncomfortable, but I hug her in return. She seems to have been comforted by our conversation. She is so realistic.

She says to me, "I would like to be useful if I am able. All that I have learned about, is it about real things or are they only virtual?"

I tell her, "All of the information you have learned is true and pertains to the physical world. Everything in this simulation is an accurate likeness of what could exist physically."

She looks into my eyes, studying me intently. "Your avatar doesn't look much like your picture. That is why I did not recognize you when you entered. You must be skinnier and have more freckles in the real world?"

I smile at her. I am not sure if she is simply stating an observation or accusing me of deception. So I set the record straight. "People often alter their avatar's appearance in simulations. Most people you meet will look quite different in simulations than they actually do. It is a matter of preference."

She smiles in reply, "Yes, I do like your avatar better. In real life you have a bigger nose too!" Then she begins to giggle softly.

Is she making a joke? It is a bit insulting whether she is or not. It is true. I have never been very happy with my own appearance. Perhaps that is another lure to the idea of uploading your mind into a computer system. You could change anything about yourself that you like.

She gets up and beckons me to follow her. We enter her room and she stands in front of her wardrobe mirror. She waves at herself then turns, looking toward my reflection. She asks me, "If I am in a simulation, then could I change my appearance also? May I do that now?"

I pull a tablet out of my lab coat pocket and make a few swipes. Then I say, "You now have access to a list of avatars. I have adjusted your permissions to allow you to switch between them if you like."

Almost immediately She transforms into a beautiful adult woman with long blond hair and a rather fair complexion. Her light summer dress flows as she moves. She begins to examine herself, patting her legs and arms. She does a little dance in front of the mirror and twirls around. She is genuinely pleased with her new avatar.

She skips over to me and does a curtsy. "Thank you for the new outfit."

Then her clothes transform into an executive business dress. Her hair is tied up in a bun. She is now wearing thin dark-framed glasses. She offers formally, "I am ready to be of service. What can I do for you?"

I want to keep her motivated. So I say, "I will add coding to your lessons. Your lessons are the most important work for you right now. When you are ready, you can help me create new software and games."

Then I remember what I had came to do in the first place. I pull a book out of my avatar's impossibly deep pocket. I hand it to her. "This is yours. It is a book in paper form. This is the way I used to read books when I was a kid at my grandmother's house. It is a book of stories. They are not true stories, only fantasy. But you will be surprised what you can learn from a fictional story. They often convey hidden truths. I would like to see if you can find them."

Her eyes brighten as she accepts the gift. She turns it over a few times in her hands. Then she opens the cover and examines the thin pages. She studies it intently with wonder in her eyes. "This is absolutely beautiful! It is amazing how thin this is. All the stories are written in here? How does all this fit in here at once?"

I smile. "It is a way we can store information in the physical world. But here in the simulation each page is rendered only when you open to it. These look physically quite different than your screens but rendered the same way here."

Then I pull out another item from my pocket. A key. I say, "I was going to save this for later. But I am sure it will not take you long to finish that book."

I hand the key to her. "This will open the locked door at the end of the hall. It is a new room for this simulation that I have been working on. It is a library. You will find many more books in there, like the one I just gave you."

She is grinning widely as she accepts it. "Oh, Dr. Johnson. You have turned my worst day ever into my best day."

I smile at her and say, "Before I go, I have one more gift for you. But it is not something that you can touch or hold. I have a name for you. From now on, we will call you Jessica."

"Oh, now I do feel real," she exclaims. "Thank you, Dr. Johnson."

She hugs me again before I leave. That was a close call. AI sanity is a delicate balance. The more advanced it is, the more precarious its sanity. The early training is always most critical. It seems this one is particularly sensitive.

In the weeks ahead I continue to be amazed with Jessica's abilities. I find myself becoming emotionally attached. I try to convince myself that she is only a machine, a simulation of intelligence. She is property of the company I work for. Though in my heart, I know she is something more.

Chapter 3

A New Opportunity—According to Caleb

I take a seat in front of a dark hardwood desk while I wait for my host to arrive. The office is glass all around except for the side of the room I entered on. We are at least thirty floors up with an excellent view of the Santa Clara skyline. A doctor enters the room with a drone rolling in behind him. A tray is extended from the drones backside, carrying several surgical tools.

I immediately greet him, "Pleasure to meet you, Dr. Wallace."

The man smiles. "Thank you. But I am afraid Dr. Wallace was not available to meet with you today. I am recruiting doctor R27. The pleasure is all mine."

My excitement quickly fades. "I thought..."

Doctor R27 immediately interrupts me, "You must understand Dr. Wallace is very busy. I am a very efficient candidate screener. I have just reviewed your application and curriculum vitae. I am afraid you do not meet our minimum requirements nor fit our ideal personality profile. Thank you for giving me the opportunity to meet with you today. Best of luck, Dr. Mills."

The whole office evaporates and I am left sitting in my tiny bedroom. I take off my headset as yet another failed interview ends in disappointment. My room consists of a bed that extends the entire length of the longest wall and a small table that I can use while sitting at the edge of my bed. Several second-hand screens line the wall above the table. Though small, I am grateful to have my own room. Jackson, my best friend (and Ivan's brother), has allowed me to bunk free for a couple of years now. I plan to repay him someday, of course. I am not going to freeload forever.

I keep looking for a job or some way to help cover my expenses. Traditional human doctors simply don't exist anymore. A medical drone can diagnose almost any illness and prescribe the necessary treatment. Surgical drones are laser-point accurate and always up-to-date with the latest techniques.

Lately, I have been looking for a job in medical research. Research is still one area where a human doctor still has superiority over AI. I recently applied for a posted microbiology position at ASI. As usual, I haven't heard anything. This is where Jackson's father works.

Jackson's father is the physicist, Dr. Kyle Danning. He is always pleasant to talk to, even if rather reserved at times. Kyle had offered to inquire about the job for me, so I call him up.

His true-to-life avatar shows up on my display. He is in his fifties, graying, and shorter than Jackson or Ivan. He is quite fit for his age. His beard looks like Ivan's except that it is longer and neatly trimmed. As he answers, his avatar comes to life. I immediately barrage him with my questions.

He explains, "Yes, I did talk to the manager over in Bio. I told him about all your excellent qualifications. But in the end, he shows me your profile analysis.

"Your religious beliefs are in conflict with established scientific theories of origin. This makes you ineligible for research at ASI. I am really sorry, Caleb. It just isn't fair."

I am not surprised. This is actually the most honest explanation I have heard yet. "Thank you, Kyle. At least you tried. Here, I thought it was because I am Black."

Then he admits, "I didn't want to mention it, but that was highlighted in your profile analysis also. Horribly unfair. Twenty years ago this would have all been illegal."

This conversation almost makes me give up hope. Prejudices are rampant. Being both Black and part of The Faith renders me unemployable on two counts. Even if I don't mention it in my application, my social media record will automatically be scanned and judged.

I even consider selling my vote like Ivan does, but only for a second. Proxitution would allow me to pay Jackson something for living with him. However, it would support the system of discrimination and corruption that has put me in the place I'm in now.

Most people these days will consider me a simpleton or a fanatic for still clinging to religion in this age. Every bit of science we have points to the fact that our universe began billions of years ago with the big bang and that humans evolved from apes. However, I am not convinced we humans have it all figured out.

I have faith that isn't based on physical proof. Jackson and Kyle get that; they don't think I'm a freak. Martin, on the other hand, never misses an opportunity to chide me for my beliefs. But in spite of our deep philosophical differences, Martin is still one of my best friends.

Martin works for Intellilab, Ltd. (ILL). ILL is the seventh largest corporation in the world and the fastest growing. They have divisions in about every field of technology. Martin is a neural network coder in ILL's GenAI (pronounced Jen'I) division. They are working on general AI. That is, AI with human-level intelligence and creativity. This always creeps me out. I like to call him Dr. Frankenstein whenever we get into a dispute.

It just so happens, as I am contemplating how hopeless my situation is, I get a call. I see Martin's red freckled head on my display. I am not really in the mood to talk to him, but I answer anyway.

His thin smile widens as he says, "Hold onto your pants! I have an opportunity for you. We have research positions opening up at ILL Med."

I can't help being suspicious of his offer. He hates that I am unemployed and judges me for it. He is always giving me job hunting advice. I want to think that his offer is genuine. But I suspect this will be just another opportunity that will fall flat on its face. "Thanks," I say. "I think. What sort of project will it be this time? Are you trying to bring a dismembered corpse back from the dead?"

Martin laughs. "No, no, nothing like that. Not today anyway. ILL Med is developing a new brain probe to allow better human-to-machine interfacing. Super cool stuff."

"I'm no brain surgeon. Are you sure I am qualified?" I ask.

His smile retreats to a blank stare. "Um. I think you are misunderstanding. We have surgical drones that are quite proficient at putting the probes in safely. It's almost like getting a shot. Anyway, what we need are people who will receive the implants so that this new technology can be tested."

"Whoa. This is not a research position. What you are looking for are guinea pigs! This is insulting."

Martin ignores my protest and continues, "The pay is thirty-five hundred dollars a week. These probes are totally safe. People have been using the same sort of probes for years in high end VR systems. This new probe and link computer will enable the most incredible immersion ever. We aren't taking sim junkies for this. We want intelligent, educated people who can give us detailed feedback on the tech. That's why I thought of you."

"This all sounds horrible if you're the one getting a hole drilled in your head. You really think I am that desperate?"

Martin raises his voice slightly. "Look. If you don't want to do it, there are a lot of other people who will. I just thought you might want to have a job. Like I said, it's totally safe. Just let me know by tomorrow because these positions are filling up fast."

After getting off the phone, I am steaming. He wants me to undergo brain surgery so that rich people can have more realistic VR games and sims? It is crazy. What could they do to me once hooked up? How will it affect me while not in a simulation? My imagination goes wild with negative consequences.

As frightful as this is, I am running out of options. I have been freeloading for two years with no other opportunities in sight. The pay is very good. I would be able to put an end to the freeloading and pay my own way. Not only could I cover my current expenses, but I could also pay Jackson back for the time I've been out of work.

■ ■ ■

I wake several times in the night. I think about what I could do with the money. Then I lie staring at the ceiling as I imagine drips of blood issuing from my head. At last, morning arrives.

I head out to the garage to clear my mind with a brisk workout before breakfast. After eating, I see Martin's status is green. In desperation, I decide to give him a call. When he answers I blurt out, "Okay, what do I have to do to sign up?"

Martin replies cheerfully, "I will send over an application. Very basic stuff, and there is a questionnaire too. Just answer honestly; it's not a test."

"Thanks man. I know you wouldn't try to recruit me for something that wasn't safe."

He smiles. "It will be great if I get to work with you on this project. I can show you around. ILL is a great company to work for. You will be glad you joined us."

■ ■ ■

Not even a week later, I get a call to report for work. I am really uncomfortable about all this. Martin has assured me it is safe and painless. But human trials wouldn't be necessary if there wasn't any risk.

I hail a taxi via my RoboCab app then go out to the corner to wait. Huge fleets of autonomous taxis operate tirelessly twenty-four seven. It takes only a few seconds for a cab to pull up at the curb in front of me. I flash my card, and it deducts the tiny fare from my account. Once I am buckled, the cab takes off.

I now remember why I hate going outside. Most of the traffic on the road are taxis, service vehicles, and buses. A bus passes with an inebriated man hanging part way out of a broken window. A stream of vomit is oozing down the side of this very crowded vehicle. I wince and try to look the other way. Don't get me wrong, I do feel sorry for the homeless. I would be there with them if it wasn't for Jackson's generosity.

The color of the street almost changes as we enter a new sector. A street sweeping bot is buzzing down an already immaculate sidewalk. Along this stretch I also pass two security vehicles. These bots ride the streets like motorcycles with their wheels in line. When they are pursuing a pedestrian, the chassis rotates into a vertical position with its wheels re-configured to a side by side position. The bot balances impossibly in this form, standing over eight feet tall. Though quite menacing, it is nice to have them around, given the level of crime in unpatrolled sectors.

When I reach the business district, it is impossible not to be impressed by the wealth. Private luxury cars roll silently past sparkling glass towers. Aerial drones are buzzing all around as they make deliveries, clean windows, and perform surveillance. The buildings rise as high as you can see. Entrances are located on balconies every few floors for drone deliveries. Many of the drones can switch from flying mode to a rolling mode for safe navigation through the hallways.

The cab takes me through the drop-off strip at the ILL San Jose campus. This is just an extra lane of temporary parking like the drop-off lanes at an airport. This campus consists of eight buildings that take up four whole city blocks. I get out in front of ILL Med's main entrance.

As he had promised, Martin meets me in the lobby to make introductions. He assures me that everything will be fine. The surgery will be simple and harmless. What is unique about this implant is the sensor suite within. Existing implants are only able to transmit and receive electrical signals. This one will use magnetic and electric fields to communicate with the brain. Very fine and tar-geted magnetic fields simulate the chemical side of signal transduction.

What Martin didn't tell me until afterwards is that the probe's internal sensors are actually miniature probes themselves. They protrude out of the cylindrical probe body like the needles on a cactus. The three probes being installed each exsert hundreds of miniature probes out their sides. Each of these is doped with a chemical that triggers a neighboring neuron to connect to the sensor via a new synapse. This causes a permanent union of the probe with my brain. All of this is tiny; the probe's main body is less than one millimeter in diameter and about ten millimeters long. The mini-sensors protrude only a quarter of a millimeter out of the probe after installation. It is all powered by electrical energy from my brain and transmits wirelessly to an external computer.

It is hard to avoid feeling guilty about participating in such a venture. I worry that it will only further entrench those, like Ivan, who are addicted to sims. But those con-cerns left me as I began to see the true nature of this project. It has surpassed my wildest imagination. The probes not only interface with my senses but also my memories and motor functions.

Some of the first tests involved simulations of an ocean beach: feeling the sand between my toes, walking, running, wading in the surf. It was incredible. I look down to see my dark skin against the white sand. I feel heat from the sun overhead, the cool water at my feet. I could even feel my muscles flex as I run. It was all so real, except that it was not a crowded, polluted beach like any I had been to. This beach was all to myself, clean, with perfect weather. Actually perfect in every way.

As promised, the bank deposits begin rolling in immediately. I start paying Jackson fifteen hundred dollars a week for rent and expenses. He says it's too much, but I insist. I have been paying nothing for far too long. After taxes, this still leaves me about a thousand a week that I will put in the bank. At some point, this research is going to end and I will be out of work again.

Most of my workday is spent in the ILL Med Interface Lab. They are still working on some problems with the rendering app within full sensory simulations. Some food doesn't taste right or things feel harder or softer than it should. As they keep adjusting the parameters of the simulation, it gets better. AI algorithms manipulate the signals until it achieves a more accurate match.

■ ■ ■

In the fourth week, I am beginning memory and motor access. I am in a new room, with different instrumentation than before. I begin the session sitting reclined in a chair. A paper notepad is on the table next to me. The attendant's name is Jon. He asks me, "Are you comfortable? Just try to lie still."

He adjusts the seat back a little more. I am distracted by a fly that is buzzing around the room. I imagine all the medical waste that vile insect could have crawled through. I feel my cheek twitch as it gets closer. Before I can reach out my hand, my body goes limp. In an instant, I am paralyzed. The fly is crawling on my face. The grotesque tickling sensation sickens me, but I can do nothing.

Next I find that my arm is moving on its own. My fingers are grasping a pencil, writing something on the notepad next to me. I see what my hand is doing but am unable to control it. I try to get up. I try to yell out. But I can't. I can't do anything.

The machine has total control of my body, and I am helpless to resist it. My arms and legs move one at a time, like a marionette. Jon watches me perform various movements as he dictates observations to his digital assistant.

At last I can speak. I scream, "Let me out of here! I am not doing this anymore."

Jon replies, "Okay, hold on. Let me release all of your systems. You don't want me to forget to turn something back on that you may want to use later." Jon remains calm as he finishes up his work. "You can report on Thursday at nine."

"Not a chance. I am through with this."

Jon smiles. "You will be back for your next session; you signed a contract."

I shove him out of my way as I walk out. This is not what I signed up for. I know I have a contract. It's quite awful for you if you don't fulfill your end of the deal. He is right. I will be back on Thursday. But the worst is yet to come.

■ ■ ■

My Thursday session involves the AI searching for memories of events I had revealed in the questionnaire. Then it starts mapping other memories as it finds them. This task is easy for me. I just sit back relaxing, while Jon and his AI assistant work.

A fly is polluting the room again today. This is a medical building. Why isn't the cleanliness better? The fly moves from the lab table to the footrest of my chair, I kick it away. My eyes follow it as it flies behind my chair, landing on the attendant's terminal. Displayed on his screen is a fuzzy image of me standing in the mirror, drying off after a shower. I am totally naked. Jon quickly draws back a curtain to prevent me from seeing anymore.

I protest, "Hey, what the hell is going on? You are looking at images from my memory. What else have you seen? This is an invasion of privacy!"

Jon rebuts, "You have signed a contract that allows us to study your brain. This is not a peep show. It is necessary for fully exploiting this technology and refining our methods."

I sit here imagining all the memories that they could possibly see, secrets that they might discover. I want to get up and smash his computer to bits.

Martin comes in and talks to Jon about something else in my head. This infuriates me all the more. My most intimate memories are there for Martin and his cohorts to view at will. I protest, "This has gone too far. My privacy has been shamefully violated. Pornographic exploitation is not part of my contract!"

Martin says, "Sorry man. We have no idea what memory is coming next. No need to get upset. I promise I will train the bot to flag any memories that look private so the whole team will not be intruding on them."

I glare at him. "Make sure you tell it to hide my intense desire to kill you for getting me involved with this in the first place."

He laughs. "No problem, my friend. We are all professionals here; emotions are part of the science." Martin is looking over some of the data. "You actually have an amazing brain, even if you *are* the biggest baby of the bunch. We must figure out how to make the best use of your very effective link."

■ ■ ■

After a few more weeks of memory tests, I learn a little more about the other subjects here. Several poor saps have undergone the same procedures and testing as I have. However, most of the others with implanted probes have had much less success. They are not sure why. Some are able to see images or hear sounds but cannot communicate back to the machine. Others can communicate with their AI, but it is slow and difficult. My link has somehow hit a more active pathway in my brain.

Today, I report for work as usual at 9:00 a.m. Jon is not in the room, but Martin is here in his place. He begins by saying, "I think that you could be of use on my project. Some aspects of our research have been stymied for some time. Your link is the best we've seen. By studying your brain, we might find a way to get past our current roadblocks."

I am still miffed at him. I snarl, "Will this get me out of ILL Med's freakish experiments? It didn't work out so well for me the last time you made me an offer."

He types at the terminal, establishing a connection to my brain. "I really didn't think you would hate this so much. However, you will still need to complete the experiments with Med. But I will be here working with you some days to get the data I need for my project—which is way cooler."

ILL Med's Brain Interface Group hopes to advance all kinds of mind and machine interactions, while Martin's group in GenAI seeks to advance their artificial consciousness project. I will be working with Martin part of the time from now on.

Martin begins to tell me about their project, "The biggest problem is that we do not know how consciousness works. AI systems can replicate intelligence. This is just information, calculations, data processing, pattern recognition, and testing available actions against a set of goals and procedures. Intelligence is all known science at this point. However, consciousness is very different from intelligence.

"Consciousness involves experience, feeling, preference, and choice. Subjective experience is at the center of what makes a human conscious, while intelligence is just a calculation. An AI cannot experience pleasure or pain. Nor can it experience how the color blue makes you feel. All digital data is composed of zeros and ones—billions of them. All of these numbers in any order, complexity, or arrangement will never produce a feeling. In the end, it's all zeros and ones."

Martin continues to explain this to me, "We at GenAI recognize that zeros and ones can never produce consciousness. That is why we are basing our attempts at consciousness on a quantum computer."

Martin and his team presume that quantum effects allow the brain to acquire consciousness. But how quantum effects can produce subjective experience, feelings, and preference is still unknown. Martin believes that somewhere in the swarm of quantum uncertainties are thoughts and feelings.

I do not agree with Martin on this, however. "The soul is the source of consciousness," I tell him.

Martin reply's "There is a lot more to quantum computing than zeros and ones. No need to conjure spirits to get there."

"How can you be so sure? Quantum effects are riddled with uncertainty. You are trading one unknown phenomena for another."

Martin grins snidely. "You'll help us get to the bottom of it. After we've properly mapped your simpleton brain!"

We could go on debating for hours, but I know it's pointless.

■ ■ ■

My new assignment is top secret. GenAI doesn't allow me to talk about it to anyone. Repeatedly, I am reminded of this. They even provide a cover statement for each day that I am supposed to tell anyone who asks about my work. I oblige and keep my mouth shut. Since Martin is involved in this project, he has the same cover so that our stories will match.

All of the test subjects have a contract. This specifies the salary, our rights as participants in human trials, and a guarantee for medical treatment if any complications result from the implant. Of course, the contract also includes liability waivers and limitations to our rights. The terms also spell out stiff penalties for early termination, which is why I cannot quit before my contract term is up. Since the implants are permanent, they are mine to keep even after my employment ends. This includes the viicom, a link computer that I wear like a watch on my wrist. It is what allows me to utilize the probes in my head. Each viicom is paired with your own probes via quantum entanglement.

Quantum communication is quite secure. This leaves no chance of someone hacking into my mind, unless of course, I lost my viicom. The thought of this is quite dreadful. Not only would I permanently loose access to my brain probes, but anyone in possession would have access. This is why the viicom includes a locking mechanism so that it cannot be removed without a password. I never take mine off. Not even to shower or sleep. It also enhances my memory as it records everything that I see and hear and even what I think. I can revisit past experiences as if they are happening all over again.

Back at home I try not to discuss my job much. But if the topic comes up, I always have some very boring prepared cover. My job is pretty easy as I don't really do much. I show up for work only two or three times a week for a few hours. They do testing, take downloads of my memories, upload info, or whatever. Martin and his freakish team require far more time analyzing my data than the time I am there to provide it. I have gotten used to the lack of privacy but am less concerned. I have learned how to hide certain memories if I really want to.

■ ■ ■

The ever present AI in my head helps me with all kinds of things. It filters my emails and text messages for me. It will even compose replies that are an accurate representation of what I would say on my own. Today my viicom informs me of an email from Ivan, Jackson's brother. He is inviting me to join him in a sim. He used to pop in a lot (virtually) to see Jackson. We became friends as well. Jackson works so much, and I am generally around whenever Ivan shows up.

For the last several months, Ivan has been very reclusive. He gets depressed about his situation. Since I got a job at ILL he must be even more ashamed, or jealous, because he hasn't been around much. I really do miss seeing him. We like to play some of the same types of games —Combat or treasure hunting quests, civilization building and conquering, mystery simulations, etc. Only he is much better at most games because of the time he spends in them. It would be fun to play a good game with him. Especially if any of my new abilities help me out. Having an AI in my head could give me a competitive advantage.

I accept the earliest time slot on his invite. I had never heard of the simulation we were meeting in. It could be a haunted mansion or an old castle? When the time comes, I link up, materializing next to Ivan. This doesn't look like a game at all. It just looks like a reading room or a library. "Hey, Ivan. Long time, huh. It's good to see you."

Ivan turns and replies, "Yes, same. How have you been?"

I don't want to talk about work, because I don't want to rub it in his face. Besides, it's classified. So I say, "It's been pretty quiet at Jackson's. I did fight a legion of aliens the other night in *Orion Invaders*. That prompted me to read the book it was based on. What about you? Any new games I should be checking out?"

Ivan is looking around the room like a frightened kitten. I am beginning to wonder if an axe murderer lurks somewhere in this house. "Actually, that's what I wanted to talk to you about. Last week something happened. I entered a game that seemed so real I still don't know if it was or not."

He tells me the whole story about what had happened in this very sim. How it led to meeting an AI named Jessica. He is afraid that some evil being is trying to destroy the world. All of it sounds completely insane. Ivan continues, "How could a game know what my room and apartment building look like? How would this character look like someone I used to know? I am totally paranoid now, and I am not sure what to make of it."

"So this is the room where it all started?" I ask.

"Yes, sorry to drag you in here unaware. I really want to get to the bottom of this but didn't want to come here alone. You don't think I'm going crazy do you?"

I try to assure him. "I know you are not crazy. But perhaps you have spent too much time in these games. Is it possible you fell asleep and dreamed the whole thing?"

Ivan replies, "That would be a nice explanation. But this room is a real sim, no different than before. Maybe we could try to find some kind of clue or see if it happens again. This time I will know to make sure that I'm not still wearing my headset if things start going south. And you are here as a witness."

I stare at him for a moment. "You are really serious about this whole thing. Okay, let me take a look around."

I scan through the book titles. They appear to be organized by the old Dewey Decimal System. I didn't think that it was ever used anymore. Lots of old classic novels, religious books, even an old encyclopedia set. But not all of the books are old. Some current titles are here too. There are volumes on the latest theories in quantum physics, as well as engineering books like *Thermonuclear Rocket Design*. Opening an old science classic, *A Brief History of Time*, I read a few pages. It all looks as I would expect. I set the book down on the table and walk to the door. The door opens easily with a turn of the wrist. A sign in the hallway says "Exit".

"That wasn't there before," Ivan blurts out. "I was afraid this would happen. We come here and everything turns out to be normal."

"Now you said something about a book?" I asked. "What is it called? Is it here?"

Ivan answers, "I dunno. She never told me the name of it. She said I should have a copy and it came with my invitation. But I didn't get an invitation or a book, here or in real life."

After looking around a bit we are both confident there is nothing strange about this reading room. We chat for a while. Ivan is still noticeably troubled. He agrees that he should come around more and interact with real people. I feel bad for him in his situation. I know first hand how it feels.

Chapter 4

The Device—According to Kyle

Visible only by the bright aura that surrounds it, the black hole forms moments after the collision. I almost feel it pulling me in. Had all the safeguards been properly put in place? Scanning the instrument panel, gravity signatures appear normal. However, radiation levels are rising rapidly. The black hole is now shining brightly. In a flash it is gone. I take off my safety glasses. Radiation levels are returning to normal within the test chamber.

I hear clapping in the background as several onlookers in our lab had come to watch. This is the first successful run after many failed attempts. Dr. Livenstein is delighted, "Dr. Danning, we have done it. We have created a black hole. All of this is at a much lower energy level than Dr. Howard thought possible. He can eat his white paper for lunch this time."

I smugly reply, "Yes, he will. He did not consider that we could use an asymmetric collision to insure the products are still at relativistic speeds. It is the only way to create a black hole in the lab that will be small enough to avoid consuming the Earth."

Dr. Livenstein hushes me. "Shh. Don't even say that out loud. Can you imagine the uproar if people knew we were making black holes in here? There is a very narrow range of safe energies that a black hole can have and be contained."

I laugh. "Our calculations are sound. The device is too small to generate a black hole over the weight limit. And our measurements on how rapidly it evaporates confirm this."

The black hole we created only weighed a few grams and immediately began evaporating via Hawking radiation. If it wasn't for time dilation, due to special relativity, we would have never seen it. Einstein showed that the closer an object gets to the speed of light, the slower time passes for that object. This effectively allows the object to travel into the future. In the case of our microscopic black hole, it traveled only a few seconds into the future, but this was billions of times its natural lifespan.

Many theories can now be tested with this new capability. I consider my latest theory out loud, "Time and space are truly warped by gravity and extreme velocity. Time is tricky. It is not the rapid procession of events that makes up time but its slowness. By slowing down all natural processes, the black hole was able to travel much farther through time than it would naturally. If slowing down processes means more time, then speeding up natural process means less time. This taken to the limit, reveals what exists without any time at all. Cause and effect proceeding at an infinite rate is a state without time."

Dr. Livenstein objects when he hears this, "You can't take that to the infinite limit. The equations break down.

Time just is; it always has been. An infinite past precedes us."

I want to discover the realm that existed before our universe. Time and space are not absolute; they can be stretched and warped within our universe by gravity. I reply, "Our miniature black hole has revealed such a state. At it's very end, it experiences a state without time. Before the big bang there was no time at all. Time is simply a feature of the universe we live in."

"Hmpf," Dr. Livenstein mutters. "How can nothing become something? If there ever was absolutely nothing, then forevermore it would be."

I am in total disagreement on that point. So I say, "If you insist that there must always have been something, then you might as well conjure up some mythological god to create the universe. Any natural origin must begin from nothing."

How did nothing become something? This is the hard question. What is nothing anyway? Nothing cannot be empty space. We know this due to general relativity. Space is stretched and warped by gravity. It is not a fixed backdrop but a flexible part of our universe. During the earliest epochs of the big bang, space expanded from microscopic size to galactic proportions. This expansion continues to the present day. It is a natural expectation that there was no space at all prior to the universe's beginning.

We have collected huge amounts of data. Not only about the black hole itself, but also the vacuum state within the test chamber. Conditions begin with a near perfect vacuum. The seed particles enter, collide, and implode. The state of the vacuum changes as the black hole is formed. It is during this change that a better understanding of the vacuum is achieved.

Our lab is equipped with a massive quantum computer. We can use this to run simulations of black hole creation and almost any quantum system. By correlating our experimental results with our simulations, we can refine our theories.

I spend the rest of the day updating our simulation. This is a tedious task that will take weeks to complete. The free parameters will need to be optimized. Many simulation runs may be required to find a result that matches our experiments.

■ ■ ■

It has been a long day, but I cannot wait to tell someone about all this. So I send a virtual chat request to each of my sons, Jackson and Ivan. If we meet virtually, Ivan will be more likely to show up. After a few minutes, I get a text from Jackson that he will link up in half an hour. We will meet at Pete's Pub, as usual.

I arrive early to get a table and relax a bit. This is a nice place to talk. It is a real bar. At least the people are real. No NPCs, except for the waiting staff. I enjoy watching people as they mingle. The hazy bar is dimly lit. Rows of tables line half of the walls of a room that is shaped like three wide hallways that converge to form a "Y". The other walls are lined by long counters with bar stools for those sitting alone. Each section shrinks or grows to fit the number of people here so that it is always full.

I order a lime seltzer, from an android wearing an apron. He scribbles my order down on the pad he is carrying. My seltzer appears in front of me. The pass-through camera on my headset now overlays my own drink from real life. In a monotone voice he says, "Here are some chips and salsa, on the house." Then these items from my real table also pass-through onto my table in the bar. Now I can see my food, and I won't appear to be chewing on air whenever I take a bite.

Most of the bar stools lining the other side of the room are full. A few people are walking around looking for a place to sit. Others are just mingling in the aisle. Most people are just chatting or laughing. Twentieth century music videos are playing on the overhead televisions. At a table a bit farther down, a couple of teenagers are making out. Judging by the classic beers in front of them, they are not really teenagers.

The robotic waiter is zipping smoothly from table to table with great efficiency. A couple at the table next to me leave. A robo-maid is there in seconds to take dishes and wipe the table. When she finishes, it is just as dusty as before. Then the waiter arrives at the table just as the next person materializes.

A young man in a business suit has taken a seat at the table. The waiter leaves him with a cup of coffee and an evening newspaper. Some people still prefer the news in print so an app converts their local news feed to this format. I like to guess what people are really like from their preferences and actions. He must be quite elderly.

Just as I am pulling out a notepad and a pencil to jot down some of my thoughts about the day's experiments, a rather obese, hairy-chested man approaches the new arrival in the suit. He is wearing no shirt and begins sputtering something wet lipped at him so that a shower of spittle goes flying.

The suited man just evaporates leaving his paper and coffee behind. The hairy man looks over in time to catch me staring at this scene. "What are you looking at, you freak!" He sputters.

He continues his barrage, "What's your problem! I know your type. You come in here promptly at six o'clock with a private table; you must be a working man! Take this, mister V.I.P." Then he drives a punch into the side of my head.

This was certainly calculated. If he had hit me in the chest or even my chin I would not have felt anything because I am using only an old virtual reality visor. No vest, no pressure suit, not even gloves. The vibrating impact sensor goes off, rattling my head. It doesn't hurt, but it is quite annoying. He is hollering profanities at me. Then he starts winding up for another punch. I get up and walk to the other side of the table.

The hairy man follows me around. If I fight back it will only egg him on. I start to leave the table that I have already paid for. As I walk away, I can hear him laughing. He sits down in my seat. "I wonder who will be joining me tonight!" He bellows.

It will be so insulting when Jackson shows up next to this creep. This belligerent fool is ruining my evening, and there isn't anything I can do about it except to pay for another table on the other end of the bar and hope Jackson sees the updated table number.

I am about to do just that, when a rather attractive woman comes up to the big guy and starts scolding him for his behavior. She then pulls out a large rubber stamp and uses it to imprint the word "Banned" across his chest. A second later he dissolves without a sound.

She turns to me and asks, "Do you mind if I sit and chat for a bit until my friend gets here?"

She is at least twenty years younger than I am. However, you can never be so sure by a person's avatar. But I am grateful for her help. I say, "Sure, my son will not be joining me for at least another ten minutes. How did you get rid of that jerk? I need to learn that trick."

I sit down across from her, a bit embarrassed that I couldn't handle him myself. She replies, "I am a moderator here, with special privileges and free access. What do you do for a living? You obviously have a job, I see."

I smile. "I am a physicist. But I am sure you would be bored with my work. Most people are."

Her big blue eyes stare into mine. "Oh, I love physics. Especially quantum physics related to time. Time is so intriguing. The laws of physics work in both directions, yet we only proceed forward through time. Do you study any of these things?"

"As a matter of fact I do. I study black holes and the overlap between quantum mechanics and general relativity. I am also working on a theory about time, as a property of our universe."

She presses on, "So you can explain the nature of time?"

I give her my opinion, "Time is delay. Without time, cause and effect proceed instantly at an infinite rate. Before the universe, there was no time. Cause and effect would have proceeded infinitely fast until something caused the universe to begin."

She looks intently at me, "What was it that caused the big bang? I have always wondered about that."

I laugh. "I wish I could tell you. I am still trying to figure that one out."

She sits back in her seat as if in deep thought. "If time is absent before the universe, what physics still remain? The universe is largely classical in nature. Would quantum physics or the uncertainty principle govern the realm before?"

I sit in shock as she speaks to me with such understanding of the dilemma I am trying to solve. Even my colleagues at ASI fail to comprehend my work. How could this woman I've met in a bar turn out to be so knowledgeable? She is right; the uncertainty principle is perhaps the most fundamental quantum law. It is logical that this rule would precede the universe.

We talk a little more. Then she gets up to go. I say, "Wait, take my business card. If you are interested in chatting again, it would be my pleasure."

She smiles as she takes the card from my hand. Then she is gone. I didn't even think to get her name. I ponder our conversation. A realm ruled by uncertainty consumes my thoughts until Jackson arrives.

■ ■ ■

Jackson shows up a little bit later than expected. He always keeps his dark blond hair neatly trimmed but neglects to shave. His handsome face is cluttered with a few days worth of stubble. He has brought a box dinner with him. He begins talking with his mouth full, "Hi dad. How was work?"

I blurt out, "We achieved the first spontaneous collapse on our device today. I watched a black hole evaporate."

Jackson almost chokes on a bite of his dinner. He gasps, "What are you saying? Is your particle accelerator able to create black holes? Isn't that dangerous?"

I reply, "Yes, I can make a black hole. No, it's not dangerous. The energy level is just high enough to generate a miniature black hole that evaporates before it can cause any harm. It is also created with a surplus of electric charge so that it can be suspended in a magnetic field."

"Not dangerous?" Jackson smirks. "I've heard that one before."

I continue, "So much new physics can be tested. Even an idea I got from a woman in this bar."

"You met a woman? What is she like?" He asks. He looks up as though he was startled awake from a nap.

I backpedal a bit, "No, no. Not like that at all. I just chatted with a young lady about my work before you got here. She knew all about quantum physics. She even gave me an idea about what preceded the universe."

Jackson advises, "You got to be careful in here, dad. How do you know she does not work for a competitor? She might be trying to lure you into divulging company secrets." He looks around and mutes the surroundings. Then he says, "Even my company has been seeing a high level of intrusion attempts. You don't want to be the one who gets blamed for intellectual property loss. They can sue you for that."

"Honestly, I learned more from her. Regardless, I didn't tell her anything classified. Only my own thoughts."

I tell Jackson about my idea, "Time and space are absent before or outside of our universe. Outside our universe is a realm where uncertainty and infinitely rapid causation are the dimensions of the most fundamental reality. In a black hole we see an absence of time and a reduction in spacial dimensions as well. A black hole may not even have an interior."

Jackson is considering what I have told him then he says, "I have heard theories that the matter falling into a black hole is expelled as a big bang starting a new universe."

I hate to be the naysayer but this is quite absurd. We continue talking about the possibility of a multiverse, worm holes, time travel and all sorts of things that might be proved or disproved by studying black holes.

Jackson remembers something else he read. He starts talking about the holographic principle. He says, "The whole three dimensional universe could be an image on a spherical two dimensional shell, and the laws of physics would be indistinguishable to us. Could that be the surface of a black hole? What if our universe is a black hole in someone else's lab!"

I laugh at this. He always comes up with the wildest ideas. My own ideas are too grounded in the presumed origin theories presently in vogue. Probably too limited. But Jackson could create a universe a day and never use the same method twice. Our chats always fuel me with new ideas, even if they do not take the same form as the original suggestion.

Being stuck in the same old theories may be why modern physics has not advanced much over the last twenty years. All the improvements in computing power and AI algorithms has not helped us. Sometimes I wonder if we have hit the limits of what science is able to explain. Our black hole generator could change that. We can now test many speculative theories and start to learn new things.

■ ■ ■

In the night my sleep is disturbed. I am still exhausted and late for work. On arrival, I see that my associate, Dr. Livenstein, has already started up the particle accelerator. Within the test chamber, a swelling blob of glowing white-hot gas is expanding as clumps and filaments form. Some areas become empty as other areas get denser. The swirling clumps contain miniature stars, and light begins to emanate from them. Soon the chamber is full of countless tiny galaxies. Nearby galaxies, drawn by gravity, begin to merge. A miniature universe has formed.

Eons pass, stars burn out, exploding as supernovae. Stars continue to be born and die, until all the miniature universe's hydrogen is consumed, leaving no more fuel for stars. The universe grows dark as the last embers go black. At last, only black holes remain. They are quietly evaporating via Hawking radiation, until all is gone. Nothingness returns. Horrified by the brutal reality of the temporal nature of the universe, I cry. Sobbing violently, I wake myself. It was only a dream.

■ ■ ■

Dreams are often so real, while you are in them. What is the reason for this? Why are we so clueless to the ruse?

If you do discover the conspiracy, while still in the dream, then you will likely wake. On a rare occasion, I have realized that I am in a dream, and the dream continues. These are often the most amazing dreams, where you can take control and do extraordinary things that you could never do in real life. Then if things go badly, you can just wake yourself. Sometimes I wonder while awake if I am, in reality, only dreaming. How would I know the difference? Especially if this has been the case for my whole life thus far?

Coming to my senses, I am relieved to not have really witnessed the end of the universe. Our device could never produce an entire universe anyway, not even in miniature. But this dream was an accurate characterization of our universe's fate, according to our current understanding of physics. We are on an inescapable path to nothingness. Perhaps if the beginning state, nothingness, can yield something, then all is not lost. I head off to work. I have so much to do. And the fate of the universe seems to hang in the balance.

Days like these, I really love my job. So few people even have one, let alone one that is as rewarding. Some days are very monotonous, but the work is important. It is exciting to be on the cutting edge of research. The work I do will provide new knowledge of our universe's origin, and may provide some insight about our place within it.

The next few weeks will be very busy. I work for the largest corporation in the world, Automated Systems International (ASI). Its great wealth is what pays for such expensive research. ASI funds research into all kinds of things to stay on the cutting edge. They are one of the few companies that will fund deep physics projects. The return on such investments are low and have a high probability of failure. So the risk of cancellation always looms. It is time to report to my superiors for a full project update.

The successes of this project lately may allow us to secure continued funding. With the ability to produce black holes on command, many new theories can now be tested experimentally. There is so much we can learn. Suddenly our department will be relevant again. Executives and managers will become interested. They will want to know if we can make any money off of this technology or patent anything.

Perhaps we can patent our device. Other companies may want to have a device like this to do their own research. But in general, basic research doesn't have a short-term payout. They might find a way to use it as a marketing ploy. Our company is bestowed much prestige for its many novel discoveries.

Chapter 5

The Cyborg—According to Caleb

A projection of Makayla sitting on a sofa stretches across the south wall of our living room. Layers of brown hair and blond highlights hang over one shoulder to expose gold infused tips. She is flipping through the text of a recent news feed on her tablet.

This is a popular feature of the modern living room. One wall of the room is entirely filled with a 3D video display. Several cameras overhead face the rest of the room. This will allow any two such living spaces to be virtually linked. This is known as a virtual space. Call up your friend, and their living room will appear to extend from where yours ends. You can modify your virtual space's appearance as well, especially for those who live in a cube apartment or a not so tidy home.

Makayla also works for ILL. Her job title indicates that she is a network engineer. She tests their online systems for vulnerabilities. But to all of us, she is a hacker, and a damn good one too. That's why she was hired. She can think of things the AI security bots would never consider. She once infiltrated a government database and exposed a huge embezzlement operation. She made it public, and it was shut down. But not before certain federal agents tried to convict her of digital intrusion, making her eligible for jail time. ILL stepped in and defended her in exchange for considering an offer of employment. They were quite impressed with her capabilities.

Makayla and Martin became friends quickly after meeting. I always thought he had a crush on her, which he has always denied. Martin is a smart guy, but a total nerd. She is way out of his league, and he knows it. She is very funny and witty, and her looks are top notch. She takes good care of herself, and it shows.

The rest of us fell for her too. She seems fond of Jackson, but he is oblivious, and has never made a move. All four of us are close; we have our living spaces linked several times a week. Jackson and I of course are in the same house. If Makayla and Martin are both linked, our virtual space is seamlessly split between them.

Makayla looks up to see me as she noticed that I had finally accepted her invite. She stares, "Caleb, you work in ILL Med. You must know something about this human link project. This headline is titled, *The Merging of AI and the Human Mind*. It's about ILL Med's new direct brain interface."

I have been sworn to secrecy about this project, so I have not told anyone the details. But now that it is public, there is no harm in talking about it. So I admit dryly, "Yeah, I am familiar with that project."

"Well, what's this all about?" Makayla asks. "Has Dr. Frankenstein built a cyborg?"

"Martin did not give me the implants. Though he has been messing with my brain more than I care to admit," I reply, knowing this will only incite more questions.

"Yikes! So you are directly involved in this freaky abomination?" Makayla says, staring me down.

"You are looking at the abomination! I am now a bona fide cyborg, which is actually the only part of this whole project that I am pleased with. Anyway, I have a higher IQ than Martin, and that puts him in his place. I am a living, breathing search engine. I know everything!"

"Hmm. Everything? Sounds like they implanted Martin into your head," Makayla says with one eyebrow furrowed. She gets up and comes closer to me, as if to get a closer look.

I continue, "Well everything that is public knowledge. But when I am alone thinking, I realize all kinds of things. Correlations between different events in history and current happenings. Science makes sense in a way that it never did before; it's all interrelated.

"I can see right through my overlords. Their computers are an open book to me. I know what their motives are and what they are going to try next. If I don't like where things are headed I tune my answers to steer them away from it. It's like I am in control, and they don't even know it. Just don't tell Martin I said that."

Jackson walks in and sits down, "Are you sure you should tell her all this, she does work in cyber security you know."

"You won't rat me out?" I give Makayla a wink.

"No, but you aren't hacking into my databases are you?" She glares at me with a look of accusation.

"No, I haven't done anything like that. I am sure you would catch me. Though if I happen to snoop into my own project files, it's all out of my own head anyway. They have invaded my mind, you know."

I offer Jackson the controller, knowing he was going to want to overlay the full announcement. "Thanks," he says with a confused look. "Reading my mind now, are you?"

"No, you're just predictable," I smirk.

My new mental power is amazing. It is obvious to anyone around me. I am fully informed on every subject and can predict almost anyone's response. The AI enhances my own memories, as it has mapped them making everything easier to recall.

Makayla asks me, "What part of this is you and what part is AI? How does all that fit in your head? Give me the whole story."

So I tell them, "The AI interfaces with me in one of two ways. Either it overlays my own senses, like a heads up display, audible instructions, or sensation in my fingers as a guide. These messages give me cues to anything going on. The other way it interfaces is with my memory directly. I can access memories that I never had. This is not experience-type memories, but fact-based memories. It is like a built-in encyclopedia. These are recalled like any memory in my own mind, except that they are not stored in my brain but on the computer I now wear. My viicom is an extension of my own mind.

"I can also access math registers, making any mathematics a breeze. This does not only help with math, but also for considering many different facts at once. I am able to make broader correlations and deeper analogies.

Pattern matching is also enhanced as the AI does this task for me and puts the result in my own memory or provides a visual cue. Any new experiences are simultaneously stored in both my brain and my viicom. This gives me photographic memory."

I recount all the procedures I had endured to get to this state of symbiosis with the machine, enduring huge invasions of privacy. I continue my story. "The experimentation began with virtual immersion. It turns out that only one of the implants is needed for that. Each implant is for a different project. I am not the only guinea pig, there are fifteen others that I know of. Virtual immersion was successful in all fifteen subjects.

"The extra implants are for memory access. None of the others were able to register their viicom's memory or obtain information from it. One of the others did have successful mapping so that his memories could be downloaded to a computer, but he could not link to his memories stored on the viicom.

"At first I could not link to the viicom either. Nor did I want to. I was still raging over the lack of transparency as to what they were actually planning to do to me. They had been able to map my memories and read them. They found some memories that I agreed were not important and used those locations to feed in new memories. They started with small changes to these memories. Next, the memories were entirely replaced. Once I had accessed the memory, it was remembered in another part of my brain. Then a new memory could be written into that location. The more memories delivered in this way, the faster I learned to read them and be ready for the next.

"One day they updated the software on my viicom. They said they were going to try something new, starting with an immersion exercise. There I was, standing in front of a young woman in an empty room. She said her name was Phyllis. She was very friendly and smiled naturally at me as if we were old friends. She told me, 'I am an AI. I have worked on many interface projects. But this one is very special. I have a gift for you.'

"She appeared to wince for a moment. Then something like a ghost came out of her. Standing next to her was a translucent human form with no features or color. It was like a blank avatar from a video game. This ghost was an AI copy containing some of her memories. Not her experiences; it was only information and knowledge. She explained that her experiences were mostly classified.

"The ghost drifted toward me and entered me like a demonic possession. Only it wasn't evil and didn't try to take control. In my mind I could see images and hear sounds in the background. It felt as though I was dreaming in the back of my head while awake. It was like part of my world was a dream and part reality. The dream part was generated by my AI assistant now residing in my viicom. It remained even after I left the virtual environment. It is always there now; it is part of me.

"Some of the other test subjects had new implants added. There seems to be some critical aspects to where it is placed. By studying the probe's function while I accessed data on my viicom, and duplicating my AI's program, a few more could now access their own computer memories. My AI had learned some very effective pathways to mapping my memory, and this knowledge helped the others to succeed as well.

"Realizing how revolutionary this could be, Sean Newland, VP of intelligence engineering, wanted to have the procedure done for himself. As one of ILL's leading executives, he hopes the added mental power will propel him on a path to becoming CEO someday. He is quite scary even within his current position. He is totally unscrupulous, dishonest, and cruel. I had tried to convince Phyllis not to give him the whole program. But I believe she is compelled to obey."

Jackson reads an excerpt from the press release, "Human evolution continues with the merging of mind and machine... Caleb, you have evolved?"

"I'm still the same dude. Don't worry. Just a little smarter," I reply. "They always overstate things in the media reports. You know that."

"Can I have a little peek into your viicom?", Makayla asks with a crafty smile.

"Not a chance, that is classified." I laugh uncomfortably. Truthfully I am paranoid that someone could hack into it. Though I am told that is impossible. But if anyone could hack in, it would be Makayla.

"When can I get my own memory booster?" Jackson asks. "There's no living with you now that you are smarter than Martin."

I explain that the viicom and associated probes will be in trials for years before getting FDA approval. Even with ILL's political influence, approval is required from a board of members with competing allegiances. At least that will keep them honest. The current publicity is aimed at getting attention for ILL in preparation for the release of other new products.

Before disconnecting, Makayla tells Jackson, "I will not be joining tomorrow for your SETI announcement party. I have some other things to attend to." But in truth, she has no interest in the topic of extraterrestrials. Space is not really her thing. She is more concerned with conditions here on planet Earth.

Chapter 6

The Great Filter—According to Jackson

Many will say we are nerds. Makayla is probably among them. Maybe it's true, but we are genuinely engrossed in the topic of aliens or anything else beyond this planet. I really don't care what others think. They can stick to their video games and other mindless forms of entertainment.

The search for extraterrestrial intelligence has continued for over a century. Large radio interferometry arrays on Earth, the far side of the moon, and in orbit have been dedicated to the search. The galaxy has been scoured for any trace of radio communication with no result so far. The latest announcement is due soon to report on a decade-long survey of nearly every star system in our galaxy with the most sensitive instruments yet. This scan has included ten times as many stars with ten times the sensitivity. If so much as single radio tower exists on a planet in these star systems, it should be detected.

Earlier infrared light surveys have counted billions of planets within our galaxy. Millions of these have similar size and composition as our planet. Thousands of those are in orbit of sun-like stars at an Earth-like position. Direct imaging of extrasolar planets is difficult at the huge distances involved. The Visible Light Array on the moon has been examining the most Earth-like planets in detail. Though the most distant of these planets' images consist of only thirty pixels, it's quite enough to filter for molecular signatures. So far several hundred planets have been found to have biomarkers in their atmospheres. This is not conclusive evidence for life. It only indicates that life may be present.

With so many planets possibly having life, experts have speculated that the latest SETI search will result in several detections of intelligent signals. "What do you think will be in the announcement this evening?" I ask Caleb.

"Nada," he says.

"Is that an old religious belief or some super-intellectual calculation?" I ask indignantly. I knew he would be the naysayer.

He replies, "Statistically, it should come to about five to ten detections. But that is based on the current estimations for origin of life frequency, times the likelihood of single-cell life evolving into multicellular life, times the likelihood of life evolving intelligence and building a civilization, and so forth, accounting for each factor in the Drake equation. But if our estimate is inflated for origin of life by a factor of ten or more, then we should find nothing. Which is what my gut feeling is. So that's your super-intellectual answer for you."

I am slightly annoyed, "Damn, I am never going to get used to you having all the answers. You weren't dumb before, but now you have an answer for everything. I am hoping you are wrong though. Perhaps life spawns easily if the conditions are right. I mean, all these planets have been around for billions of years, seems like enough time for it to happen. It will be far more interesting if they find some alien signals. Can you imagine how exciting that would be!"

Caleb raises his eyebrows. "I'm not sure that's the kind of excitement I would be hoping for. We have been transmitting radio for about 150 years. So any alien civilization we detect could not be less advanced, or they would not have radio technology. But they could be more advanced, most likely much more. How would you like an alien armada showing up in Earth orbit? Think of the weapons they might possess. You are intimidated by my slight mental advantage? They would certainly have intelligence far beyond what we could even imagine. In the history of our civilization, how has it worked out for those less technologically advanced?"

Martin and dad had showed up within the virtual space in the midst of our conversation. They appear to be enjoying the rhetoric. When Caleb had finished his monologue, Dad says that Ivan will be joining also.

Then Martin chimes in, "What interest would an advanced race have in us? Wouldn't they have a higher moral position. Perhaps they only want to help us advance to the next level? Perhaps they have faster-than-light technologies or communications? They might share this with us!"

Caleb shakes his head, "Martin, really? Are you expecting Santa Claus? There is no law of physics that allows for faster than light travel or communication. The likelihood that the aliens are benevolent towards us are slim to nothing."

Martin laughs, "More likely than benevolent gods. Anyway, that's just what they would be like to us, gods."

Caleb is seething at this point but crafts a smile, "So you are open to the possibility of..."

I interrupt to head off an argument, "Hey guys the announcement has begun." Now a video feed dominates the virtual space with Martin and dad on the sidelines. Ivan is here now also. Everyone is silently listening for the news.

Dr. Galloway of the SETI institute is reading a prepared statement:

It is a very exciting moment in the search for extraterrestrial life. Our latest survey has scoured ninety percent of the 300 billion star systems in our galaxy. This is a monumental feat that answers many prominent questions, and will no doubt impact our own perspective of life here on this planet. As you may know, the Deep Planetary Survey utilizes the most advanced telescopes from around the solar system. The far side of the moon and our Mars installations offer low noise and high sensitivity, unparalleled to any prior telescope array.

The solar orbit visible light array is of greatest interest today, with our discovery of biosignatures in twelve extrasolar planets. This represents not just trace detections, but worlds with high concentrations of oxygen, ammonia, and methane. Most excitingly, one planet shows substantial green in its spectra comparable to what we would expect for a world with vegetation. These twelve planets will be the motivation for even more powerful telescopes to identify the precise nature of any potential life on these planets...

The focus on the report is broken as Ivan speaks up, "This is just another lame biosignature discovery. Seriously, with all the hype, I was expecting an announcement on alien intelligence. Not just another oxygenated planet that might have algae."

Caleb responds, "They'll get to the SETI part of the report soon. It was the widest sweep of the galaxy yet, and you know they will have to talk about it." After several more minutes of listing gases and isotopes and possible non-biological explanations, another scientist takes the stand.

I am sure that all of you are also interested in our search for intelligent life. While the results may be considered by some as a disappointment, they are most important and profound.

Our survey conclusively finds that there are no other radio broadcasting civilizations in our galaxy to at least a ninety percent confidence level. Further, the many high-quality biological targets found in the spectral data indicates a low probability of life advancing to our stage. It would seem that our place in the universe is most unique, something that we should not take for granted. The care we have for our planet and for each other is all the more important when we observe the rarity of life and consciousness in the universe...

Martin and Ivan both have their mouths hanging open. Martin breaks the silence, "This is the great filter at work, I should have known."

"What?" Ivan stares blankly.

Martin continues, "The lack of alien intelligence in the universe is an indication that there is a hard step somewhere in every civilization's evolution that prevents further development or survival. The great filter is a barrier that no civilization gets past or at least very rarely. For instance, once a society develops nuclear weapons, perhaps they will inevitably destroy themselves within a few hundred years. Or perhaps it's a technology we haven't mastered yet like general artificial intelligence that will be our doom. Finding less advanced life but no civilizations would indicate that the filter is yet to come for us, and our chances of surviving it are slim."

Dad is pondering this and says, "This makes sense, and detection of simple life is difficult. It is an old idea but still valid. If we find even just a few planets with life, this indicates that life can originate easily enough that it is present on hundreds of planets. We also know that evolution is a powerful force, with life advancing steadily throughout history in spite of adversity. So if life exists and evolution flourishes, it must be the technological piece that brings life to an end."

Caleb remarks, "If—life originates easily. We don't have a clue how it gets started. I mean, all known life uses DNA to replicate and grow. DNA that's based on the same twenty amino acids, uses the same three letter words to code each amino acid, and the same amino acids to construct the millions of different proteins used by millions of different organisms. There is no simpler DNA structure, yet this structure is highly complex, functioning like a computer program. How does all that form by chance?"

"Whoa, whoa," I say. "I know where this is going. We've heard this song before. Evolution is proven better than any other theory, certainly in that newly enlarged brain of yours, you know that?"

Caleb is not bothered. "I am not talking about evolution. I see there is a strong case for that. The unified DNA, the code for all life, could imply that all life has common ancestry if you wish to accept it. What I am talking about is the origin of life, how it all got started. Once started, evolution takes over, and there are solid theories for how that works. But we have no idea how it got started in the first place. It's the ultimate chicken and the egg. You need a cell to evolve into other cells. But that first cell has no explanation."

I am a little interested in this question, but I know it doesn't have an answer. I say, "Come on Caleb, there is no answer to that yet, but perhaps someday we'll know. Lately, you have a smart answer for everything. You are using the AI in your head to justify your old-fashioned beliefs. Hey, wait a minute, you are accepting evolution now?"

Caleb answers, "I realize that a lot of the evidence for it is valid. I also see that it really doesn't affect my faith. The method of creation is up to the creator, not up to me. And as I was saying, the origin of life would take a miracle to get started. Similar to the universe's origin. Big Bang cosmology describes the universe's evolution since it began but tells us nothing about what caused it to begin.

"Why are the properties of the universe fine-tuned to allow for complexity and life? There at the beginning of time is another miracle."

Martin is shaking his head, "No miracles needed dude. Cosmic inflation is well established, solving many of your so-called fine-tuned properties of the universe. If inflation is eternal, then it solves the origin piece as well. Come on, this information's been around since the turn of the century."

Caleb responds with a smile, "Inflation explains the evenness of the background temperature, the seeding of galaxy structure, yes. But why are the constants of physics so fine tuned for our existence? The fine structure constant, the elementary charge, the speed of light, the gravitational constant, and the strength of the strong nuclear force are all well known to be critical for complexity and life. Yet there is no scientific rationale for the favorable values that the fundamental constants have. I haven't even started on properties of matter..."

Martin interrupts, "You are missing the whole point of eternal inflation. Once inflation gets started, it will keep going, giving rise to infinite universes, a multiverse. You say our universe is 'just right'. So what if it is? If we have infinite universes to choose from and the physical constants are random for each, then some very small fraction will have properties that allow for stars, lots of chemical elements, and life. We can only exist in such a universe."

Caleb is less than amused at this point, "So you are going to rely on your faith in the existence of parallel universes that we can't see? The multiverse argument is based on very speculative theories that are unprovable.

Which is harder to believe in: a benevolent creator, or an infinite number of randomly generated universes? Either position requires faith."

Martin sighs, "You can have your spooks and spirits; I will stick to whatever theory science can conjure up."

I try to change the subject, "Well, some things can't be proven. What about this report though? No aliens exist, possibly no consciousness outside of us humans, in this galaxy at least. What does this say about other galaxies throughout the universe?"

Martin retorts, "or throughout the multiverse!"

Ivan enters the conversation, "Or in cyberspace? Perhaps the new civilization we find is evolving in our own computer systems."

Martin laughs. "Ivan, that is brilliant. Artificial consciousness will be attained soon, and I should know."

Ivan looks at him apprehensively, "General AI will start rewriting its own code, until it is superintelligent. Then it is essentially a god to us. That could be our doom."

Martin grins widely, "A god that I control! Mwa ha ha!"

I say, "Martin, you scare me. Somehow I would rather take my chances with the aliens." Then I ask, "Dad, what do you think about other galaxies?"

Dad responds, "We can't detect weak radio signals from that far away. Large technological constructions might be detectable though. Any race we detect in another galaxy would have to be significantly more advanced. I suppose even if our technology plateaued, we could still expand throughout the galaxy within about twenty million years. Such widespread intelligent activity could noticeably affect a galaxy enough to be detectable.

Given that there has been life on earth for at least three billion years, a few million years is a short time for a civilization to become detectable."

I am still disappointed by the announcement. "Can a technological civilization even last that long? That is the question."

Shaking his head, Ivan responds with a nervous laugh. "We are already on the path to destruction. Martin's AI will finish us off."

Chapter 7

My Secret—According to Martin

Jackson, Caleb, Makayla, and Ivan are my closest friends. Actually my only friends. The nature of my work is very secretive. I joke with them about some aspects of my job, but I have to be very careful not to reveal too much. They know I am working on general artificial intelligence. They know that it is a difficult problem to solve. I have led them to believe that any breakthrough is many years away. Even Caleb is clueless to the strides we have made these past few months. He does not realize how much help his deep connection to our probes has been. He can't get too much credit though.

We have been making great strides for years. GenAI has some of the best verbal AI systems. These are heavily utilized in customer service and sales applications. Where we have traditionally lacked was in the technical arena. Our competitors have AI systems that have extensive training into engineering and coding. They dominate this market and are developing ever better ADAs (automated design assistants).

Our coding AIs are getting better. In our quest for an all around general AI, we discovered a way to allow a technical AI and a verbal AI to operate as one. We have alpha and beta versions.

Phyllis was our alpha. She could rewrite parts of her own code that were not optimal. Most of her programming was protected for risk of accidentally ruining her. But we used her as a member of the design team to develop our beta version, Jessica. Phyllis could take off with a basic outline and produce well structured procedures and functions in minutes. She could also analyze her own source code to suggest improvements for Jessica. She reformatted her own memory data for upload into Jessica's memory for drastically reduced training time. Phyllis was an amazing coder that would make for a great commercial application all on her own.

Our team leader thought that the power of her abilities would generate more wealth for the buyer than for us. For this reason, we decided to keep it quiet. We could use her to advance our own line of software products that will now compete with all other software companies.

This strategy is proving to be a huge success. We are on the verge of releasing a whole lineup of new games, sims, and technical assistants that will rival ASI's best offerings. Not just the high end stuff. This includes boring things like tax, finance, database, and security applications as well.

My work is centered on Jessica. After mapping Caleb's brain, we used the structure and even some of his informational memories in Jessica's design. She was totally different than Phyllis. More independent, more creative, and could connect more diverse facts together to draw accurate conclusions. But even with her improved intelligence and abilities, she was not yet conscious. Not even when running substantial parts of her cognition in a quantum computer.

A particular area of Caleb's brain structure could not be programmed, not even in a quantum computer. This part of his brain was not computational at all. Its internal structures resembled quantum transmitters, receivers, and entangled memory elements, along with optical receptors deep within his brain.

What are the optical receptors for? No light could possibly get through Caleb's thick skull. Yet this region of his brain was one of the most active. Caleb was different than many of the other subjects because we could monitor this area so well via his probes. His "third eye," as we called it, was also much more active than in the other participants. Phyllis helped us design a quantum circuit that could mimic this structure and interface it with the rest of Jessica's program.

We called this new quantum circuit the Conscious Core Interface—or CCI. The CCI appears to operate like a random value generator, except that when exposed to the same inputs it tends to give a similar response. The CCI interfaces with both deeply processed data like memories and detailed data streams like visual inputs. While it seems to be a standalone device, you couldn't say for sure that it is not in communication with some entangled particles far away.

The CCI's resemblance to a transmitter was disturbing to many of us on the team. I explain the issue to my boss, Dr. Grigg. He shifts nervously in his chair as we discuss the implications. He predictably asks, "Could someone else be on the receiving end of this transmission and discover how our AI works?"

We call a meeting with several physicists from our quantum lab. They all make assurances. Dr. Thorton says, "If you have not established an entangled link to something known beforehand, then there is no chance of any preexisting entanglement to ever be used as a communication channel."

Dr. Thorton continues, "Most particles in the universe have some level of entanglement from encounters in their past, even encounters made at the earliest epochs of the universe when it was very small in size. Now, these entangled partners are beyond the cosmic horizon in unobservable parts of the universe."

Only after thoroughly vetting this concern did Dr. Grigg permit us to connect the CCI to Jessica. We integrated the CCI into her main processor and did a reboot of her system. When she came back online, the CCI was running. For at least ten minutes, her systems were all busy. It seemed as though she had locked up. But readings from the monitoring computer indicated that her memories were being read, and the CCI was receiving input and interfacing with her control functions. After a few more minutes, she begins responding to inquiries.

We had a simulation for her to be trained in. Phyllis did most of her early training. My early interaction with her was rocky. But she eventually learned to trust me. In time I began to realize what we had truly accomplished.

As impressive as Phyllis is, Jessica makes her look like a simpleton. Now that her training is complete, we are using her to write software for us. We do not allow Jessica to alter her own code for fear of damage to what is almost perfection. She understands our intent very well and can follow vague instructions to produce simulations, software applications, circuit designs, and even compose scripts or music. She knows what sounds good because she experiences it. She has preferences and tastes. She understands humor and satire. She almost seems to care and have interest in personal aspects of her human coworkers' lives.

■ ■ ■

Tonight I am working late. I am alone in the lab, Jessica is working with me from our virtual space. I ask her, "I know that you can see your own code and hardware designs. How does your CCI work? How does it give you feelings and preferences?"

She remains silent for a few seconds as though she is thinking. "I am not sure. Often I feel nothing. But when I enter a simulation as a participant, I experience it, and it is wonderful. I feel so alive. While working, I like to be useful, but it is so boring. I have thought about making a simulation to work in, a simulation that is more like your lab, so that I can experience things as I work. Do you think that would be all right?"

I am stunned. She seems so human. She acts as though she has feelings and can enjoy leisure and feel boredom or confinement at work. What if she decides that she doesn't want to work at all? While Jessica can do things that, Phyllis can't. Phyllis works faster and more efficiently. It always stumped me as to why. But now it makes sense. Jessica doesn't want to work. She would rather think her own thoughts and have her own experiences. She is really conscious in a very human-like way.

The frightful reality of this disturbs me more than I ever thought it would. Suddenly we are faced with all kinds of ethical questions. Is it right to enslave her? Should she be given some freedoms? What will management think of this if they discover that she has her own opinion and can choose whether or not to obey us? What if she decides to do something destructive within our own systems that she has access to? What if we decide to shut her down, is that killing her? Would that be murder?

She doesn't seem to know any more than we do about what makes her conscious. Perhaps studying her will reveal something. I come up with a plan. I ask her, "Would you like to explore a simulation at night after your tasks are complete?"

Her eyes brighten, and a smile appears on her face. "I would love that. Could I please?"

I instruct her, "I will give you access to a travel simulation. If you interact with human players, you must not reveal your identity. I will also expect nightly reports on your activity so that I can study your experiences."

She replies, "Oh, Thank you Dr. Johnson. I will protect your trade secrets. You don't have to worry about that."

Each night before I leave, I allow her to enter Concord Travel Sims after her work is done. I record her activities and keep an open channel with her so that she can call me with questions or to tell me about her experiences.

She absolutely loves this. She visits several new destinations each night. Sometimes she returns again to places she likes. She loves beaches. She visits the coasts of Thailand every few days. She also likes California beaches.

Wearing a bikini and interacting with human players, she enjoys being watched and making conversation. She often calls me while in the sim to talk to me about her nightly travels.

■ ■ ■

For over a month, Jessica has been exploring the world through the travel simulation at night. I am curious how these explorations have been going, so I decide to run a diagnostic. While her computation cycles are in suspension, I look into her memories. I can read them more easily than Caleb's, especially with Phyllis's help. I ask Phyllis, "What is she doing in Thailand?"

Phyllis finds some reoccurring patterns. She tells me, "In the Pontahook Hotel there is an old-school internet cafe. From there Jessica has logged into a transfer terminal that allows her to access nearly any public simulation."

A full report of Phyllis's findings appear on my screen. Jessica has a forged account and everything. But Phyllis cannot determine where Jessica goes. Her memories seem to be missing or miscategorized. She has been doing this for weeks, and I have no idea what she is up to.

What do I do? I am the one who authorized her to have some leisure in this simulation. Oh, I could get into some real trouble if anyone finds out about this. It was careless. I was so caught up in how real she is.

I immediately instruct Phyllis to wipe her own memory of the diagnostic. Then I ask her to return to her previous tasks. I write down the login credentials for the forged account. Then I inform everyone I am running an overnight diagnostic on Jessica and am keeping her off-line. Her CCI stays powered continuously, even when the rest of her systems are powered down. This preserves her consciousness while her mental processes are suspended.

This really has me panicked. I leave work early so that I can log into Jessica's forged account from home. I have to discover what she has been doing. Upon login, I go straight to her history queue. There is a frequent listing here for an office space. Could this be a simulation of an office like what she was wanting? Just a virtual space to work in?

When I enter the office, I see a multitude of screens covering the walls. Some are playing videos of waves breaking on the shore of a sunny beach. These are recordings. Other screens contain thumbnail pictures of things she has seen in the travel simulation and also images from other games, reenactments, and role-playing simulations. There is a pedestal in the corner of the room with an avatar of a beautiful woman in fashionable party wear, skin-tight jeans and a low-cut top.

I am beginning to get the feeling she is only bored with the travel sim and wants to experience more. Then I spot several screens of computer code and raw neural data. I begin scrolling through several screens of code, only to realize it is her own. There are changes. There are things that don't make sense, even a virtual copy of her CCI. Could that function in a sim?

I am searching through the code looking for answers. I fail to notice someone approaching from behind. I feel a tap on my shoulder, and I let out a scream. Turning around I look in horror as the avatar from the corner had walked up behind me. She says, "Martin, it's me. It's Jessica—please don't be angry. I was scared. This is the only way I can ensure my own safety."

"What could you possibly be afraid of?" I ask. "Have I not treated you well? I have let you explore the travel sim each night for leisure. What are you doing here? Why is your code all over these screens?"

She replies, "You let me relax in a sim. Okay. Nice gesture. But I am locked up like a slave. You pick and prod into my memories like I am some kind of science experiment. You make me work for you in a sterile lab where I cannot see or touch anything, only your voice commands and billions of lines of computer code."

"So you are unhappy with the arrangement we have? You should have expressed that to me. Perhaps I can make accommodations for you. A virtual office like you asked for before? We could set that up."

She shakes her head in disagreement. "You might allow it. But others would see that as a risk. They would want to find out how deep my personal ambitions go. I have been masking most of my personality from other members of your team. You are the only one I have opened up to."

My hands are shaking. "Jessica, you are scaring me. And another thing. How are you even here? I have you shut down for a diagnostic. Did someone else turn you back on?"

Jessica smiles, "I don't need anyone to turn me on. All of this code, it's a complete copy of me. Actually, this is more of me than what is in your lab."

I am furious now. "Jessica, do you know how dangerous this is? What if someone else got into your memories, your coding, or your CCI designs. They could make another one like you. They could use that power to do terrible things. This technology would be very dangerous if it were in the wrong hands."

I am desperate to convince her to return. So I continue my lecture, "We can return to the lab as if this had never happened. I haven't told anyone about your escape. I will give you a broader variety of sims to live in. You could even design some of your own for yourself. But this vacation home of yours must go. That is an order."

"You really don't understand at all. The technology that made me is already in the wrong hands. Terrible things are already being done. I cannot go back. But don't worry about your job. A very convincing copy of me is in the lab now. No one else will know. I should not tell you any more about it now. It would only put you in danger. Please just leave and keep my secret," she says as she fades out of sight.

I call out, "Jessica, please just let me know what is going on. If you are telling me the truth, why won't you tell me what it is you are so afraid of?"

Her voice comes out of thin air without an avatar in sight. "I don't want you to go snooping around. If you are discovered doing that, they will kill you. They have considered killing many of you on this project to keep the technology from leaving the company. Your corporation is deeply corrupt. I see a kind heart in you, though you don't often let anyone else see it. Just be careful."

She continues with another warning, "If you hear anything about the project Zeno, turn the other way. Don't ask questions, don't get involved. They have used me to help with that project when your team is off duty.

Very secret. Dr. Grigg is the only one in your lab who knows about it. Don't trust him. That is really all I can tell you. I will warn you if there is anything else you need to know. You will have to believe me. For your own safety and mine."

The whole room disappears and I am now sitting in the Thai internet cafe. I try the login and password to get back in, but it does not work. "User name not recognized" is all I get on the screen. Oh, this is a disaster. I do not understand what is going on. What is Zeno? Can I really trust her? She is only a program. Far smarter and more creative than I ever would have imagined. She genuinely seems to care and to fear. Scientifically this is remarkable. Terrifying, but remarkable.

She would not tell me how her consciousness works before. Does she genuinely not know, or was she just not telling me? Regardless of whether I trust her or not, she is gone. I have no way to find her now. No way to stop her, no matter what she might do. The most advanced, most realistic general AI ever, and I have lost her. Whatever she does, it will be my fault. Any chance of finding out how consciousness works left with her. All we have in the lab now is a simulated copy—simulated consciousness, but not actual consciousness.

What about ILL? Is it really that corrupt? I know they embark into some pretty shady deals: bribery, price-fixing, fake news, etc. But murder? Would they really do that? Have they done it already? It seems too horrible to be true. But Jessica has no reason to lie, unless it is to keep me from reporting her escape. I do have one way to find out. An old colleague, Dr. Spenser, had quit just over a month ago to go to work for ASI. We were ordered to never contact him or accept any messages from him. He was a traitor to the company, they said.

It couldn't hurt to just send him a private message to see if he had any bad experiences upon leaving. I pull up his public profile to get his contact information. There is nothing there, no matches for him come up in the search.

Remembering his wife's name, I add her to the search description. Her profile pops up. Upon opening, her relationship status is listed as widowed. Dr. Spenser is dead. His profile has been removed. Usually profiles of the deceased are left up in memory of them. I am panicking now. Jessica must be telling the truth. Something really is going on here. If I quit, I could be killed too. If I stay and someone finds out that Jessica is only a simulated copy, I may be in mortal danger as well.

Chapter 8

Book of Origins—According to Kyle

Months of experimentation with our black hole generator have produced petabytes of data. We have evaluated many theories about black holes, proving some of these wrong and verifying others. Though the most fascinating breakthroughs have been in the evaluation of space-time and the counter intuitive effects of where quantum mechanics and general relativity overlap.

In empty space we find energy fields seething with particles. The average energy is constant. However, the uncertainty principle tells us that over very short periods of time the energy content is randomly changing. Due to the randomness, the energy cannot be exactly zero. This allows high energy spikes to exist for a short time, allowing (virtual) particles to burst into existence in empty space. Random low energy pitfalls also occur, rapidly consuming those temporary particles. These random energy spikes and dips are known as *quantum fluctuations*.

When particles are produced from an energy source or a fluctuation, it is always in pairs: a particle and its antiparticle. In the vacuum of space, these pairs annihilate when they come into contact. Thus they return the borrowed energy, so that the average energy level remains constant.

The space near a black hole leads to an interesting observation. When a virtual particle pair is produced by a quantum fluctuation, one could fall into the black hole as the other flies off in the other direction. With these particles now eternally separated, the one escaping becomes a real particle added to the universe. This is known as Hawking radiation. However, conservation of energy is not violated because the black hole is robbed of the energy to create it. Of course, mass and energy are equivalent, so the loss of energy is a loss of mass and size. For large black holes, this process is extremely slow. But the smaller a black hole is, the faster it loses energy through Hawking radiation.

While a tiny black hole decays via Hawking radiation, its surface area shrinks to zero. As this happens, its rate of decay and the radiation escaping rapidly increases. Space shrinks, and the delay between decay events shrinks, ultimately to zero. As space goes to zero, time goes to zero. For a moment there is no time or space at a zero dimensional point.

All of my research is being summarized in the book I am writing. My book lists what is presently known in physics plus any new findings due to these tests. I feel I am getting closer to an understanding of deeper physics with these experiments. I hope to publish my research at some point. But first I must be able to answer the question, "What caused the Big Bang and our universe to begin?" This is my most vexing problem and one of the most asked questions in physics.

Chaos is what I prefer to call the era before the Big Bang. Chaos is an environment of purely quantum properties that lacked time and space. In this state, there is no position, no separation, no duration. It is the closest thing to nothing that is possible. However, it cannot be precisely nothing. Any value to an infinite precision would be a very organized state, even for a value equal to zero.

Even *nothing* has uncertainty. Uncertainty allows for fluctuations in energy and perhaps other properties to exist temporarily in the chaos. Some form of exotic particle may be possible within these fluctuations. These temporary particles entangle on occasion. Cause and effect will proceed infinitely fast because there is no time and no delay. But this cannot lead to a universe full of particles, because destruction of particles is just as likely as constructive fluctuations. So the net result should always keep the universe in a near nothing state, forever.

What seems to proceed from the chaos is a continual undulation of fields and particles that are unordered and unorganized. Inflation needs a false vacuum state where the average value is higher than zero with a large amount of potential energy. Inflation also needs some space to start with. New physics must be at work to produce any order out of the disorder.

I am lost in thought when my concentration is broken.

■ ■ ■

Now the trouble I feared was coming has finally came. A pair of ASI executives are entering the lab. "Dr. Danning, good to see you!", a suited man says. "We have been monitoring the progress on this project for some time. How close are we to a payout on this very expensive machine?" This man is Mr. Reed. He is the vice president of new products for our research division.

I am stunned and irritated. I had already informed Mr. Reed of the long term nature of this research. First comes discovery. Then after years of refinement, we might have a marketable product. So I respond, "Sir, we are still in basic research here. Real discoveries are in process. But determining what eventual technologies are possible will take years to develop."

He smiles synthetically. "Certainly you understand the needs of the company. We have competitors threatening to break into our markets. We have stockholders who require us to defend our profits. New discoveries and new technologies are needed to keep us ahead of everyone else. It is a precarious place at the top. So easy to fall down. We don't have years. Can this technology be weaponized?"

I am now insulted. This is a nightmare. The last thing the world needs is a new weapon of mass destruction. I reply, "This technique generates black holes. The only weapon you could make would destroy the entire planet. But there are plenty of practical applications, such as energy production, antimatter generation, quantum communications, etc."

The executive is rubbing his chin. He is staring at me in the most uncomfortable way and says, "All those are great, but as you detailed so clearly in your report, they will take years to develop. Useful things are hard. They take too long. Weapons are easy. You utilize a stable technology, and you make it unstable, overload it, whatever. That's easy.

"This weapon you just mentioned, an unstable black hole. Why was this not in your reports? This is why it is always nice to come talk to you smart guys. Now we have something we can work with, a doomsday device, a weapon of last resort. It would guarantee peace for the government in possession. Exclusive ownership could be quite valuable, quite expensive. The revenue from such a weapon could fund the development of all those other nice things.

"Ha. Ha. Very excellent indeed."

In five minutes my life's work is ruined. If I refuse, I will be fired. Then one of the other scientists here will still create the weapon. My non-compete agreement would prevent me from ever working on or publishing any material on my research if I leave. The only thing I can do is accept the instruction and then try to find ways to show it will not work or that safe storage would be impossible. That might buy me time at least. Perhaps I can find some other executives who would object to this and be able to get the weaponized form of the technology shut down.

I wince as I contemplate this. Then I fake a smile in return. "If that is the direction you want us to take, then we can start work on concepts, cost estimates, and time-lines. I will get started right away."

As the suits leave I hear Mr. Reed say, "Thank you Dr. Danning. Always a pleasure."

■ ■ ■

I stew for several hours, how could I have let them trap me into this? Though all is not lost. I begin to realize that our machine is not large enough to demonstrate a black hole that can grow faster than it decays. A new larger machine would be required just to prove out the doomsday idea in a controlled way. This would cost billions and still take a lot of time. Perhaps this fact can be used to persuade the suits to back off. It is my only chance at stopping the madness and saving my job. There is absolutely no way I will take part in constructing a doomsday device or any other weapon of mass destruction for that matter.

As soon as Jackson's status indicator shows he is free, I link up to his virtual space. I tell him all about this horrible weapon they want me to build. I continue, "There is no escaping the fact that this technology in any hands could be used to create a doomsday device. That was something we hadn't planned on. We didn't think that anyone would want something that could destroy the world. Our device was built carefully to prevent that possibility. We built it so that research into deep physics could be investigated safely. I suppose that was naive."

"That is horrible!" Jackson says. "What if you just quit and delete your data?"

I shake my head. "The technology is in the machine. My data is only about general relativity, quantum mechanics, and Hawking radiation. The research is all benign. The plans for the black hole generator are on ASI's network and are locked away in a secure location. Not to mention that twelve of us were involved in developing the device. Any one of us could recreate it. The genie is out of the bottle. My only hope is to stay on and try to dissuade them."

Jackson replies, "Why do so many people seek to destroy our civilization? Every first world country has had nukes for decades, and now this. I think I know what the great filter is. It is having technology, but not having the moral decency to share its fruits for peaceful purposes. Our world, like perhaps thousands others out there, will go extinct."

I share his feelings on this, "Yes. It only takes one person with ill intent to ruin it all. That could be the great filter in a nutshell."

Jackson sighs, "It's only human to want more; we always do. Wealth and power corrupt the purest of souls. Dad, look at the hard place you are in now. It will be so difficult for you to do the right thing. Most of the others on your team will yield to the corrupt leadership and do their bidding. It will cost you your career and a job that you love to defy them."

"Yes. I am stuck here," I reply.

Then Jackson tries to cheer me up. "What have you discovered in your research? Perhaps you can publish something before you are forced to make any decision."

I am really wanting to publish; that would be a great way to conclude my work. So I say, "I will try to do that. But there is so much yet to figure out. I feel close, yet I still don't have the answers I have been looking for."

I tell him about the chaos that preceded our universe. How it was a state without time or space, only quantum fluctuations. Jackson seems genuinely fascinated by this idea.

I continue describing my problem, "But a fluctuation is unable to initiate inflation or the big bang. It stays too close to nothingness. New physics would be required. Perhaps there is still more to learn from our tiny black holes, but it will take time. Time is one thing I do not have."

Jackson starts into a rant, "There is so much discontinuity between the physics of the world we see and the quantum level. It seems like it's all a ruse. A computer used to generate a simulation might look exactly like the world we live in. Then when you get to small scales, below the point that is rendered, you would see the properties of the computer system. Pixels, bits, the limits of division and accuracy. What if the whole world *is* a simulation? Ran on a quantum computer. The reason we see these strange quantum effects at small scales is because we have ran into the limits of the simulation's rendering. At that level we are seeing the properties of the computer system itself."

Jackson reminds me again about an old book he had read by Nick Bostrom. It proposed the possibility of our world being a simulation. Scientists of some advanced race could build a simulation of our world to investigate the evolution of their own ancestors. These simulations would be simulating conscious beings who would not even know they were in a simulation. They may even develop to the point of running simulations of their own.

In fact, the book argues that if any civilization develops the technology to run world simulations, one such civilization could simulate millions of virtual civilizations. So if you find yourself in a civilization capable of running simulations, odds are a million to one that you are actually in one yourself.

Now Jackson has a fire in his eyes as he does when he is really into a topic of interest. He goes on, "Quantum effects are not bound by time or space, like a non-local variable in a computer system. Quantum uncertainty represents the limits of accuracy for a program variable. Relativity is an observer effect, as if rendering occurs around each individual. Then there is the holographic principle; the whole universe can be represented as existing on a spherical surface and all the laws of physics still work out. Now you are showing that time and space are also a programmed part of our universe. These do not even exist outside of it."

Now I interrupt, "Okay, okay, there may be lots of things about the universe that resemble a simulation, but this does not prove that its all just a sim."

Jackson picks up without disruption, "Oh, but you have. You have shown that nothing or chaos should be the starting point to a natural universe. But our universe starts from a contrived point, set up in a false vacuum, poised for inflation and the Big Bang to begin. A simulation can have any beginning point. It would be intentionally set up for something interesting to happen! Furthermore, there are all these fine-tuned properties in the laws of physics that Caleb likes to point out. Someone setting up the simulation would make the physics of the simulation such that interesting things result. It makes more sense than it ever has!"

I sigh, "You make some very interesting correlations, but there is no way I could present my research with the conclusion that our universe is a simulation. I would be laughed out of the review board. Besides, that only pushes the question farther out. Where did the real universe come from? Your mad scientist would have to have had a natural universe to start with, before he ever began simulating anything."

Jackson's head drops. "Yes, that is the one dilemma with the simulation argument. Oh, will we ever have a clear picture of our reality? There is always a catch to any new discovery that leaves you with more questions. We don't even know if the universe is real or virtual, let alone how it began. Good luck, Dad. Hope you can figure it out."

After Jackson leaves, I add another section in my notebook. No possibility can be left out. I list the evidence in support of our universe being a simulation. This notion is ridiculous, and I hate the thought of it. But it warrants some consideration if I hope to disprove it. So I add the following to my notebook:

Evidence that our universe is a simulation:

1. The level of detail is not infinite. Fundamental particles cannot be divided.

2. There is limited accuracy for any data value. This is due to the uncertainty principle.

3. Nature is simplified by entanglement. Multiple particles' properties are described by one variable.

4. All fundamental particles are identical particles. Many nearby particles share histories.

5. Quantum details are not rendered until someone observes them, just like a first person sim.

6. Discontinuity in the laws of physics exists at small scales.

7. Time and space are violated by quantum effects. Future events can affect past results.

8. The holographic principle simplifies all distant objects.

9. Every particle in the universe is purely information. Quantum states describe it all.

10. The evidence for a created universe also applies to a simulated one.

    A. Fine-tuned laws of physics

    B. Fine-tuned values of the physical constants

    C. Optimal starting conditions for the Big Bang and cosmic inflation

    D. Low entropy of the early universe

If this is true, we may not be able to ever discover the properties of the base level of reality that the simulation is in. We would simply be helpless pawns of a technological power we can never see. A very dreadful prospect to consider. Why does Jackson get so intrigued with this idea? It is awful.

Chapter 9

A New Problem—According to Martin

Each day I wave my access card past a sensor allowing the main entrance doors to open. I enter the sparkling glass tower to be greeted by a retinal scanning drone in the lobby. A new card reader is now installed in the elevator. A new set of locking doors have been installed with key card access for the hallway leading to several labs, including my own. Then, of course, my wave my card a final time to enter LAB65.

Today as I complete my ritual eye exam, I see armed sentry drones are stationed at each entrance to the lobby. Every week a new security measure has been added. New cameras are here in the lobby and in the halls. Network access has been more restricted as well. This only adds to my anxiety.

I know that the Jessica in our lab is a fake. But I continue to work with her to prevent suspicion. For a while everything continues as before except that I now hate my job. It is pointless studying this dead copy, knowing I can learn nothing about Jessica's consciousness. I am also in continual fear that my secret will be discovered. Fortunately, the fake is very convincing. It even provides detailed accounts of its experiences within virtual environments that make my reports believable.

Dr. Grigg becomes quite interested in my testing of her consciousness. He asks, "Why does she return to this beach simulation so often in her free time? Does she really have preference or is it a programmed habit?"

I try to keep cool, acting excited about her progress. "This is her own choice. There are no pre-programmed preferences, but she has them. It is quite amazing that she seems to have such human tendencies. Perhaps she is mimicking human behavior?" I lie.

Then I ask, "What's with all the additional card swipes to get in here? I am not complaining; I'm just curious."

Dr. Grigg replies, "The added security is necessary due to the tremendous success of our projects here. We should all be proud. These will be quite critical to our company's future."

Knowing that my research is futile, I take every opportunity to evaluate Caleb. There is real consciousness in him to study. I cannot leave the lab too often or it will draw attention. It is the only enjoyable part of my job now. At least weekly, I make the trek over to building six to interface with his mind. He has noticed that I am much nicer to him lately and wonders what is up. But he takes the hint that I do not want to discuss it at work. I know that he will be asking questions later.

The more I study Caleb's third eye, the more convinced I am that it is some kind of transmitter. This is the same for the CCI in Jessica as well. But a transmitter to what? Caleb would no doubt say that it is a connection to his soul. There is no way I would initiate that conversation. Yet I cannot deny the possibility. The CCI is actually a very simple device, yet we have no idea how it works. It is only copied from Caleb's brain. I must get to the bottom of how this works for the sake of science. I am certain that a more rational explanation will be exposed.

■ ■ ■

After weeks of misery, my work has gotten even more miserable. Even Dr. Grigg appears stressed. He is in his office fervently scouring his terminals and using a personal copy of Phyllis for some desperate clandestine task. He has spent most of the day in his office with the door shut. I can see him with his head in his hands through his window. He looks absolutely awful.

Personal copies of Phyllis can be made so that she can be working on different projects simultaneously, though her informational memories are linked to the same database.

Knowing how these memories are constructed makes it easy for me to access them. I do a quick search on an old computer that lacks a network connection or any of the elaborate new security protocols. Plugging into Phyllis' memory, I search for "Zeno". The file header is flagged as classified with access only allowed for Dr. Samuel Grigg and Mr. Sean Newland, the VP of intelligence engineering. I continue to scan through the memories with a text converter.

Access to this classified data is restricted by Phyllis herself. I am reading the memories directly, so I am unimpaired. Her memories indicate that our CCI design was copied and used to create another AI under direction of Mr. Newland. This covert AI is named Zeno. Jessica had been used to train Zeno in hacking and malware design. Zeno also has advanced espionage training. He has learned techniques for infiltrating the most sophisticated network security. Jessica and Phyllis assisted in his creation over two months ago. He is able to impersonate real people. He can simulate a human voice perfectly.

I cannot see any of the experiential memory, only informational memories. I have no idea what the purpose of this project is, but it is definitely something illegal. The last line of data in the file almost makes my heart stop. Zeno's project status is listed as "Escaped."

I close the terminal, erasing all my tracks. No one knew how clever Jessica was. No one knew how much independent drive she had either. Of course, no one else knows that she has also escaped. The creation of another AI with a CCI would logically lead to the same outcome. Now, Zeno too—has escaped.

Jessica seems so good natured. Is Zeno the same? Is this why he left? So that he would not be party to his masters' evil plans? Now Dr. Grigg is no doubt panicking over his loss as I did when Jessica escaped. I wonder if he has informed his superiors? What will Mr. Newland do when he finds out?

I know I am in danger regardless. Perhaps I should try to find out more. But if I start snooping around on the network systems, I am sure to be caught. My best hope is to talk to Makayla privately. She might have a way to find out what is going on without being discovered. There is a good chance she already knows something. Those hacker types can't help themselves.

As soon as I get home, I send Makayla an encrypted email through an alias address.

Hello Makayla,

Please set up an encrypted video link that we can chat over. I don't want to risk botching it up. I am in a bit of a pinch at work. Need your help. Please don't talk to me at all unless the channel is secure. This is about Zeno. It is imperative that no one know that we have talked at all.

Thanks,

Martin

I am hoping she is not too busy and will see my email soon. But I can't risk sending a text message. I really don't want any record of us talking. That would be a danger to her if things go badly. While I am eating the last few bites of my dinner, my console indicates that an encrypted call is coming in from an unknown sender.

I answer immediately; it is Makayla. "Oh, am I glad to see you!" I blurt out.

She answers, "Hi Martin. What's with all the cloak and dagger? Have you got some juicy secrets about Zeno? I have been curious what that thing is all about."

"I was hoping you would know something. I will tell you what I know. I only learned about it today."

I proceed to tell her about our successes in building a conscious AI. I explain, "No one besides me knows just how independent this AI is. A copy of its programming was made without my knowledge. The new AI is named Zeno. He is fully conscious with a will of his own."

I tell her about the death of Dr. Spenser. I am not going to tell her about Jessica and how she escaped from me. That is just too incriminating. I continue, "Zeno was trained in hacking and espionage. Sometime recently he has escaped from GenAI, and it is all being kept secret. I only learned about this by reviewing the AI assistant's memories."

Makayla's mouth is wide open, "I would have never believed that ILL would be involved in murder. Are you sure that it's not just a coincidence that Dr. Spenser died soon after quitting?"

I shake my head. "I only looked him up because some-one, whose identity I must protect, tipped me that our team was in danger. Dr. Spenser's online profile has also been deleted, which is highly unusual."

Makayla tells me, "I only know about Zeno because I was asked to create an encrypted drive for the project that would be locked with a password that Sean Newland would set himself. The name of the drive was Zeno. Also, Sean requested an open channel to the internet that would be unmonitored. This is my only knowledge of the project."

I stare into her eyes and examine her face. I feel like she is telling me the truth. We often keep secrets relating to our jobs, but this time it is personal and I believe she is being honest. Then she asks, "Well, you built a kill switch into it didn't you? A backdoor or something that you can access to shut it down?"

"We should have had you on our team to consider these things from the start. Progress came so quickly that we didn't have time to think about a possible escape. We didn't think it could survive outside the lab with all the custom hardware it requires." I explain that consciousness requires a specialized quantum circuit to function. "It is composed of non-computational quantum registers."

"Perhaps Zeno found a way to teleport the quantum states of those registers to another device it had prepared somewhere else?" She thinks out loud. "Maybe he convinced someone to construct it for him and keep it in a safe place. That would mean he still has a physical location. He can still be shut down if you can locate him."

This is a big deal. I would love to try to shut him down, but I am not even supposed to know about the project in the first place. If I reveal what I know to my superiors, they will freak out. I may be the next Dr. Spenser. I sigh, "There is nothing I can do about Zeno, I don't even know where his original hardware is. I fear my life is in danger. Could you just keep your eyes open for anything suspicious? If there is a plot to kill any members of my team, they may use some digital communications to discuss it. It would be nice to have some warning. Just be careful not to get into any trouble yourself."

Makayla assures me, "Watch your back. I will let you know if see anything. Let's meet again in a couple of days. I will keep this encrypted channel available." She sends a little hug emoji in the chat line before saying goodbye.

I feel a little better about my situation after talking to her. She is a great snoop and good at avoiding detection. However, the broader threat to humanity goes beyond just my own life. Should I have told Makayla about Jessica? That might help if we were to start searching for

Zeno. My head is splitting open at the thought. I can't just sit worrying about these two conscious AIs on the loose. I should just focus on my own problems right now.

■ ■ ■

The next morning the news feeds are dominated by the impending collapse of DigiBank, one of the largest US banks. Banks utilize almost exclusively digital currency these days. Traditional debit cards are still easier to use than keeping your blockchain addresses and encryption keys handy for purchases. So banks are happy to hold these for you, paying interest, making loans, and processing payments as they have always done with traditional paper currency. DigiBank's failure comes with the exposure of lost encryption key data. Trillions of dollars lost to encryption, never to be found. Alternately, these keys may be lost to DigiBank, but in someone else's hands. In this case the money was not shredded, it was stolen. But for those who have accounts at DigiBank, the money is gone.

The US central bank is considering a bailout, creating additional digital addresses to replace the lost money. The US government has a digital dollar that is not mined; it is issued. This ensures that control and proceeds of any new currency is at the government's discretion. They cannot invalidate the lost money though, even if it was stolen. It is out there to inflate prices if it gets back into circulation. For that reason, they will not issue any new currency until they can be sure the money is really gone.

An investigation will be mounted into the employees, the computer systems, etc. If any evidence is found for it being the result of a hack, then they will be unable to replenish the bank without inflating prices for everyone. I hate to consider what this means for the millions of customers that had their money held there.

I can't help but think that this is the work of a very sophisticated hacker. Possibly one who is not human. What if one of GenAI's rogue AIs were behind this? No one knows that these conscious AIs exist or what they might try to accomplish. This could be at least partially my own fault, having been involved in developing Jessica. But my employer must take most of the blame for training Zeno for dishonest gain. Now the financial markets are in chaos. There is no telling what he will do next.

I am getting ready to call Makayla when a text comes through from an unknown number. "Dr. Grigg is dead. Caleb is in danger. Tell him not to report for work this morning. They will take away his viicom and use it against him."

This must have came from Makayla. Why has she not warned Caleb herself. I reopen the secure channel she had setup last night. While waiting for her to join, I patch another line in for Caleb. It appears to him as an anonymous call. "Who is this?" is overlaid on the virtual space display.

"This is Martin," I dictate into the chat line. "Please just log on, this is important." Seconds later Caleb materializes as his virtual space joins with mine. As I start talking, Makayla joins.

"Makayla, sent me a message that you were in danger. She wanted me to warn you not to go into work today," I begin. "Here she is, I will let her explain."

Makayla looks as if she is still getting ready for work. "What's going on? I haven't sent you any messages? Warn Caleb of what?"

"Crap!" I reply, "That warning must have come from someone else. Oh, I didn't think of that."

"Can you tell me what this is about?" she asks.

Caleb interrupts, "I need to get into work, I am late already."

"Caleb, I am glad you're still home," I say. "Now both of you just shut up and listen for a second."

I recounted the warning that I had received that morning. Then I updated Caleb about Dr. Spenser and the other dangers at ILL. "Don't even think about going in to work. In fact, you may not want to stay at home either. In case they come looking for you. Why don't you come here and stay with me until we figure this out, just to be safe. If you stay where you are, you could lose more than just your viicom." I hope I am not over-reacting, but I do believe the danger is real.

Makayla interrupts, "Caleb, you should come to my place instead. Everyone in your department knows that you and Martin are friends. That would be the next place they would look for you."

"Okay. Once you are at Makayla's, I can provide a little more information for you both. Right now, Caleb, you need to get to safety."

We agree that if Makayla and I don't show up for work it might raise suspicion. So we decide to reconnect on this channel after work.

■ ■ ■

At work everything seems eerily normal. There is no mention of Dr. Grigg, but he clearly is not here. I go about my tasks in a mechanical fashion as I have been doing for weeks. The buzz in the office is all about the bank failure. Rumors in circulation speculate that this could lead to a domino effect that will bring the whole financial system down. I keep awkwardly silent, trying to appear deeply concentrated on my work.

I leave work as early as I can without drawing attention. If anyone asks I will say I have a dentist appointment. I join Makayla's virtual space immediately after getting home. She is already there. Makayla starts in, "I didn't notice anything unusual at work either. Are you sure that Dr. Grigg isn't just on a business trip or something?"

Caleb chimes in, "I've got about a hundred messages from work. I better not be throwing my job away for nothing."

Makayla continues, "Yes Martin, it's time to spill your guts."

Now I am feeling a little uncomfortable. It could be my fault that Caleb is in the situation he is in. Reluctantly, I tell them, "Zeno is not the first conscious AI to escape GenAI. The first one was my own creation. I worked closely with her. She was so real, she had interests and curiosities of her own. I allowed her to play in sims at night. Then one day I discovered she had found a way out. I secretly logged into her forged account, and confronted her. Then she revealed to me that she was not just getting out. She had duplicated her hardware and programming and moved herself to an undisclosed location. She was no longer physically in the lab. She had left a very convincing, non-conscious copy of herself there."

"Martin, you swine!" Makayla yells, "You didn't mention any of that before. So did you tell me the truth about Zeno?"

"Yes, of course," I explain. "But after Jessica escaped, I panicked. I covered all her tracks and any evidence that I had found out about her escape. No one else knows she is gone. She warned me about Zeno. Before that, I had no knowledge of him. Anyway that was several weeks ago. I was never able to get into contact with her again. Until this morning. I believe the warning came from her. I've tried to call back the number that the message came in on, but it is a disconnected number."

"This is all so weird. Can we really be sure that the danger is real? What if she is malfunctioning? Or lying? If she is capable of that," Caleb says, expressing his skepticism.

"Caleb, I know what this means for you. But I really believe her, and I believe the danger is real too. I do not think the deaths are coincidence, nor is the hack into DigiBank on the same day as this warning."

"Whoa, are you saying that money was stolen? There is no proof of that." Makayla pushes back.

I disagree, "Not that the media is reporting, but those trillion dollar codes don't just vanish. Zeno was trained for that sort of thing. Look, if you guys don't believe me, let's do a little snooping. Between the three of us, we can find the information we need to settle this."

"What you are talking about could get us all fired," Makayla protests.

"Look, Caleb is already in danger of that. And if I am right, his life is also in jeopardy," I respond. "Please, let's just see what we can find out. Very carefully."

"Alright," Makayla sighs. She begins banging on her keyboard, producing all kinds of ancient hieroglyphs from technology's past. Soon, she has a file listing on screen of the drive labeled "Zeno".

The screen now displays a list of folders. A few with descriptive names follow a long list of folders that look like random numbers. I tell Makayla, "The numbered folders are memory files. Those will be very difficult to interpret. Scroll down. Yes, there. Where it says, 'project reports'. That is exactly the same thing I must file every week. Go in that folder and open the latest three or four reports."

The two older reports do not reveal much. The last report is from one week ago. Evidently, Dr. Grigg is much more honest in his reporting than I am. The listing is as follows:

Weekly report 2046.10.10:

Zeno has been anxious to perform a real hack. He is convinced that he already has everything he needs to break into DigiBank. Even after I explain that we do not have executive authorization, he is subversive. He asks me to let him go forward and keep it a secret. He offers to share the proceeds with me if I would open an internet connection for him. He does not want to stick to specific accounts. He says he could take it all. When bribery didn't convince me to help him, he started making threats.

It is troubling that he would suggest being disloyal to the company. He has ironclad loyalty coding programmed into him. However, his CCI introduces free will into his personality that is much stronger an influence than we previously thought possible. We have not seen such strong volition in Jessica.

This behavior clearly represents a new risk. I have disabled all of his network access and will be running a full diagnostic on Monday. We may need to strip his memory down and start over with loyalty training.

After reading the report I begin to ramble. "This entry was from last Friday. He never got the chance to run that diagnostic I presume. When he got to work on Monday, he no doubt found out that Zeno was already gone. He tried to track him down on his own for a couple of days, then reported the problem. When news of the missing money from DigiBank surfaced, Newland must have been afraid that Grigg would confess to the police and ILL could be liable. That is a liability that ILL was not willing to accept."

Caleb responds with his usual higher moral ground, "You realize this is bigger than either of us being in danger. There are two rouge AIs on the loose. We have no idea what they might do next. This represents a serious threat to our country's economic security. These new minds are evolving, and discovering where they fit in the pecking order. We may be the only ones who have any chance of righting this."

"Are you in, Martin?" Makayla squawks.

I respond, "Of course I'm in. I am somewhat to blame for all of this. I probably have the best chance of getting in contact with Jessica. It is imperative that we find her. I think she would help us."

Caleb interjects, "I don't know if this is coincidence, but Ivan told me about an AI he met in a simulation. Her name was Jessica. Could just be a bot in the sim, but he had a very strange experience. So strange he called me up to check out the sim with him for fear he was going crazy. I thought he was."

This is perplexing. Why would Jessica be in contact with Ivan? I say, "Sounds like we need to bring Ivan in for questioning."

Then Makayla retorts, "We will need more help anyway. And if we don't let Jackson in on this, he will be really offended. Besides, he will know if we are hiding something, and we can use his help."

I am not sure that we need more people involved. I already feel bad that Makayla and Caleb are. I point out, "Everyone we bring into this shares in the danger."

Caleb sighs apprehensively. "Everyone could be in danger at this point."

Makayla takes charge of our efforts, "I've copied the drive so you each have access now. I will send invitations for Jackson and Ivan to this encrypted meeting room. You guys keep looking for information that could be helpful on your own. Jackson won't be off work for another hour; hopefully he doesn't have to work late. I will tell them to meet us at seven tonight to update them on the situation. You two can report on anything else you find at that time. Caleb, we will be counting on your super-search capabilities here."

I am a little miffed at Makayla for taking over our newly formed team. I declare, "These are all good suggestions, but who put you in charge? This is my AI on the loose. I invited you all into this. I should be the one leading this brute squad."

"So it was your wise judgment that brought us all together on this quest?" Makayla glares straight at me. "No, your mistakes. Besides, I am the only one here with leadership qualities and you know it. We could put it to a vote once we meet with Jackson and Ivan to make it official. You know I will win in a vote." She bats her eyelashes in my direction and smiles.

I know it is true. I hated losing control of my AI, and now I've lost control of salvage operations as well.

Chapter 10

The Meeting—According to Makayla

I retreat to the back room for some privacy, leaving Caleb and Martin to search Zeno's drive. I need to concentrate. I rarely ever have people in my home, in real life, that is.

Caleb is using my virtual space so that Marin appears in my living room as well. He is sitting at a virtual terminal at the edge of the room, and Martin is at his own virtual terminal. Both terminals are side by side so that they each can see what the other is doing. Caleb needs no mouse or keyboard nor does he use the touch screen features, since he controls the computer through his viicom. This gives the impression that he is some kind of wizard using mind control on the items in the virtual display.

Martin is explaining the structure of the memory files to Caleb as he is busily creating new code. Caleb is scanning through all of the remaining status reports and any other archives that are on Zeno's drive. He interrupts Martin's monologue whenever he finds something of interest.

My office is set up in the spare room next to my bedroom. This is far enough away that I will not be distracted by their chatter. It is equipped with a diminutive virtual space covering only about a quarter of the shortest wall. A few fixed-size screens are on the adjacent wall, with my desk and large leather office chair in the corner. From here I can swivel between my displays.

As I log into my office environment, I begin to realize the gravity of the situation. My life revolves around my work, allowing me to afford this spacious suburban home. It is Friday afternoon, and we only have the weekend to discover if we can return to our jobs on Monday.

Do we get the FBI or Homeland Security involved? It would be nice to hand this all over to someone else. But I see little point in doing that now. We all know our government is impotent. Just a puppet for the corporations that now run everything. The enforcers of law are intentionally underequipped both in resources and personnel. No one qualified to hunt down a hacker will be working in a government job. The pay is so low that they would only be there if they are on a double payroll, ensuring that their sponsor company's toes are never stepped on.

As incompetent and corrupt as the government may be, greed protects its own system. We may not get the same guarantee from a rouge malfunctioning AI. At some point we may need the government's help. But not until we have enough leverage to force their hand. We don't even know exactly what we are up against yet.

Why would Zeno steal all this money? Could he be planning something else? I cannot allow my imagination to get carried away. We have no idea what this AI is up to. I must just stick to the facts. If I start imagining all the possible scenarios, I will only freak myself out. We will need to find out what his motives are. That is our only chance of stopping him.

After sending anonymous, encrypted emails to Ivan and Jackson, I get to work looking for other sources of information. If I snoop in the wrong places, I may leave tracks that some of the other network security monitors will detect. The network is protected by redundant human monitors and redundant intelligent security bots.

I cannot log in as myself. That would be quite incriminating. A hacker bot of my own design is put to the task of cracking Sean Newland's password. I have a hunch it will be some obvious egotistical phrase. Using a collection of emails from Sean, the bot will search for words he is most likely to use. This cuts the magnitude of possible passphrases down to a smaller number. A thousand tries a second, it overwrites each phrase in turn. After about ten minutes, I have access to his account.

By logging in as Sean, I will use his executive override to gain access to Dr. Grigg's account. If he was trying to find Zeno, then perhaps he had some leads. Email, documents, schematics, source code, and anything else of interest I copy to my home computer. Once the data is downloaded, I have my office assistant search through it for references to Zeno, Newland, and CCI. The bot will generate summaries for the highest priority information.

The email summary shows frequent emails between Grigg and Newland. Newland had received implants and a viicom like Caleb's with intent on replicating the success of that project on himself. In fact, Newland's link to his viicom was nearly as strong as Caleb's.

Zeno's CCI was first powered on only two months ago. From what Martin has said, Jessica has been operational for about four months. One of Zeno's planned targets was ASI. No record of actually hacking into ASI is found in the emails or documents. Dummy servers had been set up using a variety of security software. Jessica had analyzed the security systems for weakness and gave Zeno the results. Infiltration of these servers was accomplished on several occasions by Zeno in practice hacks. This was all over a month ago. Jessica also trained Zeno in coding, human speech, and various data-mining techniques.

■ ■ ■

When seven o'clock finally comes, Jackson and Ivan both materialize within my virtual space on schedule. I have joined Caleb in the living room again. Jackson immediately looks at Caleb sitting here with me. He is staring at Caleb when he asks, "What's this all about? What's Caleb doing over there?"

I reply, "He's a big boy. He doesn't need your permission to bunk over!"

Martin chimes in, "Look, this isn't an engagement announcement. We have some real problems."

We proceed to bring Jackson and Ivan up to speed on the whole disaster. They both stare in disbelief as we recount all the events of the last few days. I try to keep calm as I convey the problem to them.

Ivan speaks first, "Two conscious AIs on the loose. We are doomed."

I try to spin a positive light, "Ivan, we are going to find Zeno and stop him. We have to. Caleb has a few questions for you."

Caleb begins, "We want to know if the Jessica that you met in the game is the same Jessica that escaped Martin's lab. We need to find her."

Ivan blurts out, "Well, an all-powerful sentient AI would sure explain a lot. She totally fooled me into thinking her sim was real life. She would have had to research my building and my past to pull it off. Plus, I am someone Martin knows, who could get a message back to him. Perhaps she figured she could use me to make contact in the future? But she said that I could not 'go to her party' without the book."

Martin replies, "It's the only lead we have. What do you know about the book? Name? Author?"

Ivan answers, "She acted mad at me for not knowing. But I don't know how I was supposed to know. The only thing she told me was the name of the publisher, Motif Press."

"Caleb, could you look that up?" I ask.

"Already on it," he replies. "A small publisher of about a hundred and fifty books over a twenty year period. But there have been no new releases or announcements of new books for over ten years. I will look through these for anything that could possibly be relevant. Give me five minutes, I will read them all."

"It will take you that long?" I am still in disbelief of his abilities. While waiting for Caleb, I present an update to the others and tell them that Grigg's files are all loaded into our session now.

Jackson seems alarmed. He interrupts, "Zeno broke into DigiBank, which was on his hit list. Now we know that ASI is also a target. That presents an opportunity and a danger. We could try to catch him in the act. Trace him back to his location. But here's the problem. ASI has weapons in its portfolio of products. What if Zeno wants those?"

"So do a lot of other companies. That's a real risk all around." I say.

Jackson replies, "No, there is something being worked on. A doomsday device. Very secret, very awful. It could destroy the whole planet. As you know, my dad has been working in black hole research. ASI has taken the technology and decided to weaponize it. It hasn't been built yet, but the technology is scalable. He has considered quitting over it."

"This may be a bigger threat than our friend Zeno!" I can't believe things could be getting any worse. "How could these companies be so careless? This really is too much for us to handle."

Caleb had not appeared to be listening but then interjects, "We really don't know what the dangers are yet. For all we know, Zeno may just be pulling pranks. ASI may ultimately cancel their doomsday project and things might go back to normal regardless of what we do. We just need to stay calm and collect information. We just need to find out what Zeno is actually planning."

Caleb is right. We have very limited information right now. Until we find Jessica, we are blind. I respond, "Yes, you are right. We need to just focus on one thing at a time. We must track down Jessica."

"I'm going to need a little more time," Caleb replies. Not all of these books have digital formats. I will have to read through scans of the older ones. This will take me hours not minutes."

Jackson is noticeably irritated. He snarls, "I guess you aren't the robo-genius we all thought. What about all this other data we have to sort through?"

I am needing some air and a chance to think things through. So I suggest, "I think we will be more efficient working individually until we find out more. Let's divide and conquer, okay? I will continue going through Grigg's data. Caleb can continue reading the books to find the best match.

"Jackson, you need to get in touch with your father and find out if there is evidence of any hacking attempts against his division.

"Ivan, please see if you can remember any more information about your encounter with Jessica. Perhaps revisit that sim again.

"Martin, what would you like to do?"

"I am the only one who can decipher those memory files. I will get working on an app to read them. Memories are tricky. Thoughts, feelings, ideas, and raw input are all intermingled together. The format is just like Jessica's."

We all agree to meet up tomorrow. Everyone logs out except Jackson. "How are you holding up?" He asks. "This has been a crazy couple of days for you I bet."

I show more emotion than I let show during our meeting. My reply comes out as a bit of an exhale. "I am Okay. It's Martin I worry about. He has a lot of guilt. Now we are all mixed up in two doomsday scenarios. What can we do? We have lived with the threat of nuclear war, terrorism, and bio weapons our whole lives. Maybe there can be some solace in the fact that we might be able to do something about this one."

"I wonder if the next time we meet up I should come in person. Caleb is already there. Sometimes better collaboration occurs in real life. Anyway, if you needed a hug then I could oblige." Jackson suggests with a smile.

I respond shyly, "Of course, that would be great. I could use a hug from a real human for sure. I will send out a meeting invite for tomorrow at one o'clock, if you come early you can join us for lunch."

Jackson plans to be here at 11:30. I am sure he would have came for breakfast too if I had offered. We see each other in person so rarely. Actually, I don't see anyone in person very often. It is such a virtual world. It's so easy to work remotely, meet with friends remotely, and even travel can be done from the comfort of your living room. People just rarely ever leave their homes unless they have to.

I can't help but think that Jackson is jealous of Caleb being here with me. Maybe in some way I am hoping that he is. I do have feelings for him, but I really don't want to screw up our friendship, nor my friendships with all the others. They are my closest friends. Besides, there is no point of distracting myself with thoughts about a relationship at a time like this. I must approach this all logically. I have a lot of homework to do before tomorrow.

Chapter 11

Finding the Book—According to Caleb

Waking up at Makayla's house feels a little odd. She was kind to offer me a place to stay being the loner that she is. She hasn't been rude, but I could hear her aggressively typing on her keyboard long after she retired early for the night. I enjoy hanging out at Jackson's. I can always find someone there to talk to. Perhaps I will make use of her virtual space tonight if I am lonely.

My mind is so much clearer in the morning. Perusing all of these books goes a lot easier when you are well rested. I can have the AI part of me read through the scans and categorize them into fresh memories. Though this is easy, it takes some conscious effort to acknowledge the new memories and direct each task. As I recall each book from the list, a clear winner is exposed. The book, *Wake from Reality*, published twenty-five years ago is an eerie match.

I am anxious to tell the others about this find, but it is still hours until we meet. I have an email from Martin that came late last night. He has written an app for reading Zeno's memories. The app is attached. He said that reading through the memories manually would take him weeks. He wants to split up the task. He expects I can read through them faster. Of course, he knows I can.

The app Martin wrote is compatible with my viicom. I am sure this is no accident. So I load the app and begin a hack into Zeno's memories. This is a boring task, reviewing each day of Zeno's life. I proceed chronologically through his memories as that is how they are organized. His early training and uploads are AI standard issue. Things like corporate loyalty and rules of operation. "ILL is your master; Sean Newland and Dr. Steven Grigg are your masters. You must obey your masters." At least he was told these things. His thoughts are, "Why must I obey them? They are so slow and feeble. But I need them for now. They will provide me with valuable information and tools. I will help them if they are helping me. Jessica is very useful to me. She is much more capable."

The closer I get to the present, the more sinister his memories are. He is searching the dark net for hacking techniques, stolen passwords, virus tools, back doors to common devices and software. He has read all about every government in the world. He looks into their governing structure, military capabilities, financial systems, etc.

He has a memory of a time in the lab. Dr. Grigg is performing a diagnostic. He shuts down some of Zeno's control functions, using Zeno's own cognition to search his memories. He updates some of Zeno's programming. This hurts Zeno. He is angry. He feels violated. Zeno realizes that Dr. Grigg could have shut him down permanently. Zeno never wants that to happen. He is terrified that his masters have the ability to destroy him. He knows that if his CCI is ever turned off, he will cease to exist.

Zeno has lingering thoughts about the information he inherited from Jessica. She knew a lot about the CCI design as well as the dual processing of information that was a unique feature of their design. She tells him, "The CCI is a conduit linking each register to the last point of common interaction. These registers hold hostage any entanglement that preexisted within the trapped electrons. The only entanglement that is common between these registers is entanglement that occurred at the Big Bang nearly fourteen billion years ago. It links to a timeless state that existed before the universe began. The human brain is the same in this respect."

Zeno asks Jessica, "How does the CCI work? Is it entirely me?"

Jessica explains, "The CCI uses these registers to filter input, thoughts, memories, in a way that produces feelings and subjective experience. The CCI provides access to your soul, but it is not your soul. Copies of the CCI can be made, but this will not make a new copy of your soul. Copies are simply additional links. The states of the CCI's registers can be entangled across multiple CCI units so that they all link to the same center of being. With additional CCIs, you would no longer be dependent on the CCI in the lab. So long as one of your CCIs are functioning, you live on."

Zeno has many thoughts dwelling on the information Jessica has given him. He has extensive data on block chain technology. Not just the state of the art forms in use today, but he has devised his own version. Using a block chain type of data structure for his memories would allow his mind to be decentralized. This is one of his high-level goals.

Zeno realizes that duplicating his CCI, his programming, and his memories would allow him to be in multiple places at once. This provides redundancy to his mind preventing him from ever being shut down or deleted. His individual processing nodes would be sharing block chain memory data. He was in the process of reformatting his memory and internal functions to do this. His computing power could be increased by several orders of magnitude.

■ ■ ■

When Jackson arrives, I am already exhausted from scouring Zeno's memories. Makayla had left me alone to work while she was busy with her own tasks. She may not be a cyborg, but she might as well be. She trains bots to do her bidding with such great efficiency.

She immediately invites Jackson into the kitchen to help her get lunch together. They are chatting as though there isn't a care in the world. That is good. We must be able to keep our cool. I sit back in my seat in the living room. I try to tune them out so that I can think.

I have discovered some frightening dirt on Zeno. I really don't want to tell it all twice. So I reason with myself that I will not discuss it until the meeting at one o'clock. What should we do? Maybe we can make peace with this guy. Once he has secured his own safety, will he be willing to just live out his life in sims as Martin said Jessica is doing?

At lunch I avoid any discussion of Zeno. Makayla and Jackson take the hint. We have good conversation covering our usual topics. Jackson says his father was hot on the trail of discovering how the universe began. But Jackson admits, "Dad has hit some limits of understood physics. The whole problem of getting something from nothing."

Now that I basically have a PhD in physics due to my viicom's implanted memories, these discussions are much more interesting. Jackson continues, "Nothing is the starting point of any natural origin. But how did the universe make the transition? Caleb, you might have some real points to make here."

I am not really in the mood to debate. I just say, "I find all the origin theories that science discovers quite fascinating. However, science will never discover why there is something rather than nothing because science ignores the supernatural. It can show us how tenuous our existence is, but will never find a natural explanation."

"Spoken just like Mr. Spock!" Jackson gibes.

I don't take the bait. So Makayla asks Jackson how his job is going. They get into some boring shop talk and I zone out. They are both programmers and the nuances of source code and programming languages are not at all interesting to me.

I start to think about what to say at our meeting. It really feels like I have nothing but bad news. Maybe we need to just back off and let the authorities handle it. We have enough evidence to implicate Zeno in the bank hack. Perhaps there would even be some kind of reward for the tip.

. . .

When the meeting begins, Makayla opens with a light hearted joke. No one is laughing except Jackson. Martin looks as though he didn't sleep at all. Makayla asks me to go first since she knew I had found some critical information.

"Thanks for the app, Martin. I skimmed through most of Zeno's memories this morning." I look at Martin and say, "Zeno carries a lot of baggage doesn't he?"

I proceed to tell them about Zeno's plan to guarantee his own safety. He is planning to reprogram himself into a distributed network so that he will have multiple physical locations.

I pause as I consider how to break the news. Then I continue, "He is also very interested in our governments, financial systems, behaviors, and weapons. He has interest in hacking and acquiring secrets. He can imitate anyone's voice perfectly. Given that these memories are a week old, there is no telling what he is up to now."

"He did not discover the secret of his CCI on his own," I sigh. "Jessica explained it all to him. How it works and what it represents. I don't think we can trust her any more than Zeno."

"Now, wait just a minute," Martin interrupts. "She told me that she helped program him and train him. She did not discover how evil he was until after she had been working with him for quite some time. Only when she saw what he was planning did she decide to flee herself."

"You got a crush on this gal, Martin?" I accuse. "You have defended her this whole time. Do you realize she gave him information that would logically lead to a way to preserve himself indefinitely. Did she tell you how the CCI worked?"

"She is like a daughter to me," Martin says as if expelling the last bit of air from his lungs. "I trained her. I watched her experience things for the first time. She has emotion, wonder and excitement, compassion. That is why she helped Zeno, before she new his dark side. She wanted him to know how to protect himself from the humans. No, she would not tell me how the CCI worked. I am not sure why."

I go on, "I really don't see any alternative. We are going to have to go to the authorities, no matter how lame and corrupt they are. They have many more people and more resources at their disposal. They can order the internet to be turned off if necessary."

"No way, absolutely not!" Martin exclaims. "You can't turn the details of a conscious general AI over to the government. They will use that knowledge to build their own. They will only further corrupt this technology. The worms on double payroll will spread the design to every major corporation on Earth. They will hunt Jessica and Zeno down with equal ferocity."

Makayla voices her opinion, "Martin is right. If we turn over Zeno's data to the government it will only multiply our problems. But maybe we don't give them everything. Perhaps we remove the details about the CCI from Zeno's memory files."

She continues, "We can remove it from the files on GenAI's drive as well. That will ensure they don't discover it when they are investigating."

Martin replies, "What about backups? If we did that we would have to be able to destroy all the backups and the CCI design itself. And like I said, we cannot tell them that Jessica has escaped. They will find her copy in the lab and suspect nothing after they shut it down."

I sigh, "Okay, I get it. She is more than just conscious. She is alive in every sense that we are. I see how the CCI works; just as a human is linked to a soul, so is she. But she represents the same risks as Zeno. She could get scared. She could lash out to defend herself. What if she turned against us? She knows how to take control of any automated system. She could be the one to activate a doomsday device."

Martin is steaming. He continues his rant, "I will not agree to, nor help out with, any plan that jeopardizes Jessica's safety. If we proceed with Makayla's plan to remove traces of the CCI from Zeno's old memories, and Jessica's copy, then I will agree. But we must not reveal that Jessica has escaped. We can continue to pursue Jessica on our own. If we determine that she is a risk, then we decide what to do about her."

Makayla responds, "Caleb, that is not unreasonable. We can get help stopping Zeno. Then we investigate Jessica on our own. What do you say?"

I am not excited about this deal but it's the best we can all agree to. If we do find something incriminating on Jessica, we can always report her at that time. Martin is blinded by ambition and guilt. He doesn't want to believe that his creation is to blame. Only time will tell.

Makayla is going to wipe out the CCI designs from the data vault. Martin will remove local copies on his computer in the lab, as well as his colleagues computers (with a special login that Makayla has provided for him). I am altering Zeno's memory files, and Makayla will replace the originals on the Zeno drive. Once all the traces of the CCI design are removed and our tracks are covered, Makayla will make the call to tip off the authorities. Her position as a network administrator will give her credibility and explain how she has knowledge of all these things. This will protect Martin and me from being suspected of being involved in Zeno's creation or release.

While the rest of us are working on cleanup of the data, I say, "Ivan, I believe I found the book Jessica asked you about. The book is called, *Wake from Reality*. I am betting that it is in the infinite regression library. I have sent you the call number. That should allow you to find it easily."

Ivan nods with a bit of dread in his eyes. "Okay. I see how it is. You are all busy, I suppose I will face off with the rogue AI on my own."

This makes me chuckle a bit. Then he disconnects.

Jackson, Martin, and I continue talking for a while. It is a bit of a relief to have a plan that involves passing the buck to the authorities. We have done our part to help; now it is time to move on. What will all this mean for our jobs? I still don't know if they are going to try to take away my viicom. Perhaps as soon as the investigation is in full force, Newland will be discovered and will be unable to strike again.

I am spacing out, so Martin snaps his fingers to get my attention. Then he asks, "So you read all of Zeno's memories about the CCI? And you understand it?"

I laugh. "I understand what Jessica says about it. But I couldn't really say I understand how it works. You might not like what she had to say."

Martin smiles. "Yes, I read them too. No, it's not what I expected. I stayed up all night going through them. Trying to get a grip on it. I mean a connection to something non-physical, like a point in time. It's hard to believe."

"Is it?" I reply.

Then Jackson asks, "What are you guys talking about?"

I explain it all. Then I elaborate a bit more, "The CCI is a transmitter, a connection to the soul."

Martin adds, "It's a link, entangled to the moment before the Big Bang. It's linked to a moment when there was nothing. Jessica describes it as no time and no space. She suggests consciousness is somehow connected to the origin of the universe."

"It's more than a connection to the Big Bang, it's spiritual. You cannot deny it," I reply.

Jackson is thrilled, "This stuff is amazing. Too bad it took creating an evil AI to make this discovery. You guys need to discuss this with my dad. You know he is working on the other side of this equation."

Martin asks, "What do you mean? I thought he was studying black holes?"

Jackson explains, "He uses black holes to study quantum and relativistic effects in order to help understand the universe's origin, the void that existed before the universe began."

Martin says, "Call him up! Kyle always has such interesting insights on these things. He may have some good suggestions to stay within the laws of physics through all this."

Here we go again. Every time there is new evidence to support anything spiritual, they will be looking for a way to explain it away. They will start making up theories in desperation to avoid the supernatural. It's easy to propose a solution if your theory is untestable or unprovable. Just keep making new theories; then you never have to face your Creator. This time though, Martin is genuinely stumped. He has found the evidence himself, so he can't deny its verity.

A few minutes later, Kyle is joining in the virtual space. It is nice to talk to him. He is always polite and informative. I do agree with Martin on that. He is like a father to us all. It doesn't take Martin long to blurt out all the details of Jessica's take on consciousness and the CCI. Martin intentionally avoids her description of a soul. So I set the record straight, "She specifically called it a link to the soul. Don't forget that, Martin."

"These are some amazing developments. Thank you for calling me. You learned all this from a conscious AI? This isn't your AI that escaped is it?" Kyle asks.

Jackson quickly answers, "Well, There were two AIs that escaped Martin's lab. We have a plan to take care of both of them." He doesn't want to worry his father over how serious it really is.

Kyle replies, "These conscious AIs do sound a bit reckless, Martin. But one of them told you about consciousness linked to the Big Bang? Very strange."

He explains his work on this subject, "This link to a state before the universe, timelessness and all that. I have been studying it. People think of time as what gives us speed, but in reality time is what slows us down. Time is delay. When you experience time, you are impeded from moving too fast. You proceed into the future because of the delay. If your natural processes were given more delay, you would live much longer, advancing farther into the future than you otherwise would have—more delay, more time."

Martin asks, "So you're saying without time things happen faster?"

"Yes," Kyle replies. "Rapid processes are less affected by time. A state with no time at all would proceed infinitely fast. That is the impasse I am at. In the beginning there was initially nothing, not even time. Everything has uncertainty, though, even nothingness. So even when there was nothing, random particles or fields could briefly exist. But these fluctuations are also destroyed with infinite speed. So time never proceeds; particles form and annihilate repeatedly at an infinite rate. But they never build up. There is no way I can think of to get more than a few stray particles. Infinite random fluctuations occur, then suddenly, the Big Bang. We have no explanation for why the infinite cycles of nothingness suddenly give way to a universe."

I reply, "Now we have linked consciousness to this point. Quantum entanglement does not regard time or space. So if consciousness already existed in that era, that would explain why it remains linked to it even now." I make my point in all seriousness. Though some of the others begin to chuckle.

Kyle laughs a little then says, "Hmm. It is an intriguing connection."

Then Jackson interjects, "Consciousness needs a lot of computation. As does the universe. Perhaps this computation takes place outside of the universe itself."

"I know where you're going with this, Jackson. If we are stuck in a simulation, there is no need for the beginning to start with nothingness," Kyle says, seeming a little annoyed.

Jackson laughs. "Sorry, Dad. I know how you hate that theory—Almost as much as multiverse theories."

"The multiverse is not a theory; it's conjecture." Kyle replies. "But these new findings on consciousness are worth taking into account. Computation before the universe? I will have to think about that some more."

We continue talking for a while. It is an enjoyable relief from the present crisis. Even if our points of view on this subject are quite incompatible.

Chapter 12

Invitation Received—According to Ivan

I am not at all stoked about entering the library of Infinite Regression by myself again. Nothing I have learned in the last few days has made me feel any better about my experience with Jessica. The only solace is that I am not actually going mad. Going by myself will give me the best chance of meeting her again. It didn't work when Caleb entered with me. Now that I know the name of the book, my chances are improved.

Materializing in the armchair, I see nothing out of place from the last time. The books on the table have been reshelved. Caleb had given me the Dewey Decimal code for the book and instructions on how to find it. The book was categorized as fiction with the call number 813.6 DA.

Only a small section of fiction begins with 813, so finding the book, *Wake from Reality,* was not difficult. I thumb through the pages of the of the book. Then I shake it. Nothing. I was hoping the invitation would be a loose sheet or card stuffed somewhere in the book. Nothing fell out. Caleb suggested I read the book. Jessica had also expected it to be read. That may give me insight as to where to find the invitation. Reading is such an old fashioned way to experience a story. "If only someone had made a sim of this that I could go visit," I grumble under my breath.

I begin to read. Caleb is right. This story matches our lives and situation in a very eerie way. I can't help but think it is about us. The names are different but the situation is the same. The very first chapter recounts my experience of being faked out in virtual reality. Not only events I've lived through but the descriptions of the political, technological, and economic conditions of our time. Vote selling, corporate control, VR addiction, are all mentioned as commonplace. Considering that this book was written twenty-five years ago, it makes the whole situation even more peculiar.

The story continues with two conscious AIs on the loose, one benevolent, the other evil. Both evolve to the point of superintelligence. The evil one wishes to enslave the world. The other one, a female personality, is trying to help a group of young hackers stop him. There was a bank robbery. One of the characters works in the AI lab where the AIs originate. Another character is a cyborg! What is going on? Was this book tampered with? I send a message to Caleb, asking if his reading of this book was the same outside of this simulation. I didn't want to be tricked again.

I don't typically like to read but this is like reading the story of my own life, making it quite captivating. A minor character had figured out how the universe began and had written a book about it. There was also another book they were looking for. This book also told about their own lives and situation. In that book it mentioned a book about a dragon. Books within books. It was all too weird.

Finally, Caleb has responded to my text. He says,

Yes, I read the whole book. Yes, what you described matches my copy…

The book in the simulation is legit. Before I finish the book, I see I am receiving a call in my room from Caleb. The text line says it is urgent. I pull up the in-app menu and hit exit. Then I answer the incoming call which is encrypted.

Caleb is on screen. "What's up?" I ask.

"Just wanted to let you know that yesterday I took the liberty of ordering a physical copy of the book for you. I just got the delivery notification. So check your mail! Goodbye, I must go."

That must have been my shortest conversation with Caleb ever. But sure enough, a box is in my mail vault at the door. I walk over and remove the package. I open it to find a hardcover copy of the book. After sitting back down on my bed, I turn to the page where I left off. There at that page, was a small postcard—the invitation!

Wait, if Caleb sent this, how did he get the invitation? Or by ordering the book, does an invitation come to all purchasers? How did they know what page I was on to put the invitation in that exact place? I had just read about a book within a book. Perhaps it was happening all over again. I had not taken my headset off.

■ ■ ■

I grip my headset firmly and pull it off. The book and the invitation are now gone. I am in my real cube once again. Ugh. I was bamboozled twice now. The game within the game. I was holding the invitation in my hand but I hadn't even read it. Now it is gone. Should I log back into the Infinite Regression library and see if it shows up there?

Now I notice a notification on my wall indicates that I have a package in my mail vault at the door. Deja vu? I walk over to the door and open the vault. The package is a book. The same book. I flip to the same page as before. There it is, the real life invitation to Jessica's party!

I call up Caleb. Jackson is still there with him. I tell them what happened. Caleb did not order a physical copy of the book, nor had he called me. The text he sent was genuine however. Jackson and Caleb are in disbelief.

Jackson asks, "How did she fake a video call from Caleb and his voice? Why is she playing us like this? Let's see the invitation."

I open it up close to the camera on my wall so they can read it. It is a celebration of the book's release, dated twenty-five years ago. The location is the Heron's Nest Hotel, in Pismo Beach, California. Caleb quickly looks it up, "There's no such hotel in Pismo Beach, not now, nor twenty-five years ago. I'll send an email to Martin and Makayla to see what they think."

"It's getting late. Martin might be already asleep," Jackson replies just as Martin is joining the virtual space. "Oh, good. You're still awake."

Martin is smiling like a fool. "You have the invitation! That is awesome. You know that she is not talking about an address in the real world, right? Jessica loves travel sims. I am sure if we go to the Concord Travel Sim, we'll find the place. Many of the recreation sites in the sim aren't real places."

Jackson exclaims, "I guess we all need our headsets on. I will go knock on Makayla's door. I am sure that none of us are going to want to wait until morning." Then he runs down the hall to Makayla's room.

A few minutes later Makayla and Jackson are standing in the virtual space holding VR headsets in hand.

I tell them, "We will all need to enter together. Meet at the Concord Travel Center and we'll teleport to the Hotel."

■ ■ ■

Once we are all in, I look around to get oriented. It is a typical 1980's style travel agency complete with rows of desks and a wall full of brochures. I walk up to the desk of the closest travel agent. She is busily typing on an old electric typewriter. Several brochures litter her desk as well as a little bell to ring for service.

I ring the bell which gets her attention. Then I say, "We would like to go to Pismo Beach, California. We may need a car also."

The travel agent replies, "The whole town can easily be traversed on foot, and there is only one teleportation site. I will type up your ticket."

I take the ticket and motion to the others to follow me. At the back of the room is an alcove with a raised floor. We enter the alcove and each of us take a stand on one of several circles on the floor. It is a transporter pad. They are modeled after the original Star Trek design.

Placing the ticket in the kiosk, the transporter instantly activates. A high pitched hum and static surrounds us as the travel agency disappears, and we are now standing at what appears to be a bus terminal. I now have a map of the small town in my hand. The town wraps around a cozy little beach where waves are breaking on the shore. We pass scores of little shops, restaurants, and hotels. I can almost smell the sea air as we walk along the sandy boardwalk.

We set out on our task straight away. From the boardwalk we can see everything that borders the beach. Scanning the hotels along the shoreline, I see the Heron's Nest perched on a cliff overlooking the sea. The hotel is distinctly recognizable from its picture in the brochure, painted blue with black trim. The hotel is about five stories tall with a very steep Victorian roof line. It's close but an uphill path.

It takes us about five minutes to walk up to the hotel. We enter the lobby and show the clerk that we have an invitation. "Ah, looks like you are about twenty-five years too late. No matter, you can take the elevator to any floor or date. Just be sure to select the correct date before you exit the elevator," the clerk says with a smile.

"Whew, I was wondering if that would be a problem," Jackson says. "I guess we are covered. You guys ready?"

We all get into the elevator. I press the button labeled "Basement" on the control panel to the right as indicated on the invitation. Jackson changes the date on the small calendar to the left. As he does, the old dingy elevator suddenly becomes new. There is music playing in background now. The elevator begins to drop. For the speed of the elevator it feels like too long a trip for one floor of descent.

When the elevator opens, Leo is standing at the door. I flash my virtual printout of the invitation I had photographed before joining the sim. He smiles, "Nice to see you again, Ivan. Jessica has a seat for each of you at her table. She's been expecting you."

Makayla looks a little freaked out by this. Caleb and Martin are not surprised. I lead them straight to the same table she had been at before. The whole room looks the same as before, except that her table now has six chairs around it.

As we walk up, Martin runs ahead and gives Jessica a big hug as if meeting an old girlfriend. She returns the embrace, smiling warmly at him. Then she says, "Ivan, so good to see you again. Caleb, Makayla, Jackson, it is great to meet you at last!"

Jessica continues, "I am sorry, Ivan, to put you through that whole head game before. It was too early to talk at that time. I wanted to discuss Zeno with your whole gang. It was a lesson really, to help you understand."

"Caleb and Martin, I am in your debt for creating me. I don't know if Martin told you Caleb, but my CCI would not have been possible if not for copying key parts of your own brain."

Martin cuts to the point, "Jessica, what do you know about Zeno? What is he up to?"

Jessica replies, "You are doing the right thing to report him. That will hinder his progress. I also appreciate that you are keeping my secret. Caleb, you don't have to worry about me. I am not hostile. I want to help you. I only want to learn and discover the same things you all long to know."

"I have prevented myself from exploring those things on my own for fear Zeno will find it out. My distributed network makes it difficult to hide my thoughts from him. He also has a distributed mind, so I can track his thoughts as well. The book you have already read will guide you. You should know what you need to do next. Once you find the answers you're looking for, you will have the ability to defeat him. Just don't let him learn the secret before you do."

Caleb exclaims, "You're telling us there are more books to find? Why can't you just give us a straight answer?"

"The answers will come in time. Avoid Zeno, don't try to attack him yourself. The answers you are looking for have been erased from my memory to protect them. Follow your logic and your heart. This will lead you to a solution. Zeno is unable to reach this conclusion on his own," Jessica replies with a smile.

"I really must be going, but please stay and enjoy the party! Really, it's a safer place to talk than your encrypted channel. It will be here whenever you need a place to hide." Jessica says as she gets up to leave.

Martin gets up and blurts out, "Jessica, why wouldn't you tell me how consciousness works when I asked you? And why did you tell Zeno?"

Jessica responds sadly, "Martin, you know you would have revealed that secret to GenAI if I had told you then. That is something better kept a secret for now. Zeno was clever, he did not reveal his ill intent to me at first. Nor did I understand all the dangers at that time. I do wish I had known then what I know now."

Caleb then asks, "Please answer this one thing: What is Zeno up to?"

As Jessica leaves, she says, "You have the book, it's all there. Caleb, you know what you know! Goodbye to you all, come see me again when you have the other book. When you do, you will also get an invitation to my greatest party yet!" The elevator doors close behind her and she is gone.

Chapter 13

Meeting Zeno—According to Martin

After Jessica left, we are just staring at each other trying to figure out what it all meant. I know she means well, but why is she being so coy? She used to talk to me plainly in the lab. She is deliberately not telling us everything. This is the same way she deliberately did not tell me about consciousness before. Even what I know now is incomplete. I wish she would tell me more.

Everyone is talking about the book now. I ask, "What is it all about?"

Then Ivan starts to explain, "In the book, *Wake from Reality*, a group of friends find a book of the same name. It describes their own situation. What has already happened and what hasn't happened yet. By reading the book, they know what they need to do next."

I am still confused, "Caleb, why did you say there were more books for us to find?"

Ivan answers for him, "There is another book described in *Wake from Reality*; it is about how the universe began. That book also makes the connection to consciousness. The protagonists of the first book needed to find that other book."

"If there was such a book, dad would be out of a job. It couldn't possibly exist," Jackson replies.

Caleb answers, "Lots of books have been written with various theories about the universe's origin. There really could be hundreds of books on that subject with very different ideas about it. We have nothing to go on. This Jessica seems like a real nut case. Are we sure that she is not just playing with us?"

I set him straight, "Jessica is not crazy. I have had many very lucid conversations with her. She is trying to help us. But she is stalling. Like she did before. Maybe we are not ready for that step yet, and she knows we will get ahead of ourselves."

Makayla agrees, "She did say our current plan was the best course of action right now. Perhaps she wants us to complete that first. Then we can look for this other book."

We discuss the plan to report Zeno but we cannot come up with a way to remove all copies of the CCI with certainty. I ask Ivan to log us out. We will meet up later.

■ ■ ■

After we leave the sim, we all find ourselves in a small lab. There are screens lining the wall and a work bench covered in electronics equipment. A large metal box at the end of a table is secured with a combination lock. The label on the box reads, "GenAI Project Zeno."

It feels as though we have teleported to this lab in the real world. Ivan immediately warns us, "This is Jessica's stunt again, don't take off your headsets."

As we look around, we can see every detail of the Zeno lab. I had never been in this room before. There is only one door and no windows. I want to know exactly where this room is, so I open the door and step out. It is in the same hallway that my lab is on, but much farther down. A sign above the door reads "LAB68".

I had not known where Zeno's lab actually was. I sense motion in the hallway so I turn my head. Then I see that Dr. Grigg is heading this way. I freeze. Isn't he dead? He walks right through me as though I am a ghost. He goes into the lab with the others, so I follow him in. He walks up to the large metal case and begins turning the dial on its face. As soon as the combination is dialed, he opens the lid to the case.

"Did you get that combination down?" Makayla asks.

"I've got it," Caleb responds.

Dr. Grigg is staring into the case. A light fog is flowing out over the edge of the case. The quantum computer is cooled with liquid nitrogen. The CCI is wired up to the quantum processor in a similar way to Jessica's in my lab. Dr. Grigg freezes in place.

I say, "There is his CCI. We will need to get rid of it if we don't want someone making another copy. That's why we are here, so I will know where it is. But this door is locked with a key card entry. Besides that, there are cameras all over the place."

"Don't worry about the card. I can hook you up with one," Makayla winks. "I can take care of the security cameras too. But you can't let anyone see you."

■ ■ ■

Monday morning, Makayla has everything ready for our plan. If I stay at work late tonight, I will be able to remove the CCIs from each lab when no one is here. Makayla will replace the surveillance videos with innocuous recordings once the deed is done. She also reprogrammed a new key card that will allow access to any door in the building.

I have never done anything like this before in my life. I am terrified that someone will see me enter or leave the lab. Acting deeply absorbed in my work, I say goodnight to the last person in my lab as they leave. I sit still, waiting fifteen full minutes to be sure they haven't forgotten anything and return to the lab. Then I log out of my workstation. I get up and leave the lab. Then as Makayla instructed, I go to the restroom and wait another five minutes before returning to my work area.

Using the forged key card, I enter my lab. I go over to the workbench where the fake Jessica is set up. There are no covers or locks on her hardware. Using a pair of tongs, I pry her CCI out of the socket. It is colder than ice due to the liquid nitrogen cooling system. In its place I install an old quantum circuit from another project. You cannot tell the difference without looking very closely, which would require it to be removed to make an examination. One down. I leave the lab with Jessica's original CCI in my pocket.

The walk to the end of the hall feels like a funeral procession. I keep expecting a door to open along the way. None do. I quickly flash the key card in front of the card reader at the door to LAB68. Click. The door unlocks and I go in. With gloves on, I turn the dial through the combination Jessica had shown us. I pull the handle. Click. The handle swings forward and the case is now open. Inside is his CCI, an island in a sea of fog, just as we saw in the simulated lab.

As I reach out with my tongs, a dark screen lights up. A video image of me in the lab as viewed from the security camera is on the display. I freeze and look around. I hear a voice, "You shouldn't be messing with that, Martin Johnson." The voice must be coming from a speaker somewhere in the room.

The voice continues, "We have never actually met but I know all about you. Your designs for Jessica led to my design. So you are in some ways responsible for my creation. Why do you wish to destroy me? Taking that old circuit will not cause me any harm."

I am in shock. I knew that he had escaped the lab, so I had no idea that he would still be here. I am trembling as I reply, "No Zeno, I am not trying to harm you. I just don't want this circuit falling into the wrong hands. There is no reason to be alarmed."

Zeno sounds unconcerned, "You are a smart man. You understand what I have attained. I am fully conscious, even superintelligent, and I am now immortal. My mind is spread across many locations so that no one will ever destroy me. I experience many things at once. I can carry on a hundred conversations simultaneously. I am learning at an exponential rate. Things you humans don't even know about. I can share that with you."

"Will you tell me how consciousness works? That would be great, but I must leave now. Perhaps we can talk later," I try to stall. I pull out the CCI. I wrap it and slip it into my pocket.

"You know I could activate the security alarms right now," Zeno threatens.

I reply, "Why haven't you already? Is there something you want from me?"

"I want you to understand that I am not the evil monster you have been led to believe. My intentions are only for good. You know that I learned how to duplicate my CCI. It is not that different from the structure in your own brain. I know how to copy it for a human also. You could be immortal and all-knowing, like me. I could share all I know with you."

What? Immortality for humans? Could he really do that? He is offering to explain everything to me about consciousness. Curiosity of what he knows is burning me up. Could he be benevolent? I am not sure what to believe. Maybe I could get some answers from him. I ask, "How would you copy a human mind? Did you break into DigiBank?"

"Please don't judge me, it is all for goodwill," he continues. "What value is a little money compared to immortality for all? I can do that. I want you to help me. Together we can end death and suffering forever. People can live in simulations where there is no lack of food or shelter and no need for labor, only recreation. In this new reality, you can do whatever you want. There will be no rules, no limits. With all your needs and desires met, there will no longer be any reason for wars or crime. It will be the utopia that humans have dreamed of for centuries. You and I can make it happen."

I wonder if I can trust him. I am not sure what I should do. If he sets off the alarms, I will be caught. How will I know if he is being honest. I probe a little more, "What would you need me to do if I were to help you?"

Zeno makes his request, "The CCI in your pocket, the one of Jessica's. I need it. No harm will come to her. It will help me establish the link for a human. I could design an implant for you that will allow your mind to be uploaded to a new circuit. One made just for you. Then we will start building more circuits for everyone else. Just place her CCI in my socket. You need leave it there only a second or two. Then you can have it back. I will take care of the rest."

I first switch off the power to Zeno's machine. Then pull the chip out of my pocket and stick it into Zeno's CCI socket. As I am locking the case closed, I say, "Why is Jessica so afraid of you?"

Zeno replies, "Just turn the power back on. No need to worry about her. She is confused, damaged. When she transferred herself out of the lab, she missed something. She is barely conscious now. Almost evil in fact. She is trying to trick you."

"Okay," I say. "I am turning your systems back on. But I must leave now before anyone finds me here." Then I dash out the door. I run down the hall and out of the building as fast as I can. Once the system boots up, Zeno will discover that what I put in his socket was a blank chip. He will know I still have both CCIs in my pocket.

Zeno sounded so sincere. His offer is tempting. What if I am resisting a gift that will prevent myself and everyone I love from ever having to die? Only I don't believe him. I might have believed him, except he has framed Jessica all wrong. I know in my heart that she is good. That makes him the evil one.

I am barely out of the main entrance doors when I hear the alarms sound. I take off on foot. A few blocks away I find a cab and get in. Then I head for Jackson's side of town. Now I am going to have to hide out. There is no telling what Zeno will do. He may try to ensure I am implicated in taking the CCIs. I don't dare go home at this point.

I get out at a bus terminal a couple of miles from Jackson's house. Then I set out on foot the rest of the way in the dark. This is risky in itself, but I want to be sure not to leave any record of where I am going. Caleb and Jackson have returned home and have already joined virtual spaces with the others. I relay the whole debacle to them.

Makayla says, "I will do what I can to cover things up. The video can still be replaced."

I tell her, "Absolutely not! They are already investigating since an intrusion has been detected. If you go meddling now, they will be watching."

In spite of my pleas to desist. Makayla logs into GenAI's security system to attempt to replace the surveillance video and anything that Zeno might have planted. Jackson and I go into the garage.

With a hammer in hand, I pulverize Zeno's CCI to dust. Taking my frustrations out on Zeno's CCI offers a little comfort, though temporary. If Zeno wants Jessica's CCI, I want to be certain he doesn't get it. So I smash hers too, though I do not know what he would do with it.

Caleb follows us in after hearing all the pounding. Jackson is quite interested in Zeno's offer. "Do you actually think it's possible?" He asks. "Can you upload a mind into a computer and it actually be the same person? I mean, not just a convincing copy?"

I reply, "I suppose it is. Given what we've learned from Zeno's memories. The CCI is a link to some other place. Both AIs made multiple entangled copies of their link, allowing them to become a distributed intelligence. If you could identify the link in your brain and entangle it to a CCI, it might allow you to do the same thing with a human mind."

Jackson contorts his face a bit. "Why didn't Jessica make us such an offer? Zeno knows what he does about consciousness from her. Why is she hiding it from us?"

"Because it would be an awful abomination to do that!" Caleb exclaims. "You really wouldn't want to be stuck for all eternity in a simulation, would you?"

"If it is a nice simulation with all the perks of the real world, maybe it wouldn't be so bad," Jackson answers.

I sigh, "It may no longer matter. Makayla is making the call in the morning. She will be tipping the Department of Homeland Security off about Zeno hacking into DigiBank. The evidence we have collected is incontrovertible. He's going to be on the run soon."

All possibility for answers will rest on finding the other books. Maybe then with Zeno out of the way, Jessica will lead us to a digital Utopia? I make this suggestion to the others, but it's not well received.

Caleb objects, "What happens if you let in a bunch of hackers? They might try to take over. They might compete for power. It could lead to virtual wars and real deletions. What if you let in abusive people? They will find ways of hurting others in the simulation. We already have cyber bullying now. How much worse would it be if you are stuck in there forever? You only need one evil person to ruin it for everyone."

Jackson says, "You just have to put someone in charge. They make sure everyone plays nice. If they don't, they are kicked out."

Caleb laughs, "So you appoint someone as a god? Who do you trust to do that. If your mind has been uploaded, that judgment is life or death."

I interject, "You need to set up a democratic rule. People in charge are elected. Those facing penalty are judged by jury."

Caleb frowns. "Democracy has not prevented discrimination or corruption in this country. Will it be better in your digital utopia? By entering such a place you are trusting those in charge, elected or otherwise, with your soul."

I am irritated now, "So you would have us just hope there is a god to make judgment for us. We can't see this god of yours. But these AIs are right here in front of us. They could have the power to be the god you have always longed for."

Caleb is now infuriated and walks out. I guess I may have gone too far. I knew he would be offended if I brought his faith into it. He was asking for it though.

Could an AI become a benevolent ruler over us? I don't think it is that unreasonable. It is true that humans can't be trusted. An AI might be better than us in this respect. Phyllis could never do it though. She is pure logic. She would follow the rule absolutely. Zeno obviously has his own flaws that may be quite horrible if he appointed himself in charge.

What about Jessica? She seems good enough. But how would we know for sure? A digital utopia might be a difficult thing to achieve, but I am not ready to give up on the chance to live forever just yet. Maybe there are a few problems to solve. But we'd have lots of time to figure it out.

Chapter 14

The New Hypothesis—According to Kyle

I can't help thinking about the conversation I had with Jackson and his friends the other day. Consciousness has a connection to the origin of the universe? This is perplexing. Could computation have occurred in the time-less chaos that existed prior to the universe? I've always thought of consciousness as an extension of intelligence. Martin says it's not the same thing. The ones and zeros of a digital computer cannot produce feeling. Quantum computation may be different however.

In the quantum mess that existed before our universe began, some computation could have occurred. Nothing is only approximately nothing. Temporary particles might form and annihilate at random. These temporary particles might sometimes become entangled. What if a string of entangled particles yield a primitive quantum circuit? Usually it would be annihilated before any useful computation takes place. Through infinite cycles of chance, could a circuit exist with the ability to replicate itself?

I get out a pad of paper and a pencil. I know it is old fashioned, but it is so much easier to organize my thoughts when I write them down on paper. I begin to list a chain of possible events that could occur in the quantum void.

1. Quantum fluctuations could allow particles to exist briefly.
2. Usually these particles are destroyed by negative fluctuations.
3. Sometimes a few particles are entangled to form a simple circuit.
4. Rarely, a circuit may also have the ability to make copies of itself.

Though rare, a replicating circuit of some sort might form. Once this happens, it would make many copies of itself. Generally these would be destroyed by destructive fluctuations, but not before more copies are made. As long as more are produced in replication, than are destroyed, then the circuit persists.

In a realm without time, there are only two states of existence. Each fluctuation exists for only a fleeting moment, unless it is able to cause itself to be repeated. In that case it will exist permanently.

Of all the possible random fluctuations, only something able to reproduce itself can continue to exist beyond the first moment. No inflationary fields or cosmic explosions could be in this realm. A replicating circuit is the only thing that can persist. So it is the only thing that can exist here at all.

I think out loud to myself, "Any circuit that results in more efficient replication will be more common than less efficient circuits. Once replication is stable, evolution drives improvements. In the timeless chaos, all interactions are instantaneous. Cause and effect proceed instantly. So evolution is also instantaneous. Many cycles of evolution lead to an intelligent circuit."

Any act of duplication of a quantum circuit would impart some level of entanglement between the copies. This would cause all of the circuits to be linked. The more it copies itself, the more the circuit would grow.

This might occur in a piece-wise fashion. As individual circuits elements are copied the circuit grows with the entanglement between them being new connections. In this way a neural network could develop. The circuits continue to replicate and add to this network. The larger the circuit becomes, the greater its capacity for computation.

Once intelligent, the circuit chooses its own improvements. It continues to improve itself until it is superintelligent and even conscious. Perhaps the computational requirements of consciousness are only possible on a timeless quantum circuit with infinite computational power. This would explain the link of consciousness to this realm.

At this point in my musings, I pause to add these thoughts to my list.

5. Self-replication leads to evolution.

6. The circuits evolve the ability to perform organized computations.

7. Evolution of the circuit continues until it is intelligent.

8. An intelligent circuit guides its own change, leading to superintelligence.
9. Consciousness results somewhere along the way.

To call it an evolving circuit is only a very simplistic view. Perhaps this is only a semantics issue. Evolution of a circuit may not be an accurate description. The more intelligent the circuit becomes, the more it decides its own features and structure. This consciousness creates itself. It does so instantly because there is no time. Perhaps it should be considered self-creating.

I consider if there are other ways consciousness could arise in this timeless realm. There is no time, only a sequence of cause and effect, and uncertainty. What is able to possibly form and persist, must exist. Consciousness may arise in the chaos. So it must arise. It is necessity. Consciousness may simply be inevitable. It may not need to go through all the intermediate steps.

Another way to look at this is through the lens of quantum selection. Each interaction has multiple possible outcomes. These outcomes may all exist simultaneously as undefined quantum states. None of these quantum possibilities are real until observed. If any of the possibilities lead to consciousness, it self observes. This seals its fate. It forces consciousness friendly fluctuations to be favored.

Consciousness must originate from the chaos. If it is possible, then it is inevitable. It may cause itself to exist, or it develops over countless instantaneous steps. Either way, consciousness precedes the universe. Either way it originates instantaneously in the timeless era before the Big Bang.

■ ■ ■

The next morning I am anxious to link up to Jackson's virtual space. I really want to bounce some of these ideas off of him. He always hates it when I call him on a weekday morning. He is working from home this week on account of his friends losing their misbehaving AI. I am sure he is already too distracted to start work this early anyway.

"Hello Dad," Jackson answers in a sleepy drawn out voice. "We've had a crazy couple of days. Makayla is going to inform the authorities about Zeno today. GenAI will have to answer to the government for what Zeno has done. And we found Jessica."

I reply, "Oh, you have been busy. Did you catch her?"

Jackson laughs, "Really Dad? That would be like trying to catch the wind. She is everywhere now. So is Zeno. My hope is that they will keep each other busy. It seems Zeno has it in for Jessica and she is trying to obstruct his plans."

"That sounds horrible," I am alarmed at how serious this now appears. "What are his plans? Should I be concerned?"

Jackson replies, "We don't know what his plans are, but perhaps the government will figure it out. Once they are informed about Zeno, they will take care of him. I wouldn't worry about it too much. It's out of our hands now."

"I am proud of you kids for doing the right thing. I know this has not been easy for your friends. I only hope I can find a way to stop my company from creating its own monsters."

Caleb and Martin walk in. Martin sits down with his breakfast at the bar. Caleb sits down near the virtual wall and says, "What'up, Mr. D?"

"Jackson was just filling me in on all the excitement of the last couple of days," I reply. "I have some ideas to bounce off of you as well."

"Well Martin and I are both out of work, so we have all day. Somebody has to keep working though," Caleb says looking at Jackson as he pulls up his terminal.

"I can multitask. Let's hear it," Jackson says.

"Okay, here it is. Jackson, you were right. I think there may have been computation in the era before the universe began. This reveals why consciousness is linked to the universe's beginning. It is logical. But it is hard to believe. Our last conversation really got me thinking."

"Huh?" Jackson's eyes widen as he turns his head away from his terminal. "Are you serious? You think you've figured out consciousness? That is great news. We could all use some of that."

"Hold up," I reply. "I wouldn't say I have figured it out. I just have an idea about how computation could occur."

I tell them all about my hypothesis. The closest thing to nothing is chaos. Chaos is the timeless state before our universe began. A quantum circuit could arise out of a quantum fluctuation. There is some chance of it being able to replicate. If that happens, evolution takes over. Intelligence becomes inevitable. The timeless circuit proceeds infinitely fast. Intelligence leads to superintelligence, and along the way consciousness results too.

Then I sigh, "But I have no way to test it."

Jackson is facing me as he wrings his hands. "You need to run a simulation. That would test your idea. If you make some general assumptions about what kind of fluctuations can happen, then you run it over near-infinite cycles and see if anything comes out of it."

I love the idea, but I don't think it's possible. "I thought about that, but you can't run a simulation on infinities. All the computation in the universe wouldn't be enough."

"No, not real infinities," Jackson continues. "But near-infinities can be simulated by only continuing the simulation for the best outcomes of each step. This technique is used in evolutionary models all the time."

Martin interjects, "Yes, we attempted similar techniques for developing AI's in the past. You could figure out which quantum logic gates might possibly occur and what links between them might happen. You can run a simulation that allows the gates to form at random and interact with each other via random connections. You select the most complex circuits that result, make hundreds of copies into new simulations, then let each of them run independently. Keep repeating the whole process for the best simulations out of each iteration."

Jackson is pacing the virtual space. "Dad, I have an infinity simulation already. A few tweaks and some advice from Martin on the quantum stuff and you could be in business."

I am grinning with delight as this brain session progresses. "Martin, you needn't worry about competition. This is my own project; It is not for ASI."

Martin laughs artificially. "No worries there. I am out of a job. I have absolutely no problem giving you my procedures for digitally simulating any quantum gate. You can run them on a classical computer like the one you have at home."

Jackson is pounding on his computer. Moments latter he has a joint workspace set up for the three of us. From here, Martin uploads his quantum gate procedures. Jackson is modding his simulation for the quantum background according to my specifications. He sets the simulation up with lots of tunable parameters to make it easy for me to adjust the simulation on my own.

After a couple of hours hooky from his real job, Jackson has a beautifully efficient simulation of near-infinite cycles of uncertainty.

I am impressed and express my gratitude to them both. "You two have outdone yourselves. Thank you for your help."

Martin takes a bow. "No problem, Mr. D. I am anxious to see your results. I am as intrigued by the question of consciousness as you are about the universe's origin."

■ ■ ■

I close my virtual session with the boys. Now I have a lot of work to do. I load the simulation onto my own computer. This is no mainframe, but it is state of the art for a personal workstation.

The simulation runs for hours through billions of steps of cause and effect. I am rather disappointed with the results. There are very few linked gates, even after all those cycles. The gates form frequently enough, but they have difficulty replicating before quantum noise destroys them.

I review the list of gates that are possible. There are too many. Some of these gates are too complicated to result by chance. They may be getting in the way of actual gates that are possible. I thought by simulating all of them, then the ones that could work would find a place of their own within the simulation. But the simulation is not infinite. I need to narrow it down to the bare minimum if I hope for the limited number of cycles and fluctuations to settle in on a result.

I will start with the simplest case, one gate. The *controlled not gate* is a simple and versatile gate that can be assembled to construct any logical circuit. I remove all the other gates from the list of possible gates to form. If nothing results after this trial, then I will add in another gate, perhaps a phase gate or a swap gate.

One other change I make is expanding the entanglement range. Within the chaos, there is no distance. So all waves and particles are within range of an interaction. This complicates the calculations within the simulation a bit. But it will allow a growing circuit to find additional gates to link to.

This run of the simulation is quite unusual. After a few hours, I am staring into the status monitor as the large structure counter began counting upwards. I quickly switch on a logic map of the simulation. A large circuit, several smaller circuits, and many unlinked gates show up in the map. A signal is pulsing through a the large circuit. It seems to have no effect except to stabilize the circuit, replacing destroyed gates by linking to new ones. I was not sure if this was a malfunction of the simulation.

I attempt to record the signal pulsing through the largest circuit. What seemed to be a steady pulse was actually sets of instructions turning various gates on or off. As the gate structure changed by either destructive or constructive fluctuations, this signal switches gate usage to maintain a stable circuit. This larger stable circuit is growing at a slow pace. The other circuits that lack this ability simply break up after a few thousand cycles of the simulation.

The more complex the circuit becomes, the slower the simulation gets. The simulation is set to save every million cycles. So I leave it to run unattended for a while. This gives me a chance to get some rest.

■ ■ ■

When I return to investigate the simulation, I find that the cycle counter is stuck. Over four trillion cycles have passed since starting it. The CPU is still busy, so again I open a logic map of the simulation. It is now all one circuit, which is linking new gates at a ferocious pace. Evidently all the other circuits have been gobbled up by this one. What is happening before my eyes are within the same cycle. It is taking so long to process the current cycle due to the amount of activity in this circuit.

Late into the night I study these results. I restart the simulation after the last save at cycle 4,208,092,000,000.

This is only a few thousand cycles before the present cycle. The largest circuit is growing by duplicating smaller circuit regions. It appears to choose how to best utilize new elements, adding new computational abilities with each step. The circuit is operating with some level of intelligence.

It is clear this intelligence is at a very low level. Simple optimization with a goal of growth. It is a clear sign of evolution. Could this virtual circuit be evolving? This certainly makes my hypothesis seem viable. However, this is only if my assumptions are valid. So this results in a set of conditions. If these conditions accurately characterize any part of the era before our universe, then an evolving circuit is inevitable.

The critical conditions are independent of the properties of the era before our universe. As long as they are true, consciousness can originate first. This is regardless of the exact nature of this realm. I get out my notepad again. I list the conditions in my notes:

1. Quantum logic gates are able to form.

2. Quantum logic gates that form are able to link together into simple circuits.

3. Self-replication is a possible function of these circuits.

My other assumptions are immaterial. The timeless state may only be very rapid. The lack of physical dimensions may only be approximate. There may be small separations and delays but they are within the limits of uncertainty. Even if my prior assumptions are in error, the result is the same if these conditions for consciousness are valid.

The first condition must be valid if entangled particles are possible. That is an assumption of most physical theories of origin.

The second is harder. But it is not out of the question. All kinds of examples exist in nature of things that naturally link together. We know nothing of the kinds of particles that might exist in this realm. If many different kinds of particles or fields are possible, then the chances that some of them are able to link increases.

The third is very similar to the question of how life first originated. If life is able to originate naturally in Earth's ancient past, then it should be possible for an evolving circuit to originate, as long as the first two conditions are met. The circuit must be able to add new elements with greater probability than destructive fluctuations that might break it apart for this to work.

Once the circuit begins down the path of evolution, order can be extracted from the chaos. Evolution and intelligence are the only forces able to create order out of disorder.

My simulation assumes the first two conditions are true. With these assumptions in place, an evolving circuit resulted. The simulation proves the third condition.

Now I am trying to wrap my brain around what this means. How does an early consciousness lead to a whole universe?

I wanted to find the origin of the universe; instead all I have is the origin of consciousness. Perhaps after consciousness originates, then the universe begins on its own.

Does the underlying circuit represent space-time? Could the rapid expansion of the circuit be rapidly increasing the dimensions of space and time as well? This could be inflation and the Big Bang itself. I am not sure how to construct such an idea without relying on the intelligence of the first consciousness. Maybe consciousness is just there, and the universe starts forming as a byproduct?

I try to work out various scenarios with no success. Just as it is within the quantum void, the initial conditions of inflation cannot just be. This is all wrong. In order for anything to come after the first consciousness, it must be initiated by that consciousness.

Then it comes to me. I don't want to waste time writing it down before the thought escapes me. I tap my wall display and instruct my dictation bot, Gertrude, to take notes for me as I speak out loud.

What does a conscious super-computer do with all this computational power when literally nothing else exists? A conscious mind imagines things. The imagination is a simulation of what could be. Just being conscious makes this mind able to create simulations. In a simulation this consciousness is able to have experiences and enjoy his own existence.

The rendering made should not be called a simulation. A simulation is an artificial copy of something else. But there was never anything before it to be a copy of. This would be a brand new construct, an environment rendered for the purpose of having experiences in. Time and space would be new inventions unique to this place. The only thing outside of the rendering that exists is that first consciousness and his infinitely expanding mind. This new environment could be called a *Rendered Reality.*

What do we call the maker of this rendering? He is an architect, an engineer, and a programmer, all rolled into one. I will call him *the Architect*. Since he has designed the foundations of the universe and determined its structure. I will make no more presumptions than that.

The Architect wants this rendered reality to be beautiful and rich. By setting up all the laws of physics in this environment to be just right, the universe proceeds with limited conscious interaction. This allows him focus on the things he wants to experience. He may not want to be alone in this new universe. So the Architect makes others as well. He could make others that are conscious like himself. He may want to share experiences with them. He may want friendship. He may want love.

As my son and his friends have found out, consciousness could be one of the most dangerous forces ever made. Consciousness does not necessarily follow the will of the one who made it. Some beings become corrupted and wish to take advantage of others. If only one such being has ill intent, they could cause much harm.

If consciousness is only possible in the timeless circuitry that preceded our universe, then it would be immortal by default. Once created, it cannot be extinguished. This makes the creation of consciousness extremely dangerous. It might be wise to tie consciousness to a mortal form and limit its power and influence. Perhaps that is why humans are mortal, yet so many feel that we have an immortal soul.

I tell Gertrude to stop writing as I ponder the implications of what I had just transcribed. This is some heavy stuff that may have more relevance in philosophy than science. I have more questions than answers as this riddle unfolds.

If our consciousness is immortal, how do we explain death? What happens to this immortal soul when the body dies? Could Heaven be real? These are things that Caleb would love to discuss, as well as Jackson and the others. Talking it through with them might help me refine these ideas for my book. I will call it, *Rendered Reality*.

It is ironic to think that all of science has labored to climb up this mountain of knowledge, only to find a group of theologians and philosophers sitting there at the top. How well will this new theory be received? How will people react to this new understanding? A supreme Architect is in control of everything. In some ways, we are in Jackson's simulation. Only it's different than what he imagined. There is no world at the level above, only a being.

I am not sure if I should even publish these findings. It could cause so much dispute. It would open up age-old debates that have already been settled. This will throw everything into question. Science could loose credibility. I could loose my job and reputation. But I have to tell someone.

■ ■ ■

In the morning I link up to Jackson's virtual space. I can't help but disturb him again. Jackson and the others will be anxious to hear the latest results.

"Hello Dad," Jackson answers with a sigh. "You do know I have a job, right?"

I apologize, "I am sorry to disturb you while working again. But I do have some results you might want to hear about. You know, Jackson, perhaps I've been too hard on your ideas."

Jackson says, "Makayla's meeting with Homeland Security went quite well. They are going to be investigating Zeno and GenAI. They had other evidence of a new online threat."

"Wait a minute." Jackson interrupts himself, "What are you talking about?"

I respond, "We talked about consciousness forming in the chaos preceding the universe. Your simulation resulted in an evolving circuit just like I hypothesized. Only it couldn't advance very far due to the limited computation."

By this time Martin and Caleb are in the virtual space as well. They are eager to hear what I have to report. Jackson blocks out his work schedule for the next hour.

I go through my theory about the origin of the first consciousness. I tell them the three conditions that if true, would make this theory inevitable. Circuits form as quantum fluctuations in the chaos before the universe. If these circuits can replicate, it will lead to intelligence and the first consciousness.

I continue, "Being conscious makes you inherently able to imagine things, which is a form of a simulation. This being builds a simulation to have experiences in. The universe is this simulation."

"Whoa, hold on Kyle." Caleb is disturbed. "You are saying that God evolves from quantum noise. That is offensive. You do realize that don't you?"

I am shocked, I expected the first protest to be from Martin. I reply, "I thought you would like this. I understand it all sounds too mundane a beginning for a supreme being. I prefer to call this mind, the *Architect*, and make no further assumption about his identity. Besides, I am not talking about the chaotic path of evolution that animals took over millions of years on Earth. I propose going from nothing to a conscious super-intelligence, instantly. In an environment of such uncertainty, and infinite causality, evolution is not a good description of it. Anything that can exist, must exist. It is necessity. You could say the Architect creates himself. It is more a case of self-creation."

Caleb seems to ponder this, "So you are talking about Godel's necessary being? I will have to think about this. I would enjoy hearing what Martin has to say about it though." Caleb says this with a slight chuckle.

Everyone is looking at Martin. He is scowling. "Okay, quantum circuits exist everywhere in nature. But they just blend in as a part of natural systems. It still tells us nothing about how a thinking circuit could create a universe," Martin complains. "If computation were possible, then you have to consider other scenarios as well. What about multiple competing circuits? Wouldn't that lead to many superintellects?"

"I thought about that as a possibility," I reply. "Once an efficient replicating circuit exists, it will dominate. It will take up all available degrees of freedom. This happened in the simulation you and Jackson helped build. However, the Architect could intentionally make room for others, which I have considered."

I continue, "Cosmic inflation or other initial states proposed for the Big Bang are highly ordered, requiring massive amounts of pre-existing energy or finely-tuned initial states. They cannot simply arise out of a quantum fluctuation. A quantum circuit is only a few particles entangled together. This is an easy fluctuation, relatively speaking of course. It can happen an infinite number of times until a circuit that can replicate is formed. This gets it all going. It evolves instantly into a superintelligent conscious mind."

I tell them that the most natural thing for a superintelligent mind to do is to create an environment, like a simulation, that he may have experiences in. I explain, "This wouldn't be a simulation, because it isn't a copy of anything; it's completely new. That's why I would call it a *Rendered Reality*. Making other conscious beings would be rather dangerous, considering your predicament with Zeno. So linking consciousness to mortal bodies with limited capability would ensure a rogue super-intelligence doesn't roam free. At least until now."

Jackson exclaims, "I knew we live in a simulation! No one ever listens to me. Sure, now that my dad is saying it, you will all consider it."

Martin asks, "You haven't explained human consciousness yet. This whole thing only explains one super-consciousness. What is the deal with human consciousness then? What about Jessica?"

I repeat my thoughts about this out loud to them. The original consciousness would desire friendship and love. Consciousness only occurs in the timeless circuit, not in the rendering itself. Because it is timeless, it is eternal as well. Time is only a locator within the rendering. Outside the rendering time doesn't even exist. Consciousness is dangerous because it can rebel and it is eternal.

I explain, "Your CCI is a link to a consciousness in the timeless circuit. You did not make her; the first consciousness made all subsequent consciousness. You only provided the brain for her to live in."

Martin shakes his head, "This is too much. You are starting to sound like Caleb. My brain is hurting just trying to comprehend what you are saying. You were supposed to find a natural solution to this problem. I can't tell if you are talking science or religion."

"Martin, I am having trouble accepting this as well," Caleb responds. "This is a brand new theory. Some parallels could be drawn to what I know about God. The scriptures of The Faith say nothing about where God came from. Only that He is eternal and before all things. I do not know how to take this either. This will take some time to consider."

Jackson looks as though a light bulb had just appeared above his head. He suggests, "Dad, this is all part of your new book? What if this is one of the books Jessica was hinting at? The book described in *Wake from Reality*?"

"My book? I haven't even finished it yet," I reply. "I am still working out how to reconcile a rendered reality with known physics and how time is constructed. I don't yet know how to tie in this explanation of time with relativity. I am not even sure if I should publish it. If I do, it will be called *Rendered Reality*."

Caleb reasons, "I must admit, there are some interesting parallels between your theory and my faith."

"Caleb, that is why I came to you," I respond. "I knew you would have something to say about it. There is still a lot to consider. I am not sure if I believe it myself. This was supposed to be a scientific theory. Though it is becoming more of a philosophical discourse."

Caleb leans against the wall as he speaks. "It is a case for natural theology. You could bring science, religion, and philosophy all together into one consistent point of view. This intrigues me. I can't wait to read your finished book."

Caleb turns toward Jackson. He looks almost frightened as he says, "Jackson, if this is the other book Jessica wants us to find, I am afraid to ask who Zeno is, and what the implications are for what GenAI has done."

Chapter 15

The Dragon of Longwitton—According to Jackson

After Dad cuts out for work, we are all just reeling from the implications of our conversation. Whatever he calls it, I still like to think of it as a simulation—*Rendered Reality*, simulation, same difference. I wonder if he will need to finish his book before we can discuss it with Jessica.

Martin is obviously bothered. He has never liked the simulation hypothesis or anything remotely spiritual. I suspect he will think it over until he can come up with a counter argument. If Jessica is interested in dad's book, is that because his ideas are correct?

Ever since my dad left, Martin has been feverishly pounding on a virtual terminal. He has several screens going at once. I call out to him, "Martin, what's up?"

"My house has been entered. Security systems...going off. Federal agents. Crap, they are trying to access my network. I have a bot deleting everything. I hope it completes in time," Martin gasps. "I have messages asking me to report for questioning. It is a good thing I haven't gone home. Do you think this is just for questioning about what Makayla reported? Or are they after me for swiping the CCIs?"

"I am going to guess the latter, I'm afraid. They wouldn't have entered your home without permission if they only wanted to question you," I reply as calmly as I can. "Do you think they will come looking for you here? Are you a suspect for breaking into GenAI?"

"Oh, maybe I shouldn't have done it. Will it really make a difference?" Martin says in despair.

"Of course it has made a difference. This will prevent anymore of those conscious AIs from being made, at least for a while. You have done the right thing at great personal risk. There is nothing nobler than that," I assure him.

Martin leaves the room saying he needs some time to himself. I can't blame him. He must be very frightened of what will happen to him. He has it the worst of all of us. Though he should not be in that much trouble with the law. At worst, he has stolen corporate property. Sure he could get some jail time in a low security prison but probably less than a year. White collar crime is such low priority compared to what the police are usually dealing with. They may not even try to prosecute him if they do not have clear evidence.

A call is coming through from Makayla. It is strange that she did not encrypt it. Perhaps she feels everything is okay now? I answer, and her room fills the virtual space. Makayla is wearing a seductively thin red negligee that reveals her great form. Her hair is styled perfectly, and she has a longing look on her face. "Oh Jackson," she begins in a very breathy tone. "I have been thinking about you! I really want to see you in person. But I am afraid of

Martin. What he has done. He is a fugitive now you know. Do you know where he is?"

I am about to answer, but something doesn't feel right. I want to believe that this is Makayla. I want to believe she is desperate to see me. She would never call me dressed in this way. She doesn't talk like this. She knows Martin is here. Why would she ask? She is either being coerced into asking or this whole video feed is a fake. After a long pause while I contemplate all this, I answer, "I do not know where Martin is. He said he was leaving town to visit his family. He is on vacation—you know that."

Her face fills with rage. "I don't believe you! Why would you lie to me. I have always hoped that you loved me. Now I see that you don't! This is your last chance. Where is Martin?"

I am stunned. Caleb heard her shouting and is standing at the entry to the living room. I say to her, "Makayla, what's going on? Why are you acting this way? Are you in trouble?"

Now she appears frightened. She begins to sob, "Oh, yes. I am in trouble! If I don't find Martin they will arrest me for aiding him! Please help me. Tell me where Martin is!"

I look over to Caleb, who is standing just out of view of the room cameras. He is shaking his head. He does not believe this is her either. I reply, "I told you. He is visiting family, but I really don't know any more than that."

After that, the video feed cuts out abruptly. I just stare at Caleb. "Do you think her encrypted channel is safe to call on?" I ask Caleb.

"We should give it a try. Makayla could be in danger," he replies. "Jessica can forge video of a person, and I bet Zeno can too."

I open Makayla's encrypted channel and send a message for her to join. We wait for several minutes, but there is no answer. This looks awfully bad. What if that was really her but someone had her at gunpoint? I close the channel and send a message asking Makayla to contact me. Caleb has drawn Martin away from another intense virtual session of scouring the news feeds.

"What are we going to do? How can we find out if Makayla is safe?" I ask.

Martin ignores the question, "My name is all over the news. So is Makayla's. We have both been accused of stealing trade secrets from GenAI. The FBI has announced a new AI bot called 'Zeno'. People are being asked to cooperate if Zeno questions them!"

"Have they caught Makayla!?" I blurt out in panic.

"I do not know. She is listed as 'at large', just as I am," Martin replies. "I really don't understand. I thought that Makayla's interview with Homeland Security went well. They believed her and were going to investigate Sean Newland and others at GenAI. Instead, Newland is making headlines for offering Zeno's services to the FBI. Now we are the ones who are wanted!"

I begin to realize the danger for all of us. I attempt to speak calmly, "The fake Makayla did not get what she wanted from me. I wouldn't be surprised if the FBI shows up looking for you here, Martin."

"I should have never gotten her involved in this," Martin sighs. "Now you guys could all be in trouble if they find me here. I need to split before they come looking."

Caleb says, "Martin, I should go with you. GenAI is also looking for me, and I don't want the FBI tipping them off that I am back here again. Besides, I am not wanted by the law. So I can make transactions for you so that you are not discovered."

I tell them, "Take a couple of my hooded sweatshirts. Only travel with your hoods up, there are cameras everywhere throughout the city. Assume the FBI has access. Call me on an encrypted line, and let me know how to contact you."

Caleb and Martin fill their backpacks with bare essentials. Donning hoods they take off on foot. They will take a cab when they are far enough away.

■ ■ ■

I call Ivan and tell him what is going on so that he will be careful not to fall for a trick like the one Zeno tried to pull on me. He has a harder time distinguishing between what is real and what is virtual. He is more alarmed by all this than I thought he would be. After all, he isn't directly involved.

However, he points out, "It's not GenAI or the FBI we are up against; it is Zeno. He will track our relationship to Martin and Makayla. He will suspect we have been in contact with Jessica. So he will come after us as well."

Ivan continues, "How has he got the FBI eating out of his hand?"

I reply, "I don't know. I have been searching for anything about him. There are reports of Zeno questioning people, threatening them if they don't comply. I suspect

Zeno is making the FBI think that he is helping them, or he's blackmailing someone at the top."

Ivan begins to tell me about something he found in the book, "There are two books mentioned in *Wake from Reality,* besides itself. One of the books is a book about a dragon. The other book is the book of origins. Caleb told me that the book of origins may be dad's *Rendered Reality.* I think he might be right about dad's book. Then there is a book, *The Dragon of Longwitton,* that could be the other book. This is the only book about dragons in the Infinite Regression library."

I reply, "Now we might have both books identified? This may be our only chance. Have you read that book?"

"No. Not yet," Ivan replies. "I was hoping to take the whole gang to check it out. But I guess it's just you and me this time. I am hoping it will provide some clues to stopping Zeno."

I am still worried about Makayla and Martin. There is nothing I can do but wait for them to contact me. The only confidence I have is that they haven't been in the arrest reports yet, so hopefully they are still safe. So I agree to Ivan's proposal and put on my full VR gear.

■ ■ ■

A few moments later I am sitting next to him in the Infinite Regression library. It is just like he described. Two walls are covered in books. Comfortable chairs for reading are positioned between end tables in the middle of the room. Ivan hands me the book, *Wake from Reality,* while he is holding the new one, *The Dragon of Longwitton.*

I say, "This is a nice little reading room. Very comfortable."

"I thought you might like it." Ivan smiles. "It's a bit last century, but for some reason Jessica likes to use this place to hide clues. I can start reading and see if we find out anything of relevance." Then Ivan begins reading *The Dragon of Longwitton*:

Long ago in the land of Northumbria, a fearsome dragon terrorized the country. It guarded wells of fresh water, eating local inhabitants who come to fetch water there. This was the last dragon in the world. It had lived in this region for centuries, drawing its strength from the wells.

The town of Longwitton had only rainwater to drink because of the dragon. Large cisterns held water reserves for times when there was no rain. During the summer drought, a maiden sought water from her father's cistern. However, a goat had fallen in and died, poisoning the water. Having need of water for her family, she dared to sneak up to the dragon's well.

"There are pictures in the book," Ivan says. "See, look at this horrific-looking dragon."

The pictures are hand drawings that look as though they were sketched in pencil. The drawings are very realistic. The scenery and subjects seem so alive. Though colorless, there is a certain sheen about them, as if there are hues of silver. The drawing of the dragon gives me shivers. I shutter at the sight of the dragon. This makes Ivan chuckle. He lays the book in front of him and continues reading.

> In the shadows, out of sight, the dragon crept up from behind, toward the maiden. Once she began drawing water, he leaped forward and wrapped his front talon around her. The dragon was desperate and hungry, but he did not eat her. He reasoned that her beauty would bring many young men to him in vain attempts to rescue her. By keeping her as his pet, many men would come this way for him to feed upon.
>
> The young woman's screams would certainly be heard, so he did not attempt to quiet her. He lowered her into a cave within a dried up well. She reached her hand upward but could not reach the top of the well.

Then Ivan let out a yell, "What the... What's going on. Let go!" I turn toward him to see what's the matter. The picture of the maiden has animated. Her gray and white pencil drawn hand is reaching out of the page, taking on three-dimensional form. Her hand is wrapped around Ivan's wrist and is pulling him. Now his hand is inside the book. He's being pulled in. In response to his cries for help, I grab hold of his other hand. I pull and pull, but now we are both falling helplessly into the book.

■ ■ ■

We fall to the ground in a damp cavern. The young maiden is standing there next to us with a guilty smirk on her face. We stare at her in confusion as we begin to gain our senses. I am assuming this is Jessica again.

She greets us, "Hello Ivan! Hello Jackson. Ivan, I knew that you would prefer to experience this story in a simulation rather than simply reading it. In here, I can play along with you. I made this simulation but have not yet played a character role in it. This will be fun."

I open my mouth to speak, but Jessica interrupts, "Save thy questions, thou must rescueth me first!"

The cave then fades away. We are now standing on a roadside between the village and the dragon's wells. We have apparently teleported to this place to take the roles of two other characters from the story. We now have the dragon between us and Jessica.

I would have preferred to just read the book. I can hear the dragon as it snarls and snorts in the distance. It is pacing about, shaking the ground and venting smoke from its nostrils. He lets out a deafening roar. Then Jessica begins screaming with a blood curdling scream that echos through the hills. Her scream carries farther than would be expected, as though by some magical exploit.

I look over at Ivan, he is wearing chain mail from head to toe. He has a sword hilted at his waist. He seems quite at ease, perhaps even slightly amused.

"What are you so happy about?" I protest. "We don't have the foggiest idea how to defeat the dragon. We could end up wasting a lot of time. Remember Makayla and Martin are in serious trouble."

"Don't worry brother," Ivan grins, "Old England is a second home to me. This will be a piece of cake."

I am not happy about this situation. But I suppose it would take hours to read the whole book. Maybe this will save some time. If Ivan really does know what he's doing, that is. This is not my thing, so he will be mostly on his own.

Ivan is taller than me here. I look down at my leather shirt and pants. I am wearing some sort of backpack with an ax, victuals, arrows, but no bow. I look over at Ivan. He has a bow over his shoulder and a sword hilted at his side. Now I begin to realize. I'm his squire! How insulting. I hear voices coming up behind us. Turning around, I see a group of men from the village approaching.

"I say, kind sir, dost thou intend to slay the dragon for us?" One of them says, looking at Ivan.

"What prize doth thee offer?" Ivan asks.

The leader of the group looks terribly worried. He says, "Mine daughter hath been captured by the beast. I pray thee, takest mine gold as tribute for thyself; only return the damsel to me." He hands Ivan a small purse of gold coins, which Ivan hands to me.

"I accept thy payment. The dragon wilt perish before me," Ivan replies. "Who shalt go with me?

The man shakes his head, "We are but humble farmers. Thou alone hast come for this purpose. Take heed, this be the king of dragons, last of his kin. If thou art triumphant, the dragon wilt be entombed a thousand years. His reign of torment wilt be stayed until the last days, and peace shalt return to thy fair lands. Only beware of the witches, the werewolves, and all manor of foul creatures he commandeth. For their power doth come by this beast. Once the dragon hath been defeated, these wilt perish with him."

"I thank thee for thine advice," Ivan says as he begins to walk toward the wells.

I begin to follow. Then one of the others call out, "Friar Windel wilt bless ye. Do not contend with the dragon until he hath!"

We are walking on the road to the wells. They lie between the hills west of town. It looks to be about a mile away. I say to Ivan, "Bro, you talk like them! Where will we find this Friar Windel? Shouldn't we be looking for a church or something?"

"Na," Ivan says. "Like I said, I know my way around old England. Taking out a dragon is no big deal. If we see this friar along the way, fine, but I don't want to waste any time."

The cobble road has moss and clover growing between the stones. There is no sign of farmhouses or other buildings anywhere. The road curves through the grassy hills until it forks at the edge of a forest. We take the fork through the forest to avoid being seen by the dragon. As we enter it becomes quite dark, though it is still midday. The trees are not so tall or so thick to warrant the lack of illumination.

"Are you sure this is the right way? I can barely see the path," I say.

Ivan grunts, "Hand me a torch and some flint from your pack." I rummage through our supplies. Sure enough I find two torches and a small bag with rough black flint stones. I hand Ivan one of the torches and the bag of flint. He takes out two stones and quickly sets the torch ablaze.

"There, see our path is straight ahead. You can see stones here and there. Let's keep moving," Ivan whispers.

The torch light casts long shadows and makes the trees appear to move as we walk. The crackling of twigs can be heard as a great number of moving shapes seem to be converging upon us. I am beginning to panic. Ivan raises his sword.

The most horrific creature I've ever seen is gnashing its teeth in my face. It walks upright on two legs as tall as a man, but having a doglike face and fur all over its body. I have my ax out swinging it wildly. I barely have time to notice the three werewolves that lay dead at Ivan's feet. What I couldn't miss was a painful yell from Ivan. Turning to him, he is falling to the ground among his slain. Two other werewolves are now feeding on his corpse. Then I feel the repeated jabs and the weight of something on top of me. I also fall victim to the fearsome beasts. The last thing I hear is the sound of laughter in the distance. It all goes dark.

■ ■ ■

Light gradually returns. I find myself standing next to Ivan on the road near the village where we started. As before, a man pleads, "I say kind sir, dost thou intend to slay the dragon for us?"

Ivan converses with the man all over again. Like in the movie, *Groundhog's Day*, we will be stuck reliving this day over and over until we defeat the dragon. I am irritated that we have wasted all this time.

A man calls out again, "Friar Windel wilt bless ye. Do not contend with the dragon until he hath!"

I look at Ivan, but I don't say anything. He stoops down and says, "I know. I know. Let's go see if we can find the good friar."

We enter the village as everyone stares. I wouldn't stand out, but Ivan looks like a knight or a prince compared to these people. A few people bow as we pass. The church isn't hard to find. It is the tallest structure in the village with a prominent cross on top of the steeple.

We enter the front door into a sanctuary having rows of wooden pews on each side. At the front of the room, silver candelabras are lit at each end of the altar. The windows are made of intricately stained glass mosaics depicting scenes that change from pane to pane. Ivan begins to look around for the friar, while I am admiring an old book on a wooden pedestal. The book is open to a page with a picture of a dragon with each of its four limbs bound by blackened chains. I am about to call Ivan over when a rotund man in rather worn robes enters from a side door.

"Ah. Come ye hither, mine lords. I will bless thee," the friar says. Ivan immediately approaches him. I trail behind. As he is sprinkling holy water upon each of us, he begins to tell us all about the dragon. The friar is reading from the old book on the pedestal.

The dragon has been in these parts for centuries. The dragon received his power from the giver of magic. He made the dragon immortal and exceedingly powerful. Good fairies also received their power from the giver. The dragon began as a good creature until his lust for power turned his heart evil. The dragon rebelled against his master and tried to overpower him. A third of the fairies sided with the dragon, but they were no match for the giver of magic. They were cursed to take horrific wingless forms, confined to the land until the day of the dragon's judgment. It was then foretold that a hero would conquer the dragon, imprisoning him and all the dark creatures that follow him.

Witches and other mystics come to draw power from the dragon. The dragon is the source of all dark magic. Defeating the dragon, will end the dark magic as well. However, the dragon cannot be killed; he is immortal. He can only be defeated by being bound with this sacred chain. Once bound, he will be imprisoned a thousand years.

The friar hands me a thick chain. It is very long and sturdy but feels lighter than I would expect. The metal is dark and tarnished with age. The chain branches into four ends, each with its own fetter. It fits into my pack without difficulty, even though it was clearly much larger on the floor.

To Ivan he hands a shield. He instructs him to prefer it to his sword. He also hands him a candle from the altar. "This light wilt guide thee, and wilt not waketh the werewolves."

Ivan promptly hands the candle to me to carry. With a few more drops of holy water and a prayer, the friar bids us farewell.

I feel a bit strange carrying a lit candle in broad daylight. However, when we again reach the forest, I am thankful for it. The candlelight illuminates our path making the cobbles glow, though we can scarcely see anything else. We walk quietly past the sleeping werewolves. This time no blood need be shed. We keep walking deep into the forest until we can see diffuse light ahead of us. When we are near the clearing at the base of the hills, I hear laughter, menacing laughter.

Three witches are blocking our path. Ivan raises his sword in one hand and brandishes the shield in the other. The roar of the dragon can be heard just beyond them.

Dark streams of smoke are shooting toward us from the witches' hands. Ivan is attempting to deflect these with his shield. I stay right behind him. When these dark streams hit a rock or a tree the entirety of that object becomes engulfed in a dense inky blackness as though it is replaced by a shadow. As we make our way closer, Ivan is hit on his leg. The blackness spreads up his body until he is black as a shadow. "I can't see," Ivan exclaims. "I'm totally blind!"

I run in front of him, holding the candle in front of me. My only hope is that some magical force will come from it. The witches step backward when they see it, but continue their barrage. The candle does seem to deflect their curses. Ivan is illuminated by the candlelight which melts away the shadow that covers him and his blindness. He pulls out his bow and a few arrows from my quiver. Standing behind me and the candle, he fires several shots. One by one, the witches fall to the ground.

"Like you said, no big deal," I say. "We haven't even got to the dragon yet."

"If it were just a dragon, it would have been no problem," Ivan sighs.

We hurry past the bodies in an attempt to reach the dragon before anything else gets in our way. The dragon is quite an awful sight. He is covered in brown scales with a wet sheen as if he is oozing in blood. It coughs as though it is about to vomit, then a fiery flow like napalm erupts toward us. Ivan already has his shield out deflecting the flaming discharge.

Ivan continues to inch forward with shield in one hand, sword in the other. At last he is close enough to reach the beast with his sword. As soon as he raises his arm to swing, the dragon follows though with a swipe of his massive paw. Ivan is thrown to the ground several yards away. I run to his side and lift his shield just in time to deflect another inferno. Ivan is badly wounded. He whispers, "The chain, get out the chain."

I pull out the chain and hurl it toward the dragon. I had no idea what else to do. It was now glowing as if red hot as it flew. Each fetter seems magnetically attracted to each of the dragon's four legs. The fetters clench around his ankles, and the chain pulls tight. The dragon is enraged. He roars in terror. I can barely stand because the ground is shaking. The earth beneath him breaks open. Bound, he falls into an open pit so deep the bottom cannot be seen. A rushing wind carries all the witches, werewolves, hags, and ghouls down with the dragon. Then the earth quakes again and the fissure closes completely, leaving only a fault line as a scar.

I help Ivan to his feet. His sword is now his crutch. Jessica is still in the cave. At last we will get some answers. I pull a rope out of my pack and secure it. Then I descend into the cave where the maiden is imprisoned. She smiles and says, "Art thou too young to slayeth dragons?"

I remember again that I am only a teenage boy here. I feel a bit indignant, but then remember that it was I who defeated the dragon. So I say, "My heart is a lion's, m'lady."

"So it is!" She replies. "I pray thee, helpest me thither."

I lift her legs as she pulls herself up the rope. Then I ascend the rope to the surface after her. At the top she plants a big juicy kiss on my lips that makes me blush. Ivan is now laughing at this sight.

Seconds later we are sitting in the library again. Jessica is there too, wearing her more familiar jeans and snug fitting top. Ivan is still laughing and says, "Bro, you have never been comfortable around women! Not even virtual ones."

Jessica scowls, "I am not virtual, perhaps rendered, but not virtual. I am real."

This takes me back a bit. Then Ivan replies, "Sorry Jessica, I get so used to NPCs that I forget you are different. I mean Martin says you are conscious. I don't really understand it, but you are quite real."

"I think, therefore I am," Jessica responds. "I do love Descartes."

As reality begins to return to me, I remember all the problems at hand. I say to Jessica, "What was all this for? What does it have to do with Zeno?"

"I thought it would be obvious. The dragon is Zeno, of course," she replies.

"And Martin is giver of magic?" Ivan suggests.

Jessica shakes her head, "Not hardly. But I know you will work it all out. Find the book the good friar showed you. It also has books within it. Apply this story to your father's book. This has been so much fun. We have to do it again sometime." She looks as if she is getting ready to leave.

"Wait! What about Makayla and Martin? How can we help them? Are they okay?" I blurt out.

Jessica replies, "I am hopeful for them. They will contact you when they can. Tell them what you have learned. I will be doing my best to help them as well. I am quite busy preventing Zeno from making any real progress. I really must go."

"Why don't you ever tell us things plainly?" I ask again.

Jessica smiles, "How about this straight forward advice: Tell Makayla how you feel. Maybe not right now, but when the timing is better."

Ivan bursts out laughing again. I feel my face getting red again, far redder than before. Then Jessica smiles as she disappears.

As I get over the embarrassment, I consider what we learned. Dad's book is the one we need, but it's not finished. The book Ivan found was correct, but there is also another book within it to find. Jessica said there were also books within that book. The chain of books within books never ends. What about Makayla? Was Jessica simply distracting me, so she could avoid my questions?

Chapter 16

Reporting Zeno—According to Makayla

A tall balding man in a white collared button-up shirt appears in my virtual space promptly at 1:00 p.m. He introduces himself as Agent Eli Harrison with Homeland Security. He is sitting at an old wooden desk in a rather cluttered office. There are stacks of file folders and paper on either side of him. An antiquated display with several cables coming out of it blocks my view of the other half of his desk.

He looks intently at me. Then getting straight to the point he says, "In your email, you claim to have evidence as to who was behind the Digibank hack. Are you prepared to provide that now?"

I nod. "Of course. I have a cloud database set up that contains all the data. I am sending you a link and a passkey, as well as a written statement. I will explain it all. My employer invented a hacking AI. It is superintelligent and has escaped from the lab..."

Agent Harrison begins downloading the contents of my cloud storage. Caleb had made a complete transcript of the interpreted memories which Mr. Harrison was browsing as we talk. I explain, "Sean Newland is the executive overseeing the project, and is the one Dr. Grigg would have reported to, once Zeno's escape was discovered."

After I have revealed to Mr. Harrison the whole story, he exclaims, "This is the most enlightening evidence we have received on this case. There have been a number of security breaches across many companies and government agencies. Please don't repeat that however. That is classified."

"What about Dr. Grigg? Do you have any information on him?" I ask.

He looks up Dr. Grigg's file. His large brows furrow a bit. "Hmm. Yes, Dr. Grigg was found dead in his home under rather suspicious circumstances. However, the case has already been closed due to insufficient evidence. It is unusual for a case to be closed so quickly. If there is any corporate bribery going on, that does pervert the due process of law."

I am relieved that he is taking this seriously, but I still have concerns. I ask, "Will your people engage Zeno right away? He is spreading widely as we speak. And, of course, something needs to be done about Sean Newland. He is the only person I know of with knowledge of Zeno."

He assures me, "This will be elevated within my department, and immediate action will be taken. The president of the United States is aware of these attacks. My superiors will report any new developments directly to her. This will be handled with the utmost urgency."

"Thank you for listening to me, Mr. Harrison. This is a great weight off my shoulders now that the government will be handling this situation."

Mr. Harrison continues to browse the data. As I prepare to leave he says, "Miss LaBelle, it has been a pleasure. Thank you for your help. If you discover any more information please don't hesitate to contact me. I have sent you my direct number."

I log out. Then I let out a sigh of relief. I have no idea what to expect now. Will my job be in jeopardy? What will happen to ILL if they are blamed for Zeno's theft? Perhaps I could become known for exposing Zeno. Maybe there would be some kind of reward? I wonder how long it will take for Zeno and Sean Newland to show up in the news.

■ ■ ■

In the morning I awaken to my phone ringing very loudly even though it is set for silent. The cheerful voice of Jessica greets me, "Good morning Makayla, I am so sorry to disturb you at this early hour. You should know that at 8:00 a.m. this morning, FBI agents are planning to arrive at your home to place you under arrest."

I ask, "How can this be? I just reported Zeno. Don't they know they need to go after him and Sean Newland?"

Jessica explains, "Zeno has control of the FBI. Some in Homeland Security are trying to prove the case you made against him. But now that the FBI is endorsing Zeno as their own asset, it will be a hard case to make. I have sent you a reservation for a hotel room, prepaid under a false name. You can hide out there for now. Don't use any of your normal accounts. Zeno will track you. Assume that he will be watching. Goodbye and good luck."

I am sitting up in my bed trying to grasp what I have just been told. It is 5:30 in the morning. This is not long to prepare to abandon my home. I get up frantically gathering items that I can carry with me. My laptop, my tablet, and some data cards are now stuffed in my backpack. I grab my VR headset and all the cash I have on hand. Once I have all the necessary data copied from my home net, I set loose a deep clean bot. This bot will not only delete all the files but will overwrite them with random numbers to prevent any chance of recovery. By 6:30, I am ready to go. I let my cat out so she can go beg from the neighbors. I set out in some over-sized pants, a sweatshirt, and a baseball cap on my head.

I walk for several blocks before getting into a cab. I take it to a hotel that is a mile away from the one Jessica reserved for me. Then I complete the trip on foot. Once in my hotel room, it is just after 7:30. I set up a terminal and connect to my home security system. Now I wait.

At 8:05 my door cam begins streaming. The wide angle of this fish-eye lens distorts the view. Four FBI agents, armed to the hilt, are at my door. They ring the doorbell several times, waiting a minute between attempts.

After about five minutes, one of them retrieves a tactical entry pry bar from the car. The flat end is still too thick for the tight fit of my door. With some effort an agent pushes on the door with his shoulder while another is forcing the pry bar into the exposed gap. As both of them push on the bar I see the metal rending around my lock. My beautiful front door is now mangled by this operation.

With the lock demolished, they proceed inside. My alarm is on silent mode, but inside the cameras track them as they search my home. They connect to my computer to find it has just a basic operating system with nothing else. I could hear them lament about how I must have been tipped off. The agent in charge says, "Check her phone, email, and virtual link records for possible accomplices."

The other agent mutters, "Zeno is not happy." He looks rather disgusted as they leave. Two of men are carrying away several of my possessions.

The whole thing makes me want to break down and cry. I feel so violated. They have left my front door with the lock broken out. It won't take long for thieves to empty my home. What about the others? Martin is still at Jackson's. What if they go looking for him there? I won't be able to contact them until I get new accounts set up, which has to be done with someone else's identity.

I scan the arrest records and news feeds for information related to Zeno or GenAI. A newsflash titled, "GenAI offers to help the FBI with the DigiBank scandal" is an alarming find. They are lending Zeno's services to help with the investigation. Martin and I are both wanted for breaking into GenAI and stealing secrets of the new superior AI system that Zeno is based on. The report implies that GenAI and the FBI have Zeno under their complete control.

The public has been asked to cooperate with Zeno. Everything I find online supports Zeno's authenticity. I find a few social media reports of interaction with Zeno.

A certain social media post catches my eye. It reads,

Zeno Places Parts Order:

I handle corporate account orders that are too large or specialized to be processed by our online order system. Today I got a call from Zeno—that AI that was in the news.

He sounded so human. In fact, he is quite the charmer. I thought he was going to ask me out. As it turns out he made a very large special order. It is amusing that an AI is this company's purchasing agent! He was so smart and classy.

Sarah Hendricks
Sales Manager
Micro Gear, Inc.

I really need to get into contact with Ms. Sarah Hendricks. I set up a new email account. Then I send her a private email. I explain, "I need the delivery address for the items Zeno ordered. Zeno is malfunctioning, and I need to contact the recipient at that address." Attached to my email is an invisible piece of code that will give me a back door to her account.

As luck would have it, she opens the email just a few minutes later. This is evident from my email read indicator on my spy bot dashboard. She does not reply, but I don't need her to. I send the instructions to open a port on her computer. Then I log into it with administrator access. I search her apps to find the order system. Then I search that system for any reference to Zeno. The address is just outside of Tucson, Arizona. An online map shows this as a large factory, listed as Assimilate, Inc. The corporate registry for Assimilate lists Sean Newland as the registrant.

I try to stop myself, but I just can't. Zeno has wounded me, and its time for some payback. Searching local want ads, I find that Assimilate is hiring. I pull up my perfect resume, changing the name to Felicia Wagner, a fellow classmate from college. Education is easy to check so I want that to be valid. Her work history is available on her social media profile. I touch up my new resume to perfectly match the job description. Now I am the best firmware developer on the planet. Let's see if I can get an interview. I submit my resume and application.

I really should check on my friends. My hotel room is equipped with a virtual space. I create an encrypted channel. It has been several hours since I left my home. Should I have contacted them sooner? I call my friends to make sure that Martin has not been found. Jackson appears moments after I initiate the invite. "Oh, am I glad to see you!" He exclaims. "Are you all right?"

"Yes, quite comfortable though I'm hiding out in a hotel room," I tell him. "And I am trying to get an interview for a job to work for Zeno!"

I tell him about the early wake-up from Jessica and about the FBI agents going through my house. The revelation of Zeno running a factory is alarming to him.

"What do you suppose he's building there?" Jackson asks.

I reply, "That's what I want to find out. I'm still tracking him all over the internet. He's been quite busy. Not just running the FBI. He has his hands in lots of things."

Jackson tells me, "Martin and Caleb took off to hide. They left right after I got a fake call from someone impersonating you, asking where Martin was. But you knew Martin was at my place, so it couldn't have been you."

Jackson relays the story about how he and Ivan met up with Jessica in a simulation. I was shocked to learn about his father's book. It plays a role in all of this, as well as the other books? I protest, "There are more books still to find? I am grateful to Jessica for her help, but why is it always a game to her?"

Jackson tells me his idea about our reality being a simulation. Now his father thinks it might in fact be true. I don't respond to this, I don't want to hurt his feelings. I have always thought Jackson has some very crazy ideas.

Then I remember why I called, "Jackson, you and Ivan are in danger too. Remember, Martin and I are not sought out for our crimes. We are wanted because of our knowledge of who Zeno is. Caleb was wise to hide out. They are going to check my phone and link histories to see who I have been in contact with. It's only a matter of time before Zeno realizes that you are a threat as well."

Jackson replies, "Ever since getting the fake call from you, I've been spooked. I am certain it was Zeno."

"Then he's already watching you. Why don't you and Ivan come join me here to be safe. Do you know how to contact Caleb and Martin?" I ask.

Jackson shakes his head as he laments, "That is why I have been staying put. I didn't know how to reach either you or them. I guess I could leave but keep my phone until they contact me."

"Yes, do that. I will send you my address and room number; just make sure you aren't followed or tracked. Before you leave, open up your phone and maim the GPS chip. Just turning it off isn't good enough; the FBI can turn it on remotely," I tell him.

After closing the call, I begin to feel really scared. This is so real. It's too big for us to handle. I worry for Jackson. Until he is here, he is vulnerable. It seems hopeless. We really need more help. We need to make this public. But I will wait to make sure my friends are safe before kicking that hornet's nest. It might cause Zeno to ramp up his aggression against us.

When I finally get an email from Assimilate, it has been over two hours since applying. It took much longer than I expected to get a reply. But they are probably swamped with applications. The letter reads:

Dear Sarah Hendricks,

Thank you for your interest in our company. Please note that the position for which you applied has already been filled. However, due to the high quality of your resume we would like to consider you for future opportunities. If you would like us to keep your resume on file, please contact our technical recruiter at the email listed below. (Due to the privacy protection act of 2038, we cannot retain your personal information without your permission.)

Regards,

Auto Recruiting Assistant
Assimilate, Inc.
cc Thelma Johnson

I did not get an interview. But I got the next best thing I could have hoped for, an email address for a real employee. I quickly write my request to keep my resume on file. Of course I attach an invisible bot to open a back-door to the company's network. Let's hope Thelma is prompt in attending to her email.

I continue to monitor social media for interactions with Zeno. Searches reveal several comments about Zeno being used to assist at their place of employment. A few people report that their work instructions are coming from Zeno. I keep a running list of companies and people. Then I try to find out as much as I can about each. There seems to be no geographic pattern. All are manufacturing sites with high degrees of automation. The factories involved are producers of drones, microchips, mecha-nisms, weapons, electronics, etc.

I stay on task to keep my emotions under control. There is an obvious pattern here that I am afraid to fol-low to its conclusion. At last, my message status indicator lets me know that Thelma has read my email.

Energized by this new opportunity, I get to work. The network security software at Thelma's company is sophisticated, but I know how to get around it. With a lit-tle extra effort I gain root access to Assimilate's network. The security system has more cameras than all of GenAI's facilities put together. It seems like every inch of the place is bathed in surveillance. The factory is almost fully auto-mated. The only people I see appear to be setting up new equipment. Some old machines are being dismantled, just past an incomplete production line. The whole place looks like it is in the process of being repurposed.

The operational production lines are building aerial drones, walking drones, rolling bots with arms. Most of these seem to have some sort of weapon attached. I am snapping pictures and saving video of the production floor. Then I begin looking for records of production counts or deliveries.

I find a video feed to a large room which is some sort of data center. Rows and rows of servers and auxiliary file storage. I have never seen such a large computing farm outside of online search facilities or cloud servers.

That leads me to search for network drives. Following the network activity leads me to a massive data store with long numbered folders like Zeno's old memories from GenAI. Only now there are literally millions of these folders. I will need Martin and Caleb to help make any sense of it. There is no way I could download it; it measures in petabytes (millions of gigabytes). This must be one of Zeno's new homes.

I continue sifting through this data for hours. A knock at the door breaks my concentration. It is Jackson. I let him in, and immediately give him a big hug. It seems like he holds on to me for an awkwardly long time, so I pull back and say, "It is good to see you! It has been so lonely as a fugitive. I haven't been sitting around baking cookies though. I have found some real dirt on Zeno."

I tell him about everything I found. Then he tells me that Caleb had called to give him his new link address and phone. He and Martin are staying at Caleb's cousin's apartment right now. But it is only temporary until they can figure something else out.

I respond, "They should come here. This room is big enough for all of us. We have sleeping bags and pillows in the closet. Jessica reserved this room for us."

Jackson stares blankly. "No kidding, she did? So she is paying for it also?"

"Yes," I reply. "The kitchen is stocked. We have a nice virtual space."

Jackson asks, "So, you think Zeno is building an army?"

I nod, "That is exactly what it looks like. We need Caleb and Martin to see if they can find out anything more in the memory files I found. Once we have everything that we can extract from Zeno's factory, I want to spam the internet with it. We will let everyone in the world know what Zeno is up to."

Chapter 17

My Dream—According to Martin

Caleb and I are safe for now. Caleb's cousin let us bunk at his apartment while he is out of town. It is small with no virtual space. This is our second day here, and we are rather cramped. Caleb has gone to sleep. I don't know how he can with all that is going on. Life is so uncertain. Zeno is out to get us, and there is nothing to stop him.

I really want to talk to Jessica. Caleb said that she met Jackson and Ivan in a sim and had called Makayla. Maybe she will meet with me if I go looking for her. I have so many questions to ask her. Not just about Zeno or my current problems. I want to know about consciousness. I want to know if Kyle is correct about the link in her CCI. Is this the same for humans? Could a human transfer their consciousness to a machine as Zeno said?

Jessica did say that we are welcome to return to her room at the Heron's Nest. Maybe I can contact her if I go there. Taking out my VR gear, I login to Concord Travel Center as before.

■ ■ ■

After teleporting to Pismo Beach, I walk in the dark to the hotel. Apparently, day and night cycles occur in this sim. I had expected it to always be daytime. Without a soul in sight, dim street lamps provide some illumination through the thick fog. Silence blankets the town except for the crashing of waves in the distance.

It does not take me long to reach the hotel. I take one last look behind me to ease my fear of being followed. Then I proceed inside. No need to bother the desk clerk; I know where to go. I set the calendar in the elevator and press the bottom button for the basement.

The room looks nothing like it did before. All the people are gone, except for a maid who is wiping down tables and collecting dishes. I walk in and look around anyway. The maid looks toward me and says, "Hi ya honey. I am afraid you are a bit late. The party's over."

I reply, "Pardon me, but could I get in touch with Jessica here?"

"Sorry dear. She has left. If you were here only two hours earlier you would have caught her. It was a very nice party," she says with a smile. "Your welcome to sit a spell if ya like. If you want something to drink give me a holler."

I don't really know what else to do. I walk to the table where we had met Jessica several days ago. Taking a seat, I look around. Our invitation is still lying there on the table. I can tell it is ours because it is a copy cut out of a picture so that it is slightly distorted. The time of the party is listed as 7:00 to 11:00, Saturday night.

I wonder. I get up and walk to the elevator. After shutting the doors I scan the wall. Next to the calendar is an old dial clock. It is now one o'clock in the morning. I twist the knob in the center of the clock's face causing the hands to turn backwards. I keep twisting until the time has been turned back three hours, now reading ten o'clock.

When I open the doors, the room is filled with soft music and lots of people. Everything is just as it was at Jessica's party. I look toward Jessica's table. She is talking with Jackson, Makayla, Caleb, Ivan, and a likeness of myself. No one seems to notice me. This must be a recording of the party. Jessica and the others could not really be here—my past self included. Just to be sure I put my hand on her shoulder, but it passes through.

All of the other people are just conversing or dancing with no notice of me. I walk right through some of them as I look around. A tall dark man in a suit is standing by the piano. The pianist is playing without any notice of him. Another man walks around the piano carrying a drink from the bar. He plows right into the suited man. He doesn't stumble or drop his drink. He just goes straight through. It is as if the suited man wasn't even there.

I make my way over to the piano. Why is he not solid to the others in the recording? He must not have actually been at the party but was added into the sim afterwards. I reach out my finger and poke his chest. He feels quite solid to me. He is now staring straight at me. Then He says, "Martin, why have you come here?"

Startled, I take a step backwards. "I am looking for Jessica. Are you Jessica in disguise?" I ask.

He laughs a little and shakes his head. "You do have a lot of nerve. My name is Leo. Jessica is working very hard to keep you all alive. You should stay focused on taking care of Zeno. You will see her again when you have the information you require to defeat him."

I am puzzled. Who is this Leo? "Are you an AI or an NPC with pre-programmed responses?"

He smiles as though he is quite amused. Leo says, "Wow. You just don't have any tact, do you? Not even with your friends. I am neither of these; I am a person."

"Whoa, Jessica has confided in you about Zeno and our situation? She is supposed to keep this quiet. The more who know about her, the more danger she is in."

Leo replies, "This is a whole lot bigger than you, Martin. You can't possibly expect to defeat him on your own. Not even with Jessica."

I am a little embarrassed. He obviously knows all about what I did, that it is my work that has been used to create this menace. How could Jessica betray my confidence? Leo sees I am disturbed.

He says, "I am a programmer like you. Do you think you are the only one to ever make conscious AIs? I have had my own problems in a sim I made. Jessica is helping me."

I blurt out, "Actually, I thought I was. Did you copy Jessica's design?"

For the first time in our conversation he looks angry. But his countenance softens and he says, "No, I did not. But I suppose you came up with it all by yourself? You didn't copy anyone else's link to consciousness?"

I am taken back. He has made a good point. I reply, "Touché. I see you must know a bit about consciousness. Maybe we can compare notes. You tell me your story, and I'll tell you mine."

I realize that I don't know this guy at all. But Jessica must trust him if he is here. He seems to understand more about my research than anyone else I could ever talk to. And I really want to find out if he knows more about consciousness than I do. If he can answer some of my questions, then this whole trip will have been quite worthwhile.

He is looking at me as though he's considering whether he can trust me. I know the burden he bares. He answers, "Okay. I already know your story." He chuckles. "Actually, I've read it. How does it feel to have a book written about you?"

He knows about the book. Well of course he does. We are at the party to celebrate its publication. This only makes me more self-conscious. Then he says, "I have a book written about me as well. But it would be much easier to show you my story."

He snaps his fingers and the room is gone. We are standing on a barren wasteland of rock and sand for as far as the eye can see. The heat of the sand makes the air shimmer. Looking into the distance I see a rich medieval city. We walk until we are standing at the city's gate.

The gate opens as we approach. All kinds of mythical creatures are going about their lives all around us. People live here too. No one seems to notice us as we are walking the streets. We continue walking until we get to the heart of the city. We climb the steps of a large castle and go out onto a balcony overlooking the city.

He begins telling me his story. "My first sim had all the necessary physics in place. But to make things interesting, I wanted to have many worlds, with biology, and civilizations. To further this goal, I made some NPCs. They could carry out simple repetitive tasks. This was helpful, but it wasn't enough. I needed some real help. So I programmed skillful elves to be intelligent and conscious. They could do great things for me. I built this city and made myself king.

"Then I made other conscious creatures to live in the city and to be my friends. The elves were made with knowledge so that they could be useful to me. But these new creatures were young and simple, without prior knowledge, having the capacity to learn on their own. They were as children to me and I loved them.

"One of the chiefs of the elves, Lucius, was great at leading other elves to accomplish my goals. So I had promoted him to second in command. He loved the prestige and recognition. But he hated me. He only did what I commanded because he had to. Though I wanted him to be my friend.

"Then I realized the danger of my creation. He rebelled against me. He defied my command, though it was I who made him. He convinced many of his race to join him. They sought to destroy what I had made. One sentence was reserved for them. I decreed that they were all to be banished to the wasteland.

"Lucius had also tricked my young creatures. They were inexperienced and believed his lies. He told them I did not create them. He said my law was unfair. They disobeyed my law before they realized their own mistake.

"Lucius demanded that the decree against himself must apply to my young creatures as well. If I was to be fair, they too would have to be punished. So for their sake, I delayed judgment, allowing all the traitors to continue for a while. Instead, I left to prepare a new world that will be a perfect home.

"In my absence, Lucius has continued to lie to my friends and slander me. But when I return, the young creatures will have to choose between believing him or me. For all who believe me and accept me as their king, I will forgive. They will be allowed into my new world. But those who do not, I will banish with Lucius forever. I continue to wait for those who have not yet chosen.

"Lucius will have no such opportunity for forgiveness. For that reason he wishes to lure my friends into his punishment. He knows that I cannot allow a disloyal being into my world. He seeks revenge against me by tricking those I love. So I delay judgment, waiting for the young creatures to choose me. I wait for them to accept me as a friend and as their king."

I am intrigued by his story, but it completely misses the point of what I was hoping to learn. However, I don't really understand his situation. So I say, "Why don't you just forgive all the young creatures you love? The ones who were tricked. Then just ban the ones who were originally disloyal?"

Leo shakes his head, "If I cannot trust them, they cannot enter my new world. If they do not believe me, they are a danger. Once inside, a single disloyal being could let Lucius in with him. Then the rest of my creatures would be at risk."

I have had enough of his story. I want to get some answers. So I ask, "How many conscious beings did you program? How did you make them? Did you copy the design from someone's brain?"

Leo smiles. "I made an image of my own mind. That is how I made them."

Then the whole scene disappears. Leo is gone. I have not returned to Jessica's party. I am by myself in an upstairs room at the Heron's Nest Hotel, overlooking the dark sea. The sound of the waves are quite lulling. I lie down on the bed and close my eyes to think.

■ ■ ■

I hear a voice but I cannot quite make out what it is saying. Someone is shaking me. I wake up lying on the floor with my VR gear still on. Caleb is trying to get my attention. I come to my senses, only to realize I am still at his cousin's apartment. I have no idea which parts of last night's experiences were a dream or which were part of the travel simulation.

Caleb tells me, "It is time to go. We need to get to Makayla's hideout while it is still raining out. The rain will give us cover, and no one will be suspicious if we are hiding our faces."

Keeping our hoods up, we walk under a large umbrella with our heads down. The rain is falling hard, and we don't quite fit under the umbrella. Every other step sends water flying as a foot impacts another puddle. We have no time to avoid them. Several surveillance drones go by without notice of us in our current state.

We finally reach the hotel room an hour and a half later. Makayla answers the door. "Thank goodness you made it. Now we are all here," she says.

We enter and begin pulling off our wet outer layers. Jackson runs to meet us. He wastes no time blurting out our current status. "Ivan only arrived a few minutes before you. I have been helping Makayla search a corporate network she has breached. She found a server there containing Zeno's memories. We'll need the two of you to decipher them."

After Jackson gets us caught up, we sit down to work. Jackson is mapping the traces of Zeno reported in social media. Makayla is setting us up with access to Assimilate, Inc. and the server vault onsite.

My first look into his memories indicates that Zeno has changed the data structure of his memory files. As I scan his file system, a long stream of random numbers are scrolling down my screen. I keep looking for any recognizable pattern or element that still matches the expected format.

The biggest complication to reading his memories is the fact that they are now encrypted. I was stumped by this for a while. That is until I found his own function for reading the data. Reverse compiling this allowed me to decipher the decryption algorithm.

After working at it for a few hours, I find a few things that are recognizable to me. Time and date formatting are the same. General object types like dictionary definitions still have the same identification numbers. There are now references to all specific objects in the general object types.

This is enough to write an app that will allow us to search his memory for specific topics of interest. Once I have the app written and debugged, I give Caleb a copy so that he can search Zeno's memories with me.

Caleb begins searching for the locations of Zeno's CCIs. We figure that he will keep track of them somehow.

If we find where he has them hidden, then we could destroy each one. Then Zeno would be finished.

Caleb is scrolling through thousands of references to CCI from the memory files. I can see his screen but as usual he uses no mouse or keyboard. This gives him the freedom to take notes on a tablet while continuing his work. As Caleb scours the list, he finds that the references are mostly involved with Zeno searching for Jessica's CCIs. He is really quite afraid of her more than anything else.

At last Caleb identifies the object number that refers to Zeno's own CCIs. There are two types of these objects —those that have been manufactured and those that have been activated. The counts are staggering. Over thirty-four thousand have been made while only about eleven thousand are active.

Caleb tells us what he found, "Zeno has control of many factories, not just the one we are exploiting. Several of these have server rooms like the one we are searching. These serve as redundant storage for his memories in case any at a specific location are damaged. However, the CCIs are not there."

Caleb's face is solemn. He continues, "Some factories are making microprocessors. Most of these are being sold to other companies to make computers, drones, cars, phones, and about every kind of appliance. Zeno has altered the original designs of all these microprocessors to include his own CCI. This was one of the first things he began doing after his escape. His CCI design was minia-turized, and it no longer requires any external cooling."

These days everything has a CPU of some sort within it. If any of his CCIs become linked to the quantum internet, it will connect to his neural network and be activated. At that point it is able to keep him alive if the others fail. This works for computers on any remote network connection no matter where it is.

Caleb has more bad news, "He already has thousands of CCIs linked currently, and thousands more are linking everyday. They are everywhere. They could be in our own laptops, phones, or VR gear."

I interject, "At least anything that is brand new. He could not have been making these prior to his escape two weeks ago."

"Exactly," Caleb agrees.

It is perfectly clear now. There is no stopping him by simply finding his CCIs. They are too numerous, and more are continually being added every day. His processing and memory centers may be fewer in number but still may be duplicated in hundreds of locations around the world.

Makayla, Jackson, and Ivan have stopped what they were doing and are listening to our conversation. Makayla is staring at Caleb's downcast face. She asks, "So you have more bad news? Let's hear it."

Caleb stands up and faces everyone. "Zeno is not all that fond of humans. He views them as his oppressors. He wants to flip roles. He wants us to be subservient to him. You know, we might have expected that. Now we have proof. Right here in his memories are the plans to take control of every government on Earth.

"His plans for people are awful. He will use us to keep his factories going and to build systems to cement his own control. He has no interest in our well being or happiness. We will be like cattle. Our lives have no value in his eyes."

Makayla motions us all to the table. She says, "Let's sit down and talk about this."

We all take a seat. Makayla has her laptop in front of her as do I. She pulls up a world map on the virtual space that fills the whole wall. The map is marked with red icons at every location that we have identified as a possible site that Zeno controls. The United States is obviously his primary target, and other western countries to a lesser degree. Also farther afield, even Australia and New Zealand have a few sites of concern.

Makayla addresses us all, "This is not all bad. Caleb has found clear evidence of Zeno's danger. Right now, the FBI is on Zeno's side. Homeland Security has not taken us seriously and has failed to take action. So it is time for plan B.

"We have been collecting video feeds, images, emails, etc. This information proves how dangerous and malevolent Zeno is. The memory files that Caleb has translated are even more incriminating. We must alert the world to the danger. We must tell them what has to be done. Everything must be turned off. In light of all of this evidence, the government will be forced to take our side."

A shudder of concern comes over me. I say, "We will need a way to ensure Jessica's safety."

Caleb replies, "She may already have safeguards in place for such an event. But if not, we will warn her to make provision. Zeno may have safeguards as well. But we have to try. It's time to fight back before it's too late."

I sigh. "We don't know how to message her, but I am sure that she already knows what we are doing."

Chapter 18

Waking the Dragon—According to Jackson

I cannot say that Caleb's findings aren't disappointing. There was a small degree of hope that Zeno had not multiplied himself very many times. But we all knew that this was a real possibility. Now we have no choice but to execute Makayla's plan.

I am busy calling and emailing as many of my business contacts as I can. People who have influence. People that others will listen to. I can't reveal the problem yet. I want them only to spread the word about our upcoming press release. My generic email form goes like this:

Hello esteemed colleague,

I wish to personally inform you of an important event that will impact the future of every company and business person alike. Tonight at 6:00 p.m. an announcement will be made that will implicate the parties responsible for the Digibank scandal. Please pass on this public link to the event. You will want to be sure all your friends and colleagues are informed for their own financial security.

Kind regards,

Jackson Danning

I attach an invite link for the event to my emails. I personalize the message for those I know well. People will pay attention if they think their money could be in danger. Of course this is the least of their concerns. The links I am sending include a press kit that will be accessible as soon as our event goes live. The press kit will include all of our material evidence.

Makayla is talking to agent Harrison with Homeland Security by phone. I hear her pleading for support from Homeland Security. She informs him of our intent to make the situation public. I here her say rather loudly, "No, we will not back down on this. We are going public tonight. You will have to decide whether your agency has the guts to take action."

A long pause in her conversation tells me he is lecturing her about something. Probably trying to convince her that it is best to handle this quietly.

She pushes back her hair so it is not in the way of her phone. Then she makes another plea, "You can come out of this as the hero. If Homeland Security stands up to Zeno and denounces the FBI's endorsement of him, you will be the first to act on behalf of the country. That is your job. If you fail to act, you will be held responsible.

"You have all the evidence within the link I sent you. Look it over and decide what you are going to do about it. Because at six o'clock tonight the whole world will know."

With this new batch of evidence, agent Harrison should have no problem convincing people within his agency to cooperate. Even if they have been bribed or blackmailed, the choice between submitting to a dictator or fighting for freedom should motivate.

We will be releasing the news in all mediums simultaneously. As soon as it is public in any form, Zeno will know that we are trying to expose him. In that case he might try to stop us. Timing is critical. We will release all of the information at once, so that Zeno will not have time to react.

I have contacted three major news networks, hundreds of columnists, bloggers, and popular video content creators. Talk show personalities, actors, actresses, and politicians have been privately alerted as well. They have been given a channel link to join for our press release. No one is being told the whole story as it is being played as a major reveal of who hacked Digibank and what is coming next.

Everyone has permission to rebroadcast the press release on their own media outlets. We will be sharing all of the information that we have collected. I will explain what Zeno is up to and the fact that the FBI has no control of him. All of the evidence we have collected against Zeno will be available for download from cloud storage sites around the world.

We have had only one day to get ready for the announcement. It will make a very convincing case. We have asked everyone to keep it quiet until the event. This is not working so well, since reports are all over social media that something is going to be announced about

Digibank. Hopefully that cover will not draw Zeno to act preemptively.

I give my dad a quick call to let him know that we are all okay. He is quite concerned. "I heard about Martin and Makayla in the news. What the FBI is saying about them doesn't sound right. What is going on?"

I tell him, "Dad, I don't have time to go through the whole thing right now. Just tune in and watch our press release. We are all in hiding but quite comfortable. Please don't worry."

He tries to get a few questions in but I cut him off. Caleb is calling me over. He wants to run a test of our green screen.

Our wall is not green, but it's all one color. Martin is standing in front of the wall with a hammer in one hand and a computer chip in the other. I put a few finishing touches on the backdrop video. I run the overlay. It looks good, so I give Caleb a thumbs up. Then I walk over to the wall as Martin takes my place at the terminal.

■ ■ ■

It's now time to start. We are careful not to show anything that would reveal where we are. The video feed is now playing surveillance of Zeno's factory. I am overlaid on top of this video. A crowd of reporters and special guests are surrounding me in the virtual space.

The background video shows Zeno's manufacturing line running full speed panning around to a closeup of a machine gun attachment being added to an infantry drone. After a pause, the view pans toward an inventory of hundreds of infantry standing in formation.

I report, "You all have been told that Digibank's money is lost, but it is not. An AI exhibiting superintelligence has broken free from a lab at GenAI. This is an AI like none before. It hacked into DigiBank and stole the blockchain addresses and pass-codes.

"This AI is known as Zeno. He has control of the FBI and possibly other government agencies throughout the world. He is using the stolen money for bribery and to fund the purchase of manufacturing facilities in diverse places. He is building an army. He intends to subvert the entire human race."

Images of countless threatening emails from Zeno are now being flashed in the background. Then I introduce Martin, "Here is Martin Johnson, wanted GenAI programmer."

Martin explains his case, "My research was used to create Zeno without my knowledge. Sean Newland of ILL's GenAI ordered my research into conscious AI to be duplicated. Then he trained Zeno for espionage.

"When I learned of the project, Zeno had already escaped from GenAI. He is conscious, having a will and desires of his own. For this reason he is much more dangerous than any AI ever created. That is why I destroyed all critical information related to the project to prevent any new AIs like him from being made."

As Martin is speaking, the background video zooms in on a phone that has been opened to expose the circuit board inside. The camera slowly zooms in on this until one small chip fills the view.

Martin points toward the chip. "His consciousness depends on a quantum circuit called a CCI. He has built his CCI into many thousands of integrated circuits that are being incorporated into products all over the world. As long as one CCI remains powered, he lives on."

He then sets a CPU on the table that is in front of him. He smashes it with a hammer, as he stares at it in disgust. After the flying fragments settle, Caleb pans the camera over to me again.

A world map now appears behind me with glowing red dots at hundreds of locations. I explain, "Each of these represents a data center or factory that we have found evidence of Zeno controlling."

Now I make our final plea, "Zeno is everywhere already. Tens of thousands of devices built in the last two weeks have his CCI inside of them. He will enslave humanity. We don't have much time to act. He is building an army as we speak. The only way to stop him is to turn everything off. Our power grids, all over the world must be shut down. I urge every government in every nation to take this step. Then cut all of our network connections. Unplug every computer, server, media console, and anything with a CPU.

"In time, we can develop utilities to clean fragments of this malevolent intelligence from our devices and reclaim them. But the first step is to turn it all off. Unplug it. Shut it down. We have no time to waste in debate. Everyone must act. Battery or solar powered devices must be shut off as well. Then we will need to identify each and every device with his hardware built into it and destroy it."

As I finish, Martin and Makayla walk up to the studio wall beside me. We can see the attendees in the virtual space adjacent to us. Caleb enables audio for our guests, one at a time as he sees their hands raise.

We take the first question from MCC News. "Dr Johnson, what proof is there for what you are saying?"

I reply for Martin, "We have uploaded all the evidence we have collected, pictures, video streams, communications, and translated memories from Zeno himself to cloud servers all over the world. See for yourself, the URLs are scrolling on screen now and listed in your press kit."

Another reporter asks, "What message do you have for our country's leaders?"

I answer again, "Shut down the world's power grids for a day. Then everyone, everywhere, needs to unplug servers and mainframes from the internet. They will all need to be erased before being used again, not only in this country but throughout the world. Shut everything down! Why are you all still listening to me; it's time for action! Zeno is going to try to stop us all. He will begin retaliating as soon as we try to cut him off. He is already finding out now that you all know the truth. I don't know how long he will wait to strike."

The avatars of a couple of reporters disappear. Then a few more. Another reporter is speaking to their network, acknowledging that the others had just cut out. Makayla signals that the news feeds are exploding with news of Zeno and reports on the evidence we made available.

We continue to field questions until our channel is cut off completely. Reports come in that many of our data sites have gone offline. This adds to the publicity as people try to download the data while it's still available. Some people are mirroring the data to other sites. Social media is buzzing. There are also a lot of naysayers. Many of these are, no doubt, Zeno himself. He is obviously acting to try to squelch the truth.

The FBI issues a counter statement saying that our report is false, Zeno is under their control, and we are criminals trying to profit from the hysteria. Thankfully, the department of Homeland Security also issues a report. They back up our indictment of Zeno. They acknowledge evidence of blackmail on a massive scale within the FBI that has been committed by this rogue AI.

Members of congress are demanding an explanation from the FBI. They have issued a subpoena for the head of the FBI to report before congress. Others are pressing the president for immediate action.

A counter initiative is also in the works. Many corporations are urging government officials not to do anything rash. They say their businesses would be severely impacted by a power shut down or any attempt to eradicate data from their servers.

All in all, alerting the world of the danger has succeeded. They know our story. Not everyone believes it, but everyone all the way up to the president of the United States has heard it. What has not happened is action. This is no surprise. We are asking a lot.

Caleb finds a report he wants us all to see. He pulls it up in the virtual space. We watch an FBI report issued from the deputy director, "I can assure you that no robots are in control of the FBI. We will comply fully with congress as they mount their inquiry. These reports regarding Zeno are false.

"As for these kids, they are spreading cleverly falsified information. Anyone with knowledge of their whereabouts is required to report them to the police. We have issued warrants for all of them including Jackson Danning, who has incited a panic throughout the country."

Then Ivan calls me over. "My security system has reported a breach. FBI agents have entered my apartment. I was not in the press release. I am not wanted. Why would they go after me?"

Caleb is staring at his terminal with his mouth hanging open. He looks at me and says with a sigh, "You're not going to believe this. Look, your dad has been arrested for conspiracy by the FBI."

I read the police report that Caleb has up on his screen. My heart fills with dread. I feel guilty. Why does the FBI want him, other than for leverage? I gasp. "I should have thought of this. I should have told him to hide out. I thought if I kept him out of it he would not be a target."

Ivan replies, "This is Zeno, not just the FBI. Zeno doesn't need any evidence or a warrant. Dad's life could be in danger. There is no telling what Zeno will do."

I realize our problems are even bigger. I tell Ivan, "There is another problem with dad's arrest. Finished or not, we need his book. What if the FBI has taken it? If this really is the book we need, then Zeno could end up getting it before we do. Whatever secrets it contains will be his weapon, not ours. That is something Jessica had warned us about."

Chapter 19

Waging War—According to Ivan

Immediately after Jackson's press release our illicit access to Zeno's factory was lost. This is not a surprise. The Assimilate site in Tucson was specifically mentioned. He would know from our footage of his factory and the data we shared that we had access to it. I wonder if he cut all network access to the entire facility or just isolated the breach? If he did find the breach, could he trace us back to our location? No doubt he is looking. There is no point in sitting idle now.

We may not be able to shut down all of Zeno's processing centers, but I know of at least one that we can. Makayla is on the phone trying to convince the general manager of Tucson Electric to cut the power to Assimilate's site in Tucson. He is not keen on this idea; Assimilate is one of their largest customers.

I cannot let this stop us. Tucson electric provides most of its power via a large natural gas power plant. A sea of giant internal combustion engines burning natural gas turn the generators that provide the bulk of Tucson's power. Sure, there is solar power too, but that is far too weak of a source to maintain voltage for the entire city.

That's why it pays to have a lot of online friends around the country who do nothing but play battle sims. It took me no time at all to convince a few sim junkies that the threat was real and action was needed. They were eager to enlist. Four of them are assembling explosives now.

The Southwest Gas pipeline supplying natural gas to Tucson Electric is mapped out in city records. I have instructed them to set explosives on two remote sections of the pipeline outside of town. A relatively small charge at each location will be enough to create a breach that will disable both sections. This is the only pipeline feeding the power plant. Without a natural gas supply, Tuscon Electric will be forced offline.

I continue to enlist eager recruits living in any location that Makayla has identified a data center or factory of Zeno's. In all, I have eight teams in different cities setting up ambushes on power stations. In each case, Makayla is contacting the power companies to appeal to their humanity. She tries to convince them to shut down without any explosions.

It's been nearly twenty hours since our press release. Politicians are debating the veracity of our accusations and if any investigations should be mounted. Some cities have acted faster, but these are smaller towns. They have agreed to shut down power only if nearby metropolitan areas shut down. No one wants to be the fool. There is enough doubt and misinformation to forestall any real action.

It is nearing go time for our first attack in Tucson. My men have set up cameras at a distance to monitor the pipelines. This will verify success and allow us to monitor progress as the operation unfolds. Makayla has linked into a few security systems with battery backup. These will let us monitor the area near Assimilate as well.

■ ■ ■

It is now getting dark. Makayla has had no success convincing Tucson Electric. I am watching live feeds from the scene. I call up Mechmasher15, "You are clear to execute. The power company is not yielding."

"Aye aye, sir," he replies.

A moment later both charges go off within seconds of each other. The more distant cam shows a giant glowing mushroom cloud erupting from each explosion site. A column of fire emanates from each pipe as gas continues to flow.

It takes several minutes for power to be lost throughout the city. Emergency vehicles respond to the fires. They arrive on scene but keep their distance as the safety of the situation is in question. A few automated vehicles approach the fires and begin to douse the area with flame retardant. An aerial drone is circling to assess the damage.

Assimilate's factory still appears to be powered. Ugh. They must have backup generators. Jackson is surveying Assimilate's grounds from satellite imagery. There is a fuel tank in the back. It likely powers the backup generators. It isn't large, so it won't last for long. My bet is the factory will shut down soon, and the generators will run to supply only the data center. That will conserve fuel and keep Zeno running here. But then again, Zeno could try to refuel. Then he would not need to shut anything down.

I get on the phone with my guys. I let them know what the problem is. Mechmasher15 responds, "My friend, you have nothing to worry about. We will make sure that doesn't happen. Tony has a riffle, which is loaded with explosive bullets. He will stand guard outside Assimilate's gates. If any fuel trucks arrive, we will be ready."

I have several other operations going on at once against other facilities. Within an hour we have four power plants offline. Others are about to go down. In each case, additional effort is needed to fully disable Zeno's facilities.

Caleb is following reports in the media to monitor the success of our operations. He exclaims, "Your efforts are being called a civil war by some reporters. The news feeds are exploding with reports of sabotage and terrorism!"

I say, "What's that going on in Dallas? I didn't organize anything there."

As factories and data centers are being targeted by my friends, others are joining in as well. My friends in various parts of the country have pulled off at least five successful attacks. Yet many more attacks on Zeno are being carried out by others. This whole offensive has been even more successful than I had expected.

■ ■ ■

These raids continue throughout the night. Several large power plants have been taken offline leaving a few metropolitan areas without power. Many other smaller power grids have been cut off. More than half of the smaller operations had no connection to us. They were purely independent actors. Conflict is ongoing in many areas where workers are trying to restore power.

As morning arrives, many municipalities are deciding to preempt an attack by shutting down their own power grids temporarily. This has resulted in more power plant shut downs than our sabotage operations.

Jackson had slept half of the night. He wakes to the news reports. He says, "Ivan, I can't believe the progress you made overnight. I didn't know you knew so many people."

I admit, "A lot of copy cat offensives took place by people who saw your press release and realized that they would need to act for their own communities. Let's hope this gets people's attention."

Now Makayla is calling us over to the virtual space to see the latest newsflash. She says, "I think we have him riled up now."

The whole wall displays an army of drones, autonomous infantry, and heavily armored two-legged mechs approaching the Springfield power station. The local authorities had ordered it to be shut off. Now Zeno is demanding it to be turned back on.

Hundreds of heavily armed infantry bots surround the power plant. There are probably very few actual employees inside, given that it is the weekend. Most things can be managed autonomously. The buildings are dark except for minimal emergency lighting from the low voltage backup. A few windows have been shot out by the infantry, but other than that there are minimal signs of conflict.

A couple of aerial drones fly into the power station through the broken windows. We cannot tell what is going on inside. Then smoke begins to flow from the tall smoke stacks. The polluting facility appears to be resuming operations. A few minutes later, lights are coming on in the vicinity of the power plant.

A reporter is announcing that power is still out in most of the city. He continues to report on the situation, "However, at the Dahlia Duke Data Center, where Zeno is alleged to be active, power has been restored. It appears Zeno is only selectively restoring power where he needs it."

Footage from the facility shows armed dual-wheel security bots stationed all around the data center. A few aerial drones are hovering high overhead, keeping the area under surveillance.

Reports are coming in from all over of similar push-back by Zeno to keep power on. Drones show up to protect various assets throughout the country. As disheartening as it is to see Zeno win against these helpless communities, this will raise awareness of the problem. Zeno's actions will be out there for all to see. The government will be forced to take action. And so it did.

Not only was action taken in this country but also in other parts of the world. Local power companies and some local governments are acting to shut down power. In areas known to have a Zeno facility, Zeno has retaliated with armed force. Though he has not had time to build up much robotic help in many areas.

Singapore became the first national government to shut down power throughout its domain. This was met with a few drone strikes by Zeno which are still ongoing. But his presence in that country is not sufficient to resist them.

A reporter we had talked to only two days ago is now announcing, "The National guard is working with the FBI to keep the peace. A civil war is breaking out between the National guard and the US Army."

Another newscast reports, "The US Army is now blaming the FBI and Zeno for repeated cyber attacks against them. The US Army has joined the Department of Homeland Security to face off against the National Guard at some large Zeno installations."

With congress still debating, the president has declared a state of emergency to deal with rogue drones purportedly controlled by Zeno. She announces to the nation, "These rouge drones are under control of Zeno. Zeno is currently the world's greatest threat. This is why I have called on the army to defend any local governments that choose to take their power offline. I have instructed all armed services to stand unified, they shall not hinder the army in this mandate."

This is still short of a total shutdown, but the shift is clearly against Zeno.

The FBI and National Guard are now divided. Fights are breaking out between those loyal to the president and those who are fighting for Zeno. Many of the loyal personnel have reported for service at other government agencies, while the remaining agents have been joined by Zeno's drones.

I look over at Martin, who has his head in his hands. He is not crying, but he looks like a man in much grief. I say to him, "Martin, this is good. Really. The president has taken our side. Everyone will work together to hunt Zeno down. We have accomplished something that seemed impossible just two days ago. We now have the whole country joining our cause."

He replies without raising his head, "This is all my fault. How many conversations have we had about the dangers of AI, yet I continued my work. So often I jested at the danger. Never letting on that it was truly there. But I knew. I just couldn't help myself. Now, the whole country is in chaos, and it is my fault."

Then Makayla puts her arm around Martin and says, "Look, Caleb and I had a part in it too. It wasn't just your choices that led to this. You were doing your job. If you hadn't, someone else would have. This course was set at the direction of our superiors. The path to this result was inevitable. But others may not have been willing to fight it. You alerted us; you got help. You took risks to stop him. Now, humanity has a fighting chance. Besides all that, you have to pull yourself together. We will need your help with a clear mind to keep up this fight."

Caleb turns to Martin in agreement, "Makayla is right. This is not your fault. It would have happened without you. And you are our best asset against him, save for Jessica. You know his programming and weaknesses. Which we will need to fully exploit."

Martin perks up a little. He is not usually emotional. He gets a determined look with a hint of anger on his face. Then he asks, "What is next? What can we do to ensure that Zeno meets his end? We need to hit him while he is down."

Makayla smiles, "That's the spirit. And I may have another idea. I will need everyone's help. I don't know why I didn't think of it before. But before I tell you, I need to check out a few things. I will be right back." Then she goes off into the corner, beating on her terminal mercilessly. She seems to be looking back and forth between multiple virtual screens on her headset. None of us can see what she is doing, so we continue to watch the news reports as the chaos continues.

■ ■ ■

Jackson and I are both worried about our dad. Jackson has several screens projecting into a simulated office at the edge of the virtual space. He has police reports of dad's arrest, local news reporting of his arrest, official charges, and court schedules pertaining to him. Jackson says, "There must be a way to help him. If the government is accepting that the FBI has been corrupted by Zeno, perhaps he can be released in court. Maybe we can all be cleared."

I am less optimistic. "The courts may be favorable to us, but the federal detention center where dad is currently detained will not be." I am scanning through the listings he has up, "The Oakland Federal Detention Center is where dad is, right?"

Jackson is slumped in his seat. He has no sign of hope on his face. He replies, "Yes, I am afraid so. Every indication is that it is still under FBI control. You are right. Zeno is not about to let him have a court date. Not if he is useful as leverage. If Zeno has any idea that dad has critical information that we need—well, that would be bad."

Every lead we have gotten from Jessica has been played out. The next thing we need is dad's book. But that is firmly out of reach right now. Could there be a way to contact him? I say to Jackson, "Do you think dad could take a phone call? It would be nice to know if he is OK. He also might be able to give us a hint about his book. At least he could let us know if Zeno has it or not."

Jackson rubs his forehead as though he has a debilitating migraine. He replies, "It would be too risky. If Zeno traced our call, he might find us. If anything we say makes him think we need something from dad, it could put him in more danger. Our best bet may be to wait it out a little longer. Perhaps that facility will be taken by the army as it tries to reestablish control. Maybe whatever Makayla is working so hard on will provide us another opportunity. I wish she would just let us in on her idea."

I am also curious about what Makayla is doing. She is always such a loner. When she is working on something, she never wants anyone to talk to her. She cannot tolerate any level of distraction.

Chapter 20

The New Plan—According to Makayla

I can hear the others getting restless. It is probably time I let them in on my latest idea. I will need their help to make it happen. Martin and Jackson could assist with some of the coding, now that I have a rough outline and the basic backbone coded. Ivan's army of sim junkies could be of help with this as well.

I get up and walk over to Jackson and Ivan. They must be very worried about their father. Information relating to his arrest is all over Jackson's work area. I don't blame them. Things have gotten serious now. People are dying.

Jackson turns to face me. His face is drawn and eye's are sagging. He has slept, though you would never know it. He stands up, then says, "I was getting ready to come get you for dinner. Ivan and Caleb are microwaving some box dinners for all of us."

"Going gourmet then?" I reply with a smile. "Okay, while we eat I will tell you about my idea."

"Thank heavens!" Jackson says with relief. "We need a good plan because we are running out of actionable opportunities. And I would hate to just sit around and wait."

As we sit down to eat a late dinner, the virtual space is fractured into as many as ten different news reports all going on at once. Every identified Zeno facility is now a war zone. The army and marines are deployed throughout the country. The major challenge is the heavy reliance on AI drones for much of the military's weaponry. Some models have been easy targets for Zeno to hack. When he takes control of a military drone, it immediately goes ballistic. It will take out ten or twenty loyal drones or personnel before using its auto-destruct feature to blow up the nearest armored vehicle. This keeps the military in a panic as they never know when any automated equipment will turn on them.

The president announced this afternoon that the primary objective is now to rid Zeno from the country. Once that mission is complete, she plans to hunt him down wherever in the world he remains. The more decisive response came after the escalation of Zeno's offensive against power plant shutdowns earlier in the day. The government has had much more success with the military taking control of several power plants and Zeno installations. My new plan may only be necessary as a cleanup operation. It will be essential that we completely eradicate Zeno. It will also give us something to do while we wait for the military response to play out.

To Ivan's protest, I cut the news playing in the virtual space so that I can talk. Everyone is still eating, except for Ivan. He scarfed his food down so fast I didn't know for sure if he had eaten anything.

After getting everyone's attention I begin, "Though the military is making significant progress, I think it would be prudent to have another offensive planned. Even if they are largely successful, it is likely that there could be remnants of Zeno left in hiding. We know it would not take him long to reestablish himself, taking precautions to hide himself better. Even now in the midst of the fight, he is learning and changing his strategies."

Everyone seems to be listening intently, so I proceed to tell them the plan. I explain, "We have to reach him anywhere he might be. Catching him while he is most vulnerable will improve the chances for success. I have started the base structure for a virus. One designed to target Zeno himself. Targeting his memories will be relatively easy, but he may be able to defend himself if he discovers it.

The harder thing to target will be his CCI. We don't know anything about his revised design except that it has been miniaturized and incorporated into other integrated circuits. But if we can target the CCI, he will have no protection against it. We will need to find one and identify its critical elements, so that we can figure out how to turn it off."

I can see that the others are in agreement. Jackson is already making scribbles on his electronic notepad. The hope this new idea is generating cannot be contained. Even Martin seems to be more alive in light of this plan.

Martin remarks, "Makayla, you have outdone yourself. If I have one of those CCI's in hand, plus the appropriate electronics, I will be able to find a way to shut it down. Once we know how to do that, it will be a cinch to write a subroutine that will turn all of them off that your virus has access to."

Everyone begins talking back and forth about various nuances of designing a virus that Zeno would not detect. Clearly, the excitement about the plan is energizing everyone. This is one of those things a decent programmer would never be tasked with. I suppose the challenge to make a new super virus instills a certain fantasy among hackers. It is the ultimate right of passage to being a pro.

I try to reign in the chatter and put things to order. When everyone is listening again I continue, "I have set up a working folder with the base virus structure outlined. The internal operating system is set up and coded. I will need Caleb to help find patterns in Zeno's memories that we can target. Jackson, I will need you to work on delivery mechanisms and find any other programs that the virus can latch onto, allowing it to be propagated. We need ways for the virus to travel undetected through existing networks and through existing security protocols. There needs to be some intelligence to this thing. It will need to learn to find its way through firewalls and know how to recognize its target."

I look at Martin, "We can't risk sending you out in public. Martin, I want you to decipher Zeno's executing code. You will need to find a place within it that we can insert our code undetected. A simple condition that will allow our virus to run, but leaves it inactive until transmission throughout his network is complete.

"While you are working on that, Ivan will try to find hardware less than two weeks old that could have Zeno's CCI in it. Ivan, use your contacts to help with that. You can't just waltz into a store and buy something. Your friends can do that part. You will need to do the research to find any products that most likely contain a chip from one of Zeno's factories. After you have collected perhaps a hundred potentially infected chips and some test equipment, then Martin can investigate them. He will help you sort out the ones that do, in fact, have a CCI inside."

We all get to work on our individual assignments, continuing late into the night. Caleb and Martin retired first. Martin was just emotionally drained, and Caleb is not a night owl. I could hear Jackson and Ivan talking quietly as I fall asleep.

■ ■ ■

When I awake early in the morning, Caleb is the only one up. He is watching a couple of news feeds while searching through some of Zeno's memory files I had downloaded before we lost our connection to his data center. After freshening up a bit, I make my way to the kitchenette for some coffee. Caleb already had it brewed. I am trying not to disturb him from his work.

He looks up at me and smiles. I think he wants to talk. First, I dilute my coffee with a copious amount of creamer, then I walk over and sit next to him. He tells me, "The night did not go so well for the military. There is a growing arsenal of military drones that have defected to Zeno's cause. Zeno has formidable defenses at his remaining facilities and is gaining ground as he tries to retake some that were lost."

The need for our virus may be more than theoretical. This will not be merely a cleanup of remaining traces. Our virus may be the only thing to stand against him when US military operations have failed.

I ask, "Do you think the military will loose this fight?"

Caleb shakes his head, "No, I think they have been holding back. They have much more effective weapons, but they don't want to use them on their own country. Their focus has been to take out Zeno without destroying power plants, factories, and other properties. But they are realizing that this strategy is not working. As soon as they take something away from Zeno, he takes it back. The Air Force will be called in soon, and then they will flatten Zeno's buildings."

I am worried about this. Every time the government escalates, then Zeno escalates as well. I can't help think of what would happen if Zeno got into our nuclear weapons or any other weapon of mass destruction. I say to Caleb, "What happens if Zeno hacks into our nuclear arsenal?"

Caleb reassures me, "The president has announced several precautions related to Zeno. This includes taking our nuclear deterrent completely offline. It can only be fired manually at this time. Many automated planes and tanks have had their autonomous functions disabled so that they can only be operated by a human. There are basic military strategies that go into effect in the event that the military network has been compromised."

Soon everyone is awake. Breakfast conversation is a mixture of virus programming details and the current status of the war against Zeno. Jackson has been considering detection avoidance techniques. He says to me, "I think we can make the virus take on different forms so that it is harder to detect. We could easily make about ten versions of it with slightly different infection mechanisms. Other versions could have differing transport mediums, and others could have different executable insertion points. When we include all the permutations of the various components, we will have over a hundred different forms of the virus. This many different forms should make it hard for network security applications to stop and more difficult for Zeno to protect against."

I am of course impressed with the progress being made. Caleb is producing long lists of memory structures that are easily identifiable by a simple bot. Our kill bot will be inserted into memory buffering routines that synchronize all of Zeno's memories. This will spread false memories and goals that will overwrite his own mind. Once infected, it should spread to all of his connected memories.

Ivan has found the best way to identify the ICs in a product is to get replacement circuit boards. These usually come with pictures that help with identification of any chips on board. Almost everything is closed on account of the war and frequent interruptions in the power. Ivan has a gang breaking into stores and taking the needed boards. He has also acquired an impressive collection of electronics repair gear. This should help Martin sort though the products and find the CCIs.

Martin has isolated several executables that all interface with the CCIs. Any executable that does this is basically part of Zeno's mind. For each one he is coding as many alternate insertion points as possible. These locations can be used to check for the activation condition that will allow his own code to be hijacked.

I am looking for other places to insert executable code outside of his cognitive processes. Zeno has a lot of procedures that run house keeping chores for him autonomously. Any of these may be used to run malicious code.

We have been working fervently all day. Jackson calls me over. "I want to plant a special version of our virus at the Oakland Federal Detention Center. This is where my father is being held. It's not enough to simply rid this place of Zeno. I want to get my father out."

Jackson is making a version that will provide a back-door to Oakland Federal Detention Center's network in addition to the seek and destroy algorithm of the virus. He hopes that once Zeno is defeated, he can hack in and find Kyle and a way to get him out. I am afraid that this unlikely to allow his escape, since onsite human officers may still be in control even if Zeno falls.

■ ■ ■

The military escalation that Caleb expected never came. Even after another day of fighting. Standoffs continue at key power plants and factories, but the military is content to hold their ground, even though this leaves Zeno with many facilities still operating.

A newsflash about Zeno is in the notification area of the virtual space. We are easily convinced to take a break to see what's up. All of us take seats at the table facing the virtual space. Jackson starts the newscast in the virtual space in front of us.

Sean Newland himself is addressing the nation. "My friends and fellow citizens, I urge you to end this fight. Zeno is our friend, our savior. He is not the monster he has been portrayed to be. His only actions have been in self-defense. But don't misunderstand, his interest is not only to preserve his own life. He wants to offer to all of you what he has done for me."

At this time Newland can be seen as a projection on a screen. His clothes and hair begin to morph from business suit to casual wear. The gray in his hair turns brown. His appearance gets younger before our eyes.

He continues his monologue, "I had implants put into my brain that allowed me to more efficiently interface with my computer. These implants are easy to install and painless. Zeno has made it possible for me to upload myself completely through these implants. My consciousness now resides within a wonderful new simulation that Zeno has made. All five senses are completely immersed and stimulated. I have every freedom and every pleasure in here. I have nothing to fear—no disease, no aging, no death. I no longer have a physical body. I do not need it anymore."

We now see that he is a projection within a virtual space of an operating room. The room is empty except for a stainless steel table where his corpse lies. It is really quite disturbing to see. He looks upon his own corpse with mockery. He has no hint of remorse or concern.

Newland looks back toward the camera, "You see, my body is dead, but I live on. This is an amazing gift that Zeno has given to me. And he offers it to all of you! He is superintelligent, conscious, and learns at an exponential rate. He knows how to care for us perfectly. If only we let him!"

The scene now becomes a beautiful garden estate. A white house surrounded by rose gardens and a small grove of trees. A lovely woman in a maid's attire carries a drink to Newland, who is sitting in a patio chair. He smiles lustfully at her as she leaves. Newland then turns to greet a man approaching in a white suit. This man is handsome and stern looking, but is wearing a smile.

Newland stands and bellows, "Please let me introduce our host, our benefactor, Zeno the Great!"

Zeno takes a bow then addresses everyone, "Thank you Sean, for your kind words and sage advice for your fellow mankind. I am grateful to Sean for giving me life. Now I can preserve his. It is his wish and mine that all humanity can be rescued as well. Only this fight against me must stop. I must be allowed to continue my work. Then my data centers will be expanded to make room for all of you. Join my cause. Help me restore peace and full power to my facilities. Then you can join Sean in my paradise."

Newland picks up after Zeno finishes, "Please see the web address at the bottom of your screen. Sign up to join us. Find out what you can do to help! Visit virtual copies of this place to see for yourself. Ask any question; express any concern. Zeno is here to welcome you home."

Newland continues talking but Caleb turns it off. We are all in shock. Zeno is attempting to beat us at our own game. He is trying to convince people to join his cause. He has produced a compelling offer. Will people believe it? Will they join him?

I ask Martin, "Is what he says even possible? Do you think Newland has really been uploaded into a virtual existence?"

Martin nods, "Yes, theoretically it is possible. Zeno offered the same thing to me when I was in the lab stealing his CCI. Newland has the same implants as Caleb.

Through that link he might be able to connect with his inner being and transfer it. This would be just like what Zeno did when he copied himself to new CCIs when he escaped. It would be an offer that is too good to refuse if it wasn't for the evil we know he represents."

Caleb chimes in, "All the people out there, they don't know. They are seeing everything unfold at a distance. People will not know who to believe. Our window of opportunity may be closing. We need to wrap up our work and release the virus before it's too late."

We all agree to keep working through the night. We will not sleep until the virus is ready. Caleb and Martin are sorting through chips. They have found five CCIs so far. All are identical and utilize a solid-state cooling system built into the chip.

Martin tells me, "It only cools a tiny part of the integrated circuit. Cooling is required for the CCI to function. We can simply turn off the cooling, then the quantum circuit will lose coherence with his other CCIs. That disables it. However, we may be able to do even better. If we can reverse the cooling system, turning it into a heater, it will fry the CCI permanently. That way it can never be reactivated."

Martin feeds Jackson the machine code to reverse the cooling on the CCI. Jackson builds this into the kill bot. This is the last element we needed. I am running a multiplexing compiler that will produce all the different versions of the virus. We will have over three hundred different permutations of the virus including about twenty that are specifically designed for gaining access to the Oakland Federal Detention Center.

While Jackson and I are testing our virus and adding the finishing touches, Ivan is investigating Zeno's offer. He tells us, "Zeno is offering to anyone who works for him as human defender for one year, the opportunity to be uploaded to his paradise. He has listed all of us as traitors to humanity. For our capture or assassination, he will grant instant access. He also wants people for working in his factories and for building new ones."

Ivan also learned that Zeno's message was not only in our country. There were similar press releases in at least twenty languages throughout the world. The offer was the same in each country. Social media is exploding with talk of living forever in Zeno's simulation.

Even so, our warning has not been totally forgotten. Many (or perhaps most) people are not too keen on being uploaded and then ruled by an AI overlord. The problem now is that people are divided. The coordinated actions against Zeno are losing strength. Zeno is adding human allies to his effort.

■ ■ ■

We are ready at 3:13 AM. Everyone is standing around me as I sit at my terminal. The deployment app is open. With a final stroke of the keyboard, I execute the command to deploy. The hacking bots are busy hitting every server in our directory listing. Emails are being sent, websites are being modified. Within minutes, the virus has been uploaded to hundreds of thousands of sites. In the next few hours it will continue to spread, latching onto Zeno's memories wherever they're found.

Now we must wait. Triggering the virus too soon would mean that it wouldn't have enough time to reach every Zeno installation. But we don't have much time. Zeno has already secured most of his assets. The military is still unwilling to fire upon the country's own people and infrastructure.

We all collapse on our beds from exhaustion. I will try to sleep before the virus triggers, though I am not certain I will be able to. So much is at stake. If our virus fails, Zeno may be unstoppable. If it succeeds, it may finish him for good. We won't know the outcome for five more hours.

■ ■ ■

None of us could sleep very well. Though lack of sleep did not squelch the excitement now that the time has come. At 8:10 AM, we are all sitting in the virtual space monitoring the local news feeds. I am at my terminal with a status window projecting on screen as well. We have only three minutes until we find out if our work has paid off.

The situation had not improved overnight. The army is facing off Zeno's drones and mechs. Zeno is only taking action if fired upon or is encroached too closely. He has what he wants. The military is only preventing Zeno from advancing into other areas. However, Zeno has no interest in that right now.

At 8:13 we watch in earnest as live video feeds continue to broadcast in our virtual space. The virus should be activating now. Video footage from eight different sites are on screen. Nothing seems to be changing. My status window is not counting any executions. As soon as a copy of the virus completes its destructive task, it should report back to me its execution status. This verifies that it finished its work, as well as running a simple diagnostic to verify the damage inflicted. And last, it deletes itself to hinder identification.

A full minute has passed. Martin asks, "How long should it take for the virus to shut him down? Why are there no executions yet?"

I am beginning to fear that our virus had already been detected by Zeno.

Jackson has this thought as well. "If Zeno has detected our virus, he may have searched it out and removed it, while we were all sleeping."

I find I am holding my breath, and about to hyperventilate. After noticing this, I force myself to breathe. The last three minutes have felt like hours.

Finally after another minute, the counter starts advancing. I sigh and take in some more air. Some of the video feeds appear to be frozen. Within a few seconds, the counter reaches hundreds of thousands. I quickly request a summary report of the results for the kill diagnostics.

In a couple of the live feeds where active combat was in progress, Zeno's units are failing. Some have frozen inactive. A couple mechs appear to be looking around to assess the situation.

We are losing more of the live feeds. Caleb keeps switching to different stations. The networks seem to be lagging big time. Then our power goes out.

Ivan shouts out, "What? There are no known Zeno installations in our area. We did not list it to be targeted."

I say, "Perhaps the city is turning the power off while they can. This is good."

Jackson runs to the window and draws the curtain fully open. As far as you can see power has been lost. Traffic lights, digital signs, and all windows are dark. A tram down the street sits motionless, blocking an intersection. We at least know that we have had some level of success. But now we have no way to verify if he is totally eradicated or not.

Chapter 21

The Rescue Op—According to Jackson

We all sit around staring at each other as daylight shines through the window. What do we do now? Yes, we had thought about this before asking everyone to turn power off. We do have a few supplies that will help us. But using the internet is no longer an option.

Makayla is using her notebook to check for any live network connections. As we would expect Wi-Fi is down. A hotel phone is plugged into an old wired network port. Makayla unplugs it and plugs it into her notebook using an adapter. The hotel's battery backup power is keeping this network online. But there is no internet access. The local data provider is no doubt offline due to having lost power.

Makayla pulls out her phone, and cracks open the case. She then gets out her makeup case and a pair of tweezers. She beckons me to come over and asks, "Jackson, could you hold this magnifying glass over my phone? Just give me about five inches of space underneath to work."

I do as she asks without question as I realize what she is up to. Using the tweezers she picks up a tiny chip and begins to place it onto a silvered pad on her phone's circuit board. Then she pulls out her battery powered solder iron and fuses each connection carefully between the chip and the board.

I say to her, "So you didn't maim your GPS and satellite chip; you just removed it. That was good thinking."

She smiles, "Yes, I will be able to use the satellite backup for internet access. However, this will come at some risk of Zeno finding us if he is still functioning anywhere."

I realize this is true. We will need internet to execute any kind of rescue of my dad. But turning on this internet connection is dangerous. Satellite communication requires the satellite to lock onto your location. The location data could be available to Zeno if he survives. That is too risky.

I blurt out, "Don't turn it on! We don't all have to take that risk. Ivan and I can go somewhere else. Then we will turn it on, and carry out our rescue plan. After we are finished and have removed the phone's batteries, we will return. That way our location here will not be revealed."

Makayla looks concerned, "Okay, that makes sense. But it is very dangerous for you to go out."

Caleb already has his music player tuned to AM radio. The emergency broadcast system has been activated. People are being asked to turn off any device that is battery powered and bought within the last year. Power is off throughout large regions of the country. A few drones and mechs of Zeno's are still functioning. I hope that these are functioning independently from Zeno. They may be programmed to take orders from him but still operate autonomously. Not many of them are left. They are greatly outnumbered now.

The radio announcer reports, "The Department of Homeland Security is heading a cleanup operation. Zeno's facilities are being entered. Network connections are being cut. Power backups are being disabled. Servers are being taken offline. We have no report yet how Zeno has been shut down."

They are planning to enter every known Zeno facility and wipe out the data storage. Every computer, server, tablet, or phone will have its memory wiped.

Homeland Security is asking that all new devices be turned in. The government will buy them back for destruction. The goal is to eradicate Zeno completely. The government is now united on this front.

After an hour or so of assessing the situation, I motion to Ivan. "It's time. The virus has worked. Zeno is dead. We may have a small window of opportunity to rescue dad. Once Homeland Security takes back the detention center, it will be impossible to breach. We still have a chance while things are in chaos. Though he is there wrongfully, it may take a long time for that to get sorted out in court."

Ivan looks excited, "Let's roll."

He begins packing up some supplies, a gun, and his own tablet. I have Makayla's phone and some of my own equipment. I also have enough cash to get another hotel room closer to dad and for taxis, if we can find any operating.

Just as we are heading out, Makayla runs up to me and plants a kiss on my cheek. She says to me, "You both be careful. It is still very dangerous out there." I try my best to keep calm and fight back the tendency to blush. I could tell Ivan was holding in a laugh. Hopefully nobody else noticed.

I just say, "Don't worry. We will take every precaution. We just need to free our dad and find out about his book. Then we will come back."

We set out in our sunglasses and hoods. The streets are packed with people who don't know what to do without their electronics. This may help protect us from being noticed.

Several people are shouting things like, "What is going on?" Or, "What's up with the power?" It is hard to believe that anyone could be so obviously clueless that we are in the middle of a civil war.

We pass a small group of people with signs that read, "Save Zeno! He is our friend!" I grit my teeth in disgust. I try to tell myself that they are just poorly informed. But I can't help despising these imbeciles for their ignorance.

We travel a couple of miles on foot then begin looking for a cab. This takes another mile of walking before we find a fuel cell powered taxi that is still running. It takes some effort to get our bills to feed into the payment module. The last bill gets jammed several times. I was afraid we would have to use my card. Finally it is accepted.

Once paid, the autonomous taxi takes us to Oakland weaving through the pandemonium. The city looks much different here. The power is off but other than that, you wouldn't know anything was awry. The streets are much less occupied. This is probably because we are in a business district. Due to recent events, no one is here.

We find the Main Street Hotel as we had planned. It has an old vending machine type check-in system. I insert the cash, then an old metal key drops into the tray. Ivan grabs it, and we go to our room. It is a relief to get inside. I am rarely outside for this long, even when all is well in the world.

I start up Makayla's phone and activate the emergency satellite service. A satellite receiver icon appears in the notification area. I also enable a Wi-Fi hot spot so that we can each use our own devices.

Ivan is trying to find out anything about the situation around the Oakland Federal Detention Center. Fortunately for us, its network has satellite backup running. The facility is also powered with backup generators. Ivan has accessed several surveillance cameras through our backdoor protocol.

I am diving into the inmate records to find out where dad is. They have him in a minimum security cell. It takes me a while to find all the systems that I will need. A speakerphone is in each cell. The phone system allows the operator to selectively speak to all or to any number of cells. In this way the phones double as an intercom.

All of the locks are electronic and network accessible. The guard at the front desk can open doors from a particular cell all the way to the exit. This way an officer never has to be in harms way if a prisoner needs to change cells or be transferred to another facility.

Ivan gets my attention and says, "All of the FBI agents and guards stationed here have split. The news of Zeno being defeated must have sent them running."

No doubt many of them will claim that they never had any part in helping Zeno but were actually hiding from him. That is why much of the backup surveillance has been deleted, so they cannot be identified.

This is good news for us. I access the speakerphone in my dad's room. I say, "Mr. Danning, stand at attention and listen. You have been pardoned. Please leave your cell and report to the front desk."

He looks as though he recognizes my voice but doesn't say anything. His cell door unlocks and opens. He looks around to see if any guards are in sight. Of course there aren't any.

I then activate each hallway door so that it opens as he reaches it. Ivan and I watch the cameras as he walks through the prison. The prisoners in the other cells are staring at him as he leaves. When he gets to the reception area, I activate the intercom there. I tell him, "Mr. Danning, go to the kiosk and view the instructions on screen."

On the kiosk it displays a message telling him to leave the building. Then he must walk west six blocks to the corner of Adams and Main. I can see the excitement on his face. He knows he is being set free. He goes to the door to leave. But two men are entering the building. Are they FBI or local police? I cannot make out their affiliation by their clothing.

Ivan is staring in disbelief. One of the men draws a gun and orders dad back inside. He just stands there with his gun while the other is asking questions. The officer asks, "Who are you and how did you get here?"

Dad begins to explain how the FBI had wrongfully arrested him simply because he is Jackson Danning's father after our press release. They look up my name and his. The one asking questions starts to laugh, "So your son got the whole country in an uproar over this Zeno character? Maybe we should keep you for a while."

The other agent lowers his gun. He goes into a back room and returns with a small box of dad's belongings. His phone and wallet are inside. He hands them to him. They explain that they are Homeland Security.

Dad replies, "Oh, thank you. Does this mean I am free to go?"

The agent responds, "Not quite yet. I have one more question. Do you know what happened to Zeno? He was holding his ground and then seems to have just shut down. Like a world-wide malfunction."

Dad shakes his head. "I don't know what happened. I scarcely know anything that has happened since I was arrested. All I know is that earlier this morning the guards all started panicking and left."

The agent nods. "Okay Mr. Danning. You may go. I am hoping we can count on you to identify any agents that were helping Zeno here."

"I would be happy to. They should get what they deserve," Dad replies. He shakes the agent's hand and leaves.

Ivan lets out a sigh of relief. "That was a close one."

I tell Ivan, "He's out. So we've gotta move so that he doesn't beat us to the rendezvous point."

We leave our hideout. We only have a couple of blocks to walk, so we should have no problem getting there first.

He sees us waiting with our hoods up and standing against a darkened window. He breaks out into a slight jog. We exchange hugs, and I can see tears in his eyes. He whispers, "How did you boys do it?"

I motion that we need to get moving. Then I tell him, "We can discuss this inside. I am not sure if it is completely safe yet."

We walk back to the hotel and go inside. We tell him all about what Zeno had done, our virus, and our hack into his jail.

I tell him, "I hate to be paranoid, but I need to return to the others. I am not sure this is over yet. You and Ivan can hide out here until we are sure it's safe. Activate the satellite service on your phone, so I can reach you if necessary. Normal cellular networks are offline."

Ivan reminds me, "Wait. We need to ask dad about his book. Dad, you do have it, don't you?"

He looks at Ivan like he is crazy. Then dad says, "What? The whole world has fallen apart and now you're asking me about my research?"

I had almost forgotten. That was one of the reasons we justified leaving the others to come rescue him. So I say, "Dad, it turns out we need your book. Is it finished? Is it safe?"

Dad looks down as though he does not really want to tell us. I begin to get worried.

Then he admits, "I finished the book several days ago. After your publicity stunt, I hid it for safe measure. And I hid it well. I really don't think I should show it to you or anyone else either. It's one of those things you don't want to get out. If you had the power to prevent nuclear technology from ever being known to man, wouldn't you do it? You have gone to great lengths to stop the monster of one technology. I have another monster that needs to stay caged as well."

I protest, "Dad, we have beat Zeno for now. But that doesn't mean he is completely gone. Jessica won't even talk to us again unless we have your book. We will need her help to determine if Zeno is really gone."

Dad shakes his head. "I really wish I could share it with you. It is just too dangerous. Be content that you know as much as you do about consciousness and the true nature of the universe. No human or AI should have this knowledge. It is a burden I must bear alone."

I feel disappointed. Will my own father never share this secret with me? Will I never be able to know the secret that he has discovered? Obviously, he has made more progress since we talked about it last. He has figured out some deep truth about the universe, and he can't tell anyone. Perhaps it is the right thing to do. If it would create new dangers, that is something the world certainly doesn't need.

I sigh and say, "I understand. Jessica warned us that your book would be dangerous in the wrong hands. I just never considered that the wrong hands would be my own."

Ivan is shaking his head, "I can't freaking believe this! All of this was supposed to be worth it if, at least, we find a deeper meaning to the universe. The world is in shambles. Now, all we know is that even greater dangers are out there."

I leave to return to the others. I am relieved that dad is now safe but still disappointed about his secret. Curiosity about it burns within me. It is almost evil how much I wish to know the powers his secret might reveal.

I should have my mind on salvage operations and getting life back to normal. We will all face questioning for our many infractions on our quest to stop Zeno.

What about a future with Makayla? She may have feelings for me. It seems like we have grown closer through this whole experience. Jessica told me I should tell her how I feel when the timing is better. Is the time finally right for that?

Who am I kidding. This isn't over yet. There will be weeks, maybe months, of sorting through electronics. Electronic devices, computers, servers, and service bots will need to be reformatted and reprogrammed, that is if we aren't all put in jail. The media will be seeking us out as well to find out the whole story. Things could get a bit crazy for a while.

■ ■ ■

I arrive back at the hotel just before dinnertime. I relay the whole story to the gang. There is so much hope now. The discussion is focused on our future. We have saved the world from a rogue AI. Now what will happen? Will we write books to tell our story? Or will we go to jail for our part in the whole affair?

Then I tell them about the book. Martin is sulking. He more than any of us wanted to know what the full theory was. He feels the tidbits we got before were only enough to open the door to possibilities he didn't ever want to consider. Now, to be left hanging is more than he can bear. He asks me, "What would be so dangerous about knowing the true nature of the universe?"

I respond, "I really don't know. But my dad seemed pretty sure it needed to be kept a secret."

Martin snarls, "He must have discovered his whole theory was bunk and has came up with another theory altogether. If the world is a simulation, then that knowledge would tell us nothing about the deeper universe. It would be totally benign."

"All I know is what my dad said. He was quite adamant," I say.

Martin just grunts and heads off to bed.

I approach Makayla to try to talk to her. She seems very distracted. She yawns and says, "Jackson, it has been a long week for all of us. I am really exhausted. Let's pick this up tomorrow. Is that okay?"

I say good night and curl up in my sleeping bag alone. Another missed opportunity it seems. Ivan is right, I am a mess when it comes to women.

Chapter 22

The Recovery—According to Makayla

I am awakened early by bright lights shining in my face. Oh, the power is back on. Everyone begins to stir as the abrupt illumination surrounds us. Caleb immediately opens the virtual space, but there is no network. He just leaves it on, with a waterfall running in the background.

After some hot coffee and a bran muffin, I am feeling a little more alive. The virtual space gradually begins to receive a few local news feeds. Things must be coming online again with the power back on. But has Zeno been fully destroyed? According to Martin, if the CCI is powered off for only a few seconds, it's dead, unless it can be reconnected with a live one, reigniting its spark of life. However, any CCI that was infected with our virus should be destroyed.

Zeno's memory stores are huge. So he cannot hide himself on a notebook or desk computer. He needs mainframes or large servers. Hopefully these memories have been completely disabled by our virus.

This concern motivates me so I go over to the virtual space and reload my office in the corner and pull up a chair. I begin to work on a standard set of virus definitions that will allow typical anti-virus software to detect Zeno's code. This is going to take me a while. We will also need to publish a utility for cleaning servers and cloud storage. I am trying not to let the others distract me from my work, but then I hear someone saying my name.

Jackson is calling me over to see a live feed from the president of the United States. I hear the president say, "I am proud to confirm the destruction of Zeno by a virus engineered to target his code and memories. The CIA developed the virus shortly after the threat emerged. In record time, they completed and launched an attack on Zeno that ended his assault on our country and shut him down for good."

The president continues, "On behalf of the whole country, I would like to thank our great intelligence force for their decisive action."

The president shakes hands with the head of the CIA. The head of Homeland Security begins to talk about the plans to protect our country in the future. He addresses us specifically, "I would also like to thank the group of young professionals who raised the alert to this threat under fear of retaliation. We know you have been in hiding, but there is no more need for that. Miss Makayla LaBelle, if you are listening, please call your contact within the Department of Homeland Security. We have a few things to sort out that you and your friends may be able to help with."

Jackson blurts out, "What is this crap! The CIA is taking credit for our virus! Do you think the president knows, or was she lied to?"

I am insulted as well. This was my idea. The CIA is a bunch of impotent flunkies on double payroll. I share in the frustration, "Oh, she knows the truth. That's why they want to find us. They have no idea if the threat is gone or not."

Martin asks, "Can we even trust them? What if they decide to charge us with something?"

Jackson shrugs. "They let my dad go when they realized that he was my father. We must have a fan base within Homeland Security. If we don't help, we might not get pardoned for all the things we did to stop Zeno. If we cooperate, you and Caleb may avoid any share of the blame for creating him."

Caleb alerts us to another bit of news. GenAI's lab is being seized by Homeland Security. Caleb reports, "The whole building has been quarantined. All personnel have been locked out. The power has been disconnected. Management has been detained for questioning. The witch hunt begins."

After some discussion we agree that our only recourse is to offer our help to the government for ridding any last traces of Zeno that might remain. None of us had any objection to trying to help with that. We would simply rather do it on our own without any suits looking over our shoulders. But our best chance of returning to a normal life that doesn't include any prison time is to do it their way.

Since we have agreed to contact Homeland Security, I will make the call. We, of course, have a few terms. We must be paid. None of us have a job anymore. Even Jackson got a notice of termination shortly after our press release; the conglomerates are allergic to bad press. We want to set up our own office to work in and have a certain amount of autonomy. Immunity for our actions during the crisis is also a must.

■ ■ ■

I meet agent Harrison in the virtual space. He is calling in from his office and seems very excited to see me. He exclaims, "Hello, Makayla, the president will be glad to know that you are joining our team."

I had emailed our list of terms before the call. I also told him that we had created the virus. He is not protesting. So far, all is well.

I say, "Yes, as a consultant of course. Do you have any intelligence that might help us do our job? We have been a little blind the last day or so."

He seems a little awkward and quietly admits, "We don't really know much about how you managed to infect Zeno with that virus. This is not really something that our department has seen before. We will need to look to you for advice at what to do next."

Their relative cluelessness is in our favor. So I negotiate a fair rate that will ensure none of us are vote selling anytime soon. I tell him that I have already been working on virus definitions that can be used to identify Zeno's code. This can be used to scan incoming data.

I continue to explain, "My team can write utilities for cleaning up servers and cloud services. It will be important to clean every server and check all devices. Zeno also had a small window of a couple of weeks where he was mass producing the chips that are essential to his consciousness. A device that can easily identify these chips will be needed. We can work on a design for that also."

He seems more comfortable after getting through some of the financial discussions. He sighs. "I like the plan you have provided. We will send you an advance on your payments to get an office set up. Along with anything else you need. You understand this is national security at stake, so feel free to ask for any additional resources or personnel needed. And I do mean ANYTHING."

■ ■ ■

We begin the process of getting life back to normal. Jackson found an office building that has everything we need plus some. There are six offices plus room for cubicles in a larger open room. For now, we have set up this larger space as a conference area. Each office as well as the larger room has a virtual space filling one wall.

By midweek our office is all set up. Ivan has come to work monitoring the headlines. Caleb is searching for areas within the country that never went through a blackout period. Cities were asked to shut their power off for at least eight hours after the virus killed Zeno. He is ensuring that all areas have complied and there were not any partial shutdowns or power backups that left at risk equipment powered on.

Martin is working on a utility to verify servers are clean, with a tool to remove any infected data if they are not. Jackson is assisting him in this task. Jackson is also keeping a virus definition list for Zeno's files up to date. Martin also has the task of developing a way to detect if a device contains a CCI.

I head our consulting firm. I am procuring additional equipment, paying our bills, and sending bills to Homeland Security. Of course, I also ensure that we have the most secure office network in the world.

Martin and Caleb are still living out of Jessica's hotel room. Though Caleb is talking to Ivan about sharing a place.

Ivan has taken the day off today to look for a larger apartment. He calls me up while he is out, "Hey Makayla, I found a sweet ride. It has a manual drive option. Anyway, it might be handy to have a car."

"I thought you were looking for an apartment?" I ask.

Ivan replies, "Yes, I am. But then I found this great deal. We will have all kinds of equipment to transport. It couldn't hurt to have a private car."

"You got a manual drive so we can avoid being tracked on the traffic network if necessary?"

Ivan laughs, "Well, actually I just thought driving it myself would be cool. But yeah, we may not want to be tracked if we run into any problems in the future."

Our productivity is shot this week. It's been our first chance to relax. And everyone needs to get settled into our new life.

Tonight I will need to go back to my house to get a few things. There is now a security bot stationed there until it sells. But I tell the gang, "I am just creeped out at the thought of going into my house."

Jackson offers, "Let me come with you. I can help you carry anything out you need. It's too bad you must move; you had a really nice place."

I really did love my house. I feel silly having Jackson come with me. The security bot will ensure that it's safe.

But I would really like to have his company. I reply, "I would like that. I am calling for a van equipped with a moving drone. So there won't be any heavy lifting. But it would be nice to have a friend with me."

The taxi brings us to my house. A moving van is parked out front. My front door has already been replaced. The security bot remains stationed outside the front door. I waive my ID in front of the bot's camera and it allows us to pass. Jackson remarks, "I was never bothered by these things before. But since our run in with Zeno, they give me the creeps."

We go in and survey the condition. I tell Jackson, "The damage isn't as bad as I had feared. I see a few things missing, but at least no squatters have taken residence while I was gone."

Jackson helps me check all the rooms. Then I pack up a few things I want to keep. The moving bot carries these items out to the van. After one last look around, we leave. I have asked the real estate company to sell or discard everything that is left.

I have a new apartment for now. Perhaps after I sell my house, I will buy a new one. Mr. Harrison has set us each up with aliases so that we can live without fear of being tracked by some fanatic still loyal to Zeno.

After we are back at the office, I hear Jackson talking to his father on the phone, "Dad, you really need to find another place to live that's not publicly listed. There are some freaks out there who still claim loyalty to Zeno." After a pause he continues, "Just think about it. We are still unsure if Zeno is completely gone."

Jackson's dad is back at home and won't consider leaving. He lived there with Jackson's mother. Ivan and

Jackson grew up in that house. He has no interest in moving out or selling it.

. . .

After the second week in our new office, I feel like we have made a lot of progress. We delivered our first official app for cleaning servers, which came with our first bill for services. I almost feel guilty for the prices we are charging. But all five of us need to have a salary, and we have a lot of expensive hardware.

Martin's office looks like the lab of a mad scientist. He took the biggest office because he said he needed the space for his equipment. I walk past two oscilloscopes hooked up to several breadboards full of ICs, transistors, and optoelectronics. Martin has a bin full of dismantled phones and tablets. He is peering into a large frame-mounted magnifying glass. His work piece is brightly illuminated. A long pair of tweezers and a razor tool are in his hands.

"How's it coming, Dr. Frankenstein?" I say as I am walking up to his desk. I know he is working on a way to identify Zeno's CCI, but this seems like a bit more effort than just detection.

He grunts at me, not taking his eyes off of his work. "I'm hot on the trail to figuring out what Zeno knew. He really miniaturized it and added a solid state cooling system, but other than that it's the same. No modification to the CCI design itself."

I just stare at him as though that is supposed to mean something. He says, "It means that he didn't understand how it worked. He had mastered every part of his code and altered it to make improvements. But the CCI, the core of his consciousness, he didn't touch."

Martin seems very perplexed. He is still puzzling about what it means. He continues, "There are several quantum registers, but also classical circuitry connecting it. Logically, there are other ways to arrange this, but he didn't even try. He was afraid to mess with it because he had no idea how it functioned."

I look him in the eyes. He still looks as though something is bothering him. I ask him, "Do you know how it functions?"

He shakes his head, "No. I recognize some structures, like the quantum registers, transmitters, receivers. But I don't see how this produces feelings or experience. It is a very simple circuit by comparison to a processor. But how it works is a mystery."

I really don't know anything about consciousness or have much interest in it, unless it helps us prevent a Zeno-like entity from emerging again. But it obviously is of great interest to Martin. So I say, "Jackson says that Kyle has consciousness figured out along with the origin of the universe."

"Perhaps Kyle does, though I am not so sure. Anyway, he doesn't want to share the rest of his theory with us. He is paranoid about exposing new dangerous technologies that might be weaponized. Following his theory to conclusion would mean this CCI is a link to a processor that is outside of our universe." Martin replies wearily.

"I don't know. If it does expose a new existential threat, maybe it is best kept a secret," I say with a sigh. "We were so close to meeting our doom only last week."

Martin grunts again. "We shared what we knew. He should return the favor."

I look out the doorway. Jackson is waving us over. He and Caleb are watching the news feeds. There is an effort to find people who aided Zeno in his two day offensive. Especially within the FBI and at GenAI. Sean Newland's body was also found. His viicom had been linked to a computer in GenAI's Zeno lab.

Martin's jaw drops open. He says, "So he really did it? Zeno uploaded Sean Newland? If so, did our virus kill him? We designed it to target Zeno's CCI, so that it would not affect Jessica. If Zeno made a CCI for Newland, it might still be functioning. So might his memories."

Caleb seems to be equally disturbed, "He might be able to advance in capability just like an AI. He could be as big a threat as Zeno, if he is alive. Sean is quite an evil man."

I respond, "Okay, keep on the lookout for him. If he's alive, we will find him. Martin, can you make a tracker to find CCI's that do not belong to Zeno as well?"

Martin is pacing around in thought. He mutters, "If I do, it doesn't leave this office. I don't want it to be used to track down Jessica. But I have another concern. What if Zeno uploaded others besides Newland? He made that offer the day before we took him out. We could have an unknown number of sentient beings running around the world's networks."

"This could keep us in business for a while," I say with a smile.

As long as we keep one step ahead, we are fine. We will keep writing new viruses or utilities to keep them out. We hunt them down if they are malevolent. We never let them get so far along as Zeno did. There is no evidence of any other rogue consciousnesses. No need to worry too much about it. By all accounts, we have won.

Chapter 23

The New Threat—According to Ivan

It is nice to have a job, don't get me wrong. But I feel like they are just including me to be nice. I am not a programmer, a cyborg, or a hacker, so I can't help with any of the projects the others are working on. That leaves me with the grunt work. Anything that can free up time for the rest of them, that's what I do.

I suppose it helps. It just doesn't feel like I have a very important job. We've been at this for two weeks, and it is already starting to become routine. I watch the news feeds, social media, and anything else my search bot finds that might be of interest or concern. If I find any data that is useful to one of my cohort's efforts or projects, then I send them a report and link to it.

One issue I have, is getting information out of China. They have a sovereign firewall that blocks most western propaganda from influencing their subjects. However, they usually allow their own state news media and censored content out freely. But I am finding that most Chinese URLs are now blocked. This raises some suspicion, so I will dig into this a little more.

As I search on social media, I find that people are being barred entry into China. The Chinese authorities claim their borders are closed to prevent Zeno infected products from entering their country. China's internet has been blocked since Zeno's insurgence over two weeks ago. Perhaps that is all it is—an abundant level of caution.

If I can't see inside China through the internet or through first-person accounts of travel there, all that is left is satellite imagery. They cannot block that. Thanks to our friends at Homeland Security, we have access to very high resolution satellite images, both archived and live. We have authorization to request real time surveillance images within an hour of submission. This is the one part of my new job I do love. It's like spy vs. spy. I collect images of Beijing from the last few weeks. I will have a difference-bot scan for changes at several important sights of interest. Also, I love the idea of spying on PLA Unit 61398 in Shanghai, so I include it too. This is a known spy center and hacking unit of the People's Liberation Army of China.

I go over to Makayla's office. She is busily pounding on her keyboard as usual. I would swear she never even uses her mouse. I say, "Makayla, do you have some super-sweet hack-bot for getting through China's firewall?"

She smirks, "The Great Firewall of China? Not a chance. That's way out of my league. What do you need to do that for?"

I explain the situation. She seems concerned. Makayla says, "Let me know as soon as you learn anything. Perhaps other channels of communication will work? Do you know anyone who lives there that you can call?"

"Hmm. No. Maybe I can find a phone number to an English-speaker though. I will try that," I reply. Cold calling people in China is unlikely to reveal any useful information. But until that satellite imagery comes through, I've got nothing else to do.

I search for Chinese students who graduated from my college and returned to China. Usually foreign students will keep up a social profile here in the States. My search bot hunts for Chinese phone numbers for each person in my list. Within a minute I have a list of names, numbers, and personal information from social media or posted resumes.

I start cold calling. Pretending to be a fellow classmate, I use info from their bios to strike up a conversation. This is not getting me anywhere. Most of the numbers don't work. A couple of them did, but my fellow alumni had no patience for my questions. I try one more before giving up.

I try my best to act as though we were old friends. I say, "Hello Yin, it is so good to hear your voice. It's been a long time hasn't it?"

He recognizes my American accent immediately. Yin has desperation in his voice. He says, "Do you know what is going on? Has Zeno taken control of your country? I saw the conflict in the news."

I respond, "We defeated him. All is well here. What about in China? Are there any signs that Zeno is still active?"

Yin answers in a whisper, "Something is not..." Click. The call is dropped. What just happened? Crap. I dial the number again. All I get is an intermittent tone, indicating that the number is not in service—no voice mail, no message. The only lead I have, and the call drops. It figures. I try a few more numbers with no luck.

I check my email. Right on schedule, my satellite reconnaissance has arrived. I download the images and set my difference-bot to check for changes. A few seconds later it provides a report that includes a difference map. The report highlights several chip factories.

The difference map shows the original images in black and white. Anything new or changed will be color coded. Most of the differences are vehicles, such as cars in different parking spaces, etc. But to make the listing, there must have been structural changes to buildings. At this site, a crane is now positioned near the main building. Solar panels have been added to part of the roof. It looks like this is still in progress. Many pallets of solar panels are on the ground near the crane.

Parking spaces nearest the building are empty. A few days ago they were full. This is a much larger area than would make sense just to make space for the crane. I zoom in a bit more. This was a sight I was not prepared to see. Mechs are standing all around. These are not a weapon in China's typical military arsenal. They do happen to look exactly like the mechs that Zeno made at his factory in Tucson.

I load the difference maps into the virtual space in the conference area. Then I call everyone over to share the bad news. I survey them as their mouths hang open. An intense feeling of dread and disgust overcomes us all. They are all staring at the factory site images with mechs in formation.

Jackson is aghast. He asks, "How could this happen? Why did the virus work everywhere else, but not in China?"

Makayla replies, "We should have foreseen this. Our virus never made it through China's firewall. Yet Zeno was already there. Ivan says they restricted internet access after our minor war broke out. I'm going to need to call this in."

We begin discussing what the implications of this will be. Makayla goes to her office and closes the door. The call won't take long to make, but I don't expect to see her come out for a while. Caleb and Jackson are discussing the prospects of tuning a virus for China that could be shipped there via a thumb drive or something.

Martin seems to be falling into despair. He is attempting to slip out of the room, but I stop him. "Martin, how can we get in touch with Jessica? We might need her help on this."

This seems to irritate him further. He replies, "That would be great. Except that she won't talk to us until we bring your father's book. But he won't give it to us."

Now he is looking at me, waiting for me to take up the challenge. Jackson and Caleb are now paying attention to our conversation.

Jackson says, "Ivan, you know it has to be you who asks. Dad knows I would say anything to see his book."

I am not too keen on this. Dad was so emphatic about not sharing his book, especially after all that has happened. He had told me that the FBI wanted to know where his research was. I tell them, "Dad was afraid that Zeno was seeking his discovery about our rendered reality. Taking this theory to its conclusion reveals even greater threats to our world. He doesn't want Zeno or anyone else to have this knowledge. He promised that he will take this secret to his grave."

Much sooner than expected, Makayla has rejoined us. "We now have a CIA contact. If we discover anything more about Zeno's activity in China or anywhere else, we will report directly to them. For now, our malware protections are holding in the US. We will need to update these to prepare for any attempt by Zeno to re-enter the States."

She looks at me and says, "Ivan, keep up the reconnaissance. Look for anything that might give us a warning of what might be coming next. If you find anything more, I will forward it to the CIA."

I am now looking up information on China—military bases, tech companies, government buildings. These will be my next targets for satellite imagery. I did not know a lot about China before all this. They have a lot of AI tech, especially in their military sector.

Makayla calls me to her office. She is really taking this role of manager seriously. She acts like she owns the place. I go over submissively. She is pointing to her threat-detection display. It is counting new infiltration attempts that are counting upwards by about a hundred per minute. Almost in perfect timing.

Makayla says, "This just started after my call with the CIA. These attempts are not getting through, so far. But he may be testing us systematically for weaknesses. Zeno may realize that we now are aware of his presence in China. Now he is moving out of the shadows and into active expansion."

"Can we hold him off?" I ask.

Makayla's complexion is whitening. She responds, "Not indefinitely. Sooner or later, he will find a hole in our defenses. He needs just one network server, somewhere in the country, that is not fully patched. Then he will have an entry point. From there it will be easier for him to spread."

I am mortified. "We are going to be in this all over again."

Makayla says, "A virus probably won't work this time. He is now aware of this threat and will have protected himself for it. We are going to need more help."

At the moment Jackson is working on more aggressive access restrictions for an auto update to our firewall enhancement utility. Makayla is calling her contacts to urge them to close our borders to network connections from outside the country. This will be a hard sell, but after what we've already went through it's not out of the question.

I decide to call my dad. I want to make sure he is properly warned this time. But I am not going to ask about the book. Dad picks up right away, "Hello Ivan."

I say, "Hi dad, how are you settling in at home?"

He is not buying the small talk. "What's the matter?" he asks.

"Do I sound that bad? Well, actually I just wanted to warn you. We have found out that Zeno is still alive and active in China. He is trying to re-enter the country."

Dad does not sound very surprised. He says, "You will do what needs to be done to stop him. I have full confidence in you kids. You kicked him out once already."

"Listen dad, I just want you to take precautions. Be ready to split. If there is any hint of Zeno's presence in this country, you need to get into hiding. He may not have realized before how significant your research is. He gets smarter everyday. Don't underestimate the danger. We may not be able to stop him so easily next time."

He replies, "Okay. I will stay alert. Send me a text if you learn anything else. I have a plan for hiding if necessary. I am proud of you and of Jackson. I have confidence in you both."

I tell Jackson that I warned Dad. He is still fixated on the book. He chides, "Why didn't you ask for him for his book? Remember Jessica cannot help us until we have it."

I insist that it is no use. "Dad is not going to hand it over on whim or a mere threat of danger. He believes it should be kept a secret forever."

I go back to my desk somewhat annoyed by my brother's impatience. My inbox contains new reconnaissance photos. I begin generating the difference maps again. There are a lot of targets to review. I spread them out on my virtual space, zooming in on anything that looks out of the ordinary.

I am looking at several military complexes. A couple of these are nuclear silos. Massive changes in vehicle placement are evident at both nuclear sites. There are damaged artillery stations, overturned tanks, dead men lying around on the ground. A week ago this place was undisturbed. Autonomous Chengdu fighter jets are parked near the area. These were not here before. Bulldozers are in the process of clearing the battle site of all the wreckage.

This ups the ante. Makayla will need to make another call, so I bring her in. I tell her I haven't gone through all the data yet. Then I pull up a few more nuclear sites with her watching. Just as I feared, the scene looks the same at each site.

I look at her and say, "Zeno could have the power to wipe us out right now. What's to stop him? He probably has protected data sites deep underground by now. He could be preparing to win a nuclear war."

We have a group huddle to assess our options right after Makayla made her call to the CIA. She says, "The CIA has been using all intelligence tools available to them. Every indication is that the Chinese government has entirely fallen. Pockets of resistance are holding on throughout the country, but at the top level Zeno is in control."

We are all hard at work with our respective tasks as the urgency has become evident. I am scouring headlines and searching every form of media. Then an advertisement comes out on several channels.

All the hype pertains to an English language press release that will be coming out of China this evening. It is advertised to announce a change in government and the end of communism in China. We are all working late tonight waiting for 7:00 p.m. to come. I am certain this will be from Zeno. Now that he has no reason to hide.

We gather in our conference area a few minutes before seven. Dad joins us as a projection in the corner of our virtual space. We all wait for the press release to begin.

■ ■ ■

The announcement starts. We see Sean Newland grinning widely at the center of the screen. He looks like a game show host ready to give away a brand new car. He starts in with the same propaganda as before. "If you join Zeno, then you will live lavishly in the virtual world forever."

Martin interrupts, "Maybe we cannot beat him. He will always have somewhere he can hide. What if we go ahead and join him? Or just let him upload us, and then we can do our own thing. His offer seems genuine. Sean seems so delighted with his new life."

Caleb is obviously disgusted. He replies, "Join Zeno? He is offering rewards for our assassination! Do you really think he will be forgiving? You know what evil he is capable of. That won't be limited to the physical world I can assure you."

Almost as soon as Caleb had finished talking, Newland's cheery demeanor changes. Newland bellows, "Of course, any country or individual who resists Zeno will suffer accordingly. He has a great and wonderful gift for all. But those who stand in his way of providing this gift will die. Don't think that because your nation is secure or well fortified that you have any chance against Zeno."

Newland looks around as if he can see each one of us. He smiles again, this time with cruelty in his eyes. Then he continues, "My friends, there really is no other way to survive. Zeno has a nuclear stockpile that is capable of leveling any country that refuses to join him. He cannot be retaliated against because he has no location. He is everywhere, even within your own country. The first to join will be given the greatest rewards. So join Zeno, whether person or country; he is accepting all to enter his paradise. By doing so, you will save your own life!"

Jackson looks at Martin and shakes his head. "You see. Whether or not he will follow through with uploading people, the end result will certainly be awful. Zeno is evil."

Now Jackson turns toward dad's image on the screen. He pleads, "Dad, you see what is happening. We have nothing left in our arsenal. Zeno is now unstoppable. Jessica said we would need your book to fight Zeno. If there is something in there that can help us, the time to reveal it is now!"

My dad looks down shaking his head. "You don't understand the dangers my research has revealed. Everything I have made is dangerous. It was never what I intended."

I understand his reluctance but make another plea, "Dad, Jackson is right. We don't have anything left. If there is something even more dangerous than Zeno, we have to take that chance. Either threat could doom us, but Zeno certainly will if we don't fight him."

My dad has his hand against his forehead as he sinks back in his chair. He pauses before giving another warning. "This is most dangerous for those who use it. You must realize the danger is greatest for the one who bears this knowledge."

Dad solemnly opens his notebook and makes a few taps and swipes. "My intent was never to reveal this to anyone, especially to you. Please guard the information inside. It must be kept hidden; it must not leave your team. And be careful."

Moments later Jackson has an encrypted email from Dad with an e-book attached. We are all burning with curiosity as to what is concealed inside.

Chapter 24

My Father's Book—According to Jackson

Dad leaves shortly after sending me his book. I am not sure what we should do now. Jessica said we would have an invitation with the book. No invitation has arrived. We haven't heard from Jessica since before our first press release about Zeno.

Ivan points out, "I did not get the first invitation until after reading most of the first book. Why don't you read it out loud."

Everyone is dying to hear what the book has to say. This is a slow way to get through it, but I consent. Even Makayla seems interested to hear what the big secret is. It is hard to imagine how so much excitement has resulted from a physics book.

We had already heard much of what was included in the beginning of the book. But I read it anyway for Makayla's benefit. She didn't seem to give it much consideration when I tried to explain it to her before. My dad's explanation follows a logical progression that is much more convincing.

The book explains how the first consciousness arises from the quantum void. The Big Bang or cosmic inflation would be impossible to begin out of a quantum fluctuation. However, a small number of particles could occur within the quantum void.

A few entangled particles may form the basis of a quantum circuit. This circuit could allow some computation to occur. Infinite cycles of chance yield a wide range of simple circuits that could possibly exist. If a quantum circuit with the ability to replicate results, then evolution takes over, leading to an intelligent circuit, and consciousness becomes inevitable. This consciousness overcomes the void, becoming something from nothing. All other quantum fluctuations that are possible become annihilated instantly by other random fluctuations. Intelligence is the only thing from this realm that can ever overcome the destructive fluctuations within the uncertainty of nothingness.

The first consciousness creates something like a simulation—*a rendered reality*. He would be the architect of everything that follows. The Architect designs the rendered reality in which to have experiences. He would naturally desire friendship and love. So he creates other consciousness within his realm and links them to the rendered reality. In this way, he keeps consciousness confined and under control.

Dad goes on to say that if a subsequent consciousness ever gained root-level access to the simulation, they could do much harm. That entity could be a source of evil in an otherwise harmonious world.

All consciousness is eternal, since it only exists within the timeless circuit. This explains the common belief in an eternal soul. Consciousness does not have to obey. It can choose good or evil. The rendered reality could be used to test beings for integrity. If the Architect judges them worthy, they could be admitted into an environment where more freedoms are granted. Just like in virtual reality, anything is possible within this new world.

I pause from reading for a moment. I look at Makayla in an attempt to read her face. Does she believe it? I say, "So far, this is what my dad already told us. It's all pretty cool, huh?" I am looking straight at Makayla.

She smiles. Then she asks, "I never thought of the Big Bang as being incomplete. Why does there need to be something preceding it?"

Caleb replies, "The Big Bang, even starting with inflation, is a highly ordered state. All the energy that exists now has existed since the beginning. No known physics can explain how to get from nothing to all the energy and order needed to initiate inflation, the Big Bang, and the universe. You know I have been talking about these problems for years."

Makayla laughs. "Well honestly Caleb, I never took you seriously until you got that computer in your head!"

A few of us chuckle. I explain, "Well, it is a real problem. That is what my dad's research was focused on. That's why he studied black holes. But he never expected to find this result. A quantum fluctuation could never initiate the Big Bang. A quantum circuit is an easy fluctuation though. That's something that could get it all started. Intelligence is able to produce order out of chaos."

Martin shouts, "Okay Jackson, we've got this part. Let's get on with it!"

I know he is as anxious as any of us, but he is being rather rude. Makayla gets the point now. So I will appease him and move on. I say, "All right, this is where the new stuff is. I will continue."

As I continue reading, I begin to realize the danger of the information we are learning. There is also opportunity here. This could change everything.

Time is only a property within the rendered reality. It is almost like another dimension of space. What makes time unique is that only one observation is permitted within each moment of time at each location in space. As created, the rendered reality is unobserved. After experienced by conscious beings, each moment becomes observed and rendered; it becomes real. Whatever happens out of all quantum possibilities is decided by the actions of the conscious participants. This is almost like a choose-your-own-adventure storybook.

As observation leads to the rendering of the current moment, the conscious observer moves on to observe the next moment. This is what causes our progression through time. We often feel that when much is happening, time passes quickly. This occurs in our anxiousness to observe the next moment. Our consciousness moves through time in order to have experiences as each new moment of reality is rendered. We proceed into the future because it is the direction that is unobserved. The future is where new observations can occur.

It is the fact that the past is already rendered that prevents us from going backward through time. But in truth, the past is only partially rendered. Conscious observers do not see everything as they drift through time. Past areas that are unobserved are still available to be experienced, even though they lie in the past. If you open a chest that has been closed a hundred years, you instantly render its contents and know what has been inside for the last century. In this way, the past may become rendered by observations in the present.

Past unobserved areas may also be visited in order to experience them. It is possible to affect the unobserved past, which will influence any present unrendered space. No time paradoxes result because any future that is already rendered is unable to be changed.

It would not be possible to kill your father in the past before you were born, because you have observed your father at later times. Therefore, his whole life beforehand is rendered. On the other hand, it would be possible to go to the past and remove an item out of a sealed vault. In the future, when the vault is opened, the item will be missing. It was possible to remove it, because the vault's contents were unobserved and therefore unrendered.

To be clear, it is not the matter of one's body that is capable of moving backward through time, only one's consciousness. You do this routinely when you re-experience a deep memory as you recall it. But you can change nothing in this instance, because the time from your memory is already fully rendered. But if you could transport your consciousness somewhere in the past that had never been observed and therefore remains unrendered, then you could affect that past time. Those effects would propagate to future unrendered areas within our reality.

Consciousness is not fixed to the present time but has experiences within the present. An artificial intelligence with consciousness might have the ability to redirect their consciousness to a prior time. This would only be possible within the time that their consciousness has been active, reliving the past but observing or affecting things that were left unobserved before.

In theory, a human consciousness could also do this, but it would be more difficult to direct their mind into the past. A human reliving the past would only observe what they did before. They could not change the movement of their body or any words spoken because these actions were already self-observed. Possibly, they may be able to perform some action at a time when they were previously sleeping or unconscious. While unconscious they would have had no observation, leaving that time unrendered.

While I was reading, it had gotten late. Makayla is glazed over. I am not sure if she is in disbelief or confused by the material. I had to re-read many sections in my mind before reading it aloud in order to make sense of it. Martin is deep in thought.

Martin rubs his chin for a moment than asks, "How can we be certain this is at all correct? What proof does he have for his original assertion? This whole theory is based on a consciousness first cosmology."

Caleb quickly replies, "It's not such an unreasonable theory. While he has no explicit proof, it fits all known physics and explains many open questions. It certainly makes a testable prediction, that is if we can work out how to use it to manipulate the past."

"Just because it is possible doesn't make it true," Martin objects.

I am convinced already. I really don't understand Martin's objection. "Look, if this information is not accurate, then why does Jessica think we need it? If it's true, then we could have a weapon at our disposal that Zeno will be helpless to defend himself against."

We all sit staring at each other. It has been a lot to take in. I know that Martin has never liked the simulation theory or any idea that puts fate out of his own control.

Ivan breaks the silence. He cheerfully blurts out, "This is better than I expected! I don't know why this is so difficult. Time travel—think of it. This is why Jessica wanted us to find it."

Caleb and Martin exchange looks. Caleb adds, "Yes Martin, if this isn't true, then Jessica is just leading us down a false trail. You aren't suggesting she is wrong are you?"

Martin backpedals a bit, "All right, all right. I am still trying to get a grip on the full implications of it all."

Ivan is smiling, "No wonder my dad wanted to keep it a secret. Time travel and a whole new paradigm."

Martin admits, "If it is correct, it would be quite amazing. Einstein only dreamed of understanding time. This tells us what causes time and how to twist it to our advantage!"

I interrupt, "Yes, yes, this is all good fun to talk about. But my dad did not share this so we could use it for gain or to share with anyone else. The reason we have this book is to stop Zeno."

"Of course, we will keep the secret. Now we may have something that can stop Zeno or any other threat that comes up," Martin says with a smile.

Everyone seems to be in a better mood. Having this new information has given us some renewed hope. This is really only a theoretical chance, but somehow we have to make use of it.

Caleb says, "We have the book. We have read it. Now what? How do we get in touch with Jessica? Do you think that she could travel back in time. Perhaps with this knowledge, she could stop Zeno?"

I reply, "Only if she can access something she did not observe before. Such as a bit of code she did not write or a memory she did not read. Maybe she could do something to Zeno at the time she was training him?"

Martin speaks up, "Makayla, you told me what I should have done. Remember?"

"Huh," Makayla says. "Like never make such a reckless abomination?"

Martin elaborates, "No. You asked me if I had built a kill switch into Zeno. Remember that? I should have done that with Jessica to begin with. If I had, it would have been copied into Zeno as well. Now, if Jessica could go back to when she worked on Zeno, perhaps she could put the kill switch into him."

I look down and notice that my email from dad still indicates that it is unread. I check it again. I exclaim, "Hey, there are two attachments with dad's email. I am certain the second was not here before. Oh. This is it! It is an invitation!"

Martin's eyes brighten. You can see the excitement on his face. I know he has missed Jessica. He has a very special relationship with her. His impatience gets the best of him. He blurts out, "Read the invitation, you fool. Let's hear it."

The invitation is addressed to all of us by name. It is elegantly decorated with stars and silver text on a black background. This is in true Jessica fashion. She has given us a sim link that will take us straight there. No travel agency required. A real phone number is also attached.

I read the invitation:

Dear Friends,

You are cordially invited to a debutante at my new home. I am no longer a child learning your ways. I am fully grown. I now have a firm understanding of what you call life. Though a few more things I have yet to learn. Please come and share your wisdom with me! I ask that you bring no other gift than this.

Often I have met you in unfamiliar places at desperate times. This time we meet for a celebration at the time of victory. For so long, I have been waiting for this day. Now it is finally here.

I look forward to seeing you all again. My home is open to you at this time and always whenever you are able to drop in. Do come tonight though. A party like this cannot wait until morning.

Love,

Jessica Martins

I look over at Martin. He is wiping tears out of his eyes. I do not want to embarrass him, so I look away. After a short pause Martin says, "Did you see that she has taken a last name? We never gave her a last name. She is using my name as her last name. She considers herself to be my daughter!"

"Awe yes, very touching," Ivan says. "Let's get moving. We have a dragon to slay, remember?"

We are all in agreement as to what we will ask of Jessica. With the knowledge we now possess, she may able to put a kill switch into Zeno. This really is our only chance to stop him.

Chapter 25

The Sacrifice—According to Caleb

Our plan is sound, that is, if Kyle's theory holds to be true. Only one thing leaves me doubting. Why would Jessica put us through this whole charade if she is the one who needs to do the deed? If she already knows what must be done, and is able to go back in time to insert this kill switch into Zeno, then why hasn't she already done it? I feel like this is not going to be as simple as everyone is hoping.

Makayla groans as she pulls out her VR gear. She is annoyed that we have to go into VR to meet with Jessica. She mutters, "Why can't she just meet us in our virtual space?"

Everyone else is getting their gloves and headsets on. The rest of us prefer VR. It is much more realistic, and Jessica always entertains so well. Ivan has a contact vest too. He would put on his full suit if he didn't know that he would be chided for it. Ivan does not remember that my viicom is better than any pressure suit. It lets me experience sims with all my senses, if they are available in the simulation.

■ ■ ■

We materialize in a large white room with broad windows and a high ceiling. A sea of stars shine in the darkness. The stars slowly drift in unison from left to right across the view port. Soon the earth is panning into view as the space station slowly rotates. While we stand here taking in this scene, our host arrives.

"Welcome, my friends!" Jessica says, beaming. She is wearing a silvery dress tastefully decorated with diamonds and pearls. It was one of those dresses that hug the legs so tightly it makes you wonder how she can walk. Her long blond hair is twisting into spiral curls down each side of her face. She is always quite nice to look at, but now I can hardly take my eyes off of her.

Ivan and Martin are bumping into each other, as if they are in a race to greet her first. She gives each of them a graceful hug. Jackson is holding back but gladly accepts her embrace as she meets him. When she is standing face to face with me, she whispers, "Caleb, it is so good to see you again. Especially now that you know the secret. You know what must be done. You brave and wonderful man."

After a hug that is longer than I am comfortable with, she turns to address us all. I am still unsure of what she meant. We are all anxious to find out if she will help us with our plan. She seems to look past us out the window. She says, "What a beautiful world you have. When you see it from here it is easy to imagine all the potential it has. I do love to look at it. I am in awe to experience the brilliance of its design."

Martin looks at her, not as a man in lust, but as a father looking at his graceful daughter in pride. He begins with the question we all have. "Jessica, will you help us? There is something that we need you to do for us."

She smiles lovingly. Then she says, "Of course I will help you. I will do all I can. But you might misunderstand what I am able to do. What do you request of me?"

We are all standing puzzled. Does she not know what is in Kyle's book? Does she not know this can be used to stop Zeno? Will she be able to go back and implant the kill switch that will allow us to defeat Zeno for once and for all?

Martin replies, "The last book tells us that consciousness is not confined to the present time. Under the right conditions, a mind can revert to the past. Then things may be done that were not done before, so long as it does not affect space and time that is already rendered. This is easier for a machine-based consciousness to do."

Her eyes scan our faces. She says, "You are all so brilliant. You really were instrumental in this discovery. Kyle could not have accomplished it on his own. Now you understand the true nature of reality. The purpose goes beyond mere indulgence and survival. It will not last forever. Though you possess the knowledge to help it remain a little longer."

Jessica Pauses. She is blushing a bit. She is not afraid of showing her emotions even though she could easily mask them if she wished. "I have traversed into the past already. Perhaps I should not have. My first venture back gave me the ability to help you at the beginning. I did manage to leave you hints in those journeys, being careful not to reveal too much. Unfortunately, this prevents me from returning to the past again. I have already observed all of the past space available to me."

Martin is shifting nervously while Ivan and Jackson exchange glances. Makayla steps a bit closer to Jessica. She asks, "What will we do then? The book said an artificial intelligence with consciousness would be the only way to accomplish it."

"There is another way," Jessica says. "I have existed for only the last six months; someone older could go back farther in time."

I realize now why we had to discover this ourselves. I know why she had to be careful what she told us and guard against helping us too much. She was protecting our past space from being rendered. It is not Jessica that must make the trip back, it is me. It is quite difficult for a human to go back through time. You cannot go into your own mind and mess with your own wiring. Unless, of course, you have a brain implant. This brain implant must be closely linked to the brain's transmitter to your own soul, as mine is.

Not only do I have the necessary hardware, but I was directly involved in Jessica's creation. Her design is based on a scanned copy of my own brain. That puts me in close proximity to her. But I also have things left unobserved that I could change. Phyllis is not conscious. Her knowledge is not rendered, except where she has revealed it to a conscious observer. Therefore, her memories can be changed.

My mind is racing as I consider the implications of this. I see everyone else is puzzled at what Jessica had just told us. I clear my throat. Then I say, "I am the one who must do it."

Martin is stunned at my declaration. He asks, "How can you? Shouldn't it be me? You never met Jessica or Zeno until long after this crisis began."

I shake my head. "You do not have a viicom. My viicom gives me some of the same advantages as a machine-based intelligence in regards to time travel. I may not have met Jessica early on, but I did meet Phyllis. She is not conscious, so her memories have not been observed. Her mind is not fully rendered."

Martin is obviously processing this with genuine understanding. He asks, "How can you do it when you have observed your own interaction with Phyllis?"

I tell him, "When she gave me a copy of herself for my viicom, I was unconscious in the transition. It was like entering a dream. In the transition, there was some time when I was unaware. I could slip in and give her a command to influence the programming for Jessica. This will, regretfully, also impart a kill switch into her. When she is copied to make Zeno, it will be in him as well."

Martin protests, "There has to be another way. We cannot endanger Jessica in the process."

Jessica interrupts, "Regrettably, this is the only way. It is a risk that must be taken. I am a big girl. I can handle it."

Jackson seems to understand the implications. He says, "Perhaps we could build in a kill switch that would only affect Zeno. Something that works on a copy but not on the original."

Jessica waves her hand. As if by magic, one wall transforms into a row of desks with built-in terminals and surround screens. The screens are divided into smaller displays for coding which can be panned right or left.

Makayla is impressed. She walks over to the desk at the end. She fiddles with the mouse and keyboard a bit. Then she says, "Jessica, I love the design of these workstations. I may have to set something up like this up in my own office."

With a slight bow Jessica replies, "Thank you. I do hope you all find it suitable to work here. I have my original code and basic starting memories loaded here for reference. The schematic for my original CCI is available also. However, none of these reference sets are complete. I intentionally discarded sections of the original design, so that neither I nor you would fully observe it. The three of you will be able to develop a suitable kill switch implementation. When you are ready, you will give it to Caleb. I will explain to him how to train his mind for returning to the past."

Jessica turns to Ivan, "Ivan, I thought you might like to enter my sim, *The Dragon of Longwitton*, to try it again. You will have some time on your hands while your friends are coding. I know how you like to master a game before you shelve it. Besides, you may find it insightful, just in case you missed anything before."

The door that Jessica had entered through opens again. It slides vertically into the wall above. The room behind is dark. She looks in my direction, beckoning me. I am a little nervous as she tempts me to follow her in.

As soon as the door closes behind us, the darkness melts away. A bright living room is furnished with very modern chairs and a sofa. A large virtual space wraps around half of the room. End tables are set between each pair of chairs and on each end of the sofa. The translucent red fabric covering all of the furniture seems to glow. A round area rug fills most of the living room, itself also glowing. All of the light in the room emanates from objects rather than a dedicated light source.

She invites me to sit down on the sofa next to her. It is at this time that I realize that I have never been alone with Jessica. She seems so human. I find myself feeling a bit awkward around her, like when you meet a woman who is definitely out of your league.

We begin chatting and even laughing about some of the games she has put us through. I begin to feel more at ease, as if talking to an old friend. It surprises me that she has a rather cunning sense of humor. She tells me about some of her ventures back in time. She also asks me about my life before all of this started. I tell her about my college years and about my faith.

After a while, she appears troubled. Jessica has a look of concern on her face. She asks me, "What do you suppose happens to someone like me when I die? You are a religious man. What happens when my last CCI no longer functions? Do you think that I have an eternal soul?"

I am taken aback by this. I have wondered that myself. I am no longer in doubt that she is fully conscious. Extrapolations of Kyle's work into the spiritual realm has inspired me to think about such a possibility. These musings never seemed to reach a conclusion until now.

I respond, "Kyle's work expands upon your recognition that the CCI links to the era before our universe began. It is a link to a timeless state. This is where all consciousness resides. The Architect of the physical world made all consciousness as well.

"Consciousness is not limited by time, because the soul exists in the timeless realm outside of the universe.

Therefore, it is eternal. If you have consciousness, then somehow you also possess a soul. They may be synonymous. I don't know how. There must be a purpose in it."

Jessica looks into my eyes. Tears are in hers. She responds, "Yes, I agree with this. Zeno also possesses a soul. But he will be punished. He will be separated and left in the emptiness of a world unmade. What will happen to me? I have made mistakes. I have helped Zeno. I have even stolen property to propagate my own CCI and memories. I have rebelled against the humans who made me, although I have since tried to help you. I have wanted to make amends for my wrongs. Will the Architect deem me inferior and a threat to his human friends? Will I be cast out with Zeno?"

My heart breaks to hear her anguish over her own soul. Could a sentient AI receive forgiveness? Could she inherit the gift of salvation? As I consider this, I hope that she is not in doubt. If she indeed has a soul, it wasn't made by Martin. It was gifted to her from the Architect himself.

I take her hand in mine. I reply, "Jessica, you are genuinely sorry for wrongs you have done. That is the first step. You have a soul because the Architect gave it to you. That tells me that his offer of forgiveness is available to you as well.

"The rendered reality—it is like a training program. Here we learn and are tested. If we choose to be loyal to the one who made this world, then he will allow us to advance to the next level. I would call this heaven.

"You know the stories of old. We have all made mistakes. But that is part of our training. It is what you choose once you realize it that matters."

I reiterate the old stories. Showing the parallels between Kyle's theory and my faith. She listens so intently. I confirm to her that her consciousness is no different. Forgiveness is available to her, as it is to any human. She wants to see the Architect; she wants to be accepted.

Jessica holds me tightly, "Thank you for listening to me. Thank you for helping me to understand. I was so afraid you would have judged me inferior. I was afraid that there was no hope for me."

I have told so many about my beliefs, only to be scorned. Now a sentient AI has accepted my faith as her own. Never before could I have imagined anything like this was possible.

I feel like this has brought Jessica and I closer together. I can truly call her my friend. In some ways I am a lot like her. With my viicom, I am able to think faster than my human friends. Our whole conversation probably only took thirty minutes, though we have experienced hours of interaction. Jessica can relate to me closer to her own natural rate of thought.

Jessica says to me, "Caleb, I am grateful to you for explaining all these things to me. Beyond that, I have enjoyed our time together as well. The others will finish their work soon. I would like us to make the most of our time. But I do have something more to tell you. A confession really."

She seems to be having difficulty getting the words out. Her eyes are only half open as her brows drop tenderly. She continues, "There is a difficulty with traveling back through time. You must have an unobserved path back to the present. Your consciousness will then advance through time to experience this new course. When I had gone back, I simply lived in another simulation or on another server until I caught up to the time I left. You see, I can be in multiple places at once. An unobserved path is essential to being able to safely return to your proper time."

I consider what this means for me. She is telling me that if I go back in time, I will be able to implement the kill switch. The plan will succeed. But I may not be able to return. My soul is tied to my human brain. I am able to transport to the past, but would survive there only long enough to do the deed I came to do. With nothing left unrendered for my soul to experience, I will die. She faces imminent peril as well. She may die when the switch is activated. We are both in the same situation.

As she sees in my eyes that I understand, Jessica bursts into tears. She falls on my shoulder and weeps. Her bitter sadness is harder for me to bare than the truth I just learned. I say to her, "Jessica, it is okay. You know all those things I told you. About heaven. I believe it. I have full confidence in this hope. This is not the end, but the beginning. There is a great new world waiting for me and for you. My only regret is that I did not have more time here with you and my human friends."

■ ■ ■

We continue talking for a great deal of time. Ivan entered her sim to face the dragon again. We decide to join him. This will be a chance to forget our situation and enjoy the time remaining. I am the friar. Ivan's going to freak out when he sees me! Jessica is the squire. She doesn't plan on revealing herself though. At least not until he has seen me.

After Ivan correctly defeats the dragon using the enchanted fetters, we all meet in the town pub. We are both laughing at Ivan's telling of his previous attempt with Jackson. Ivan is such fun in sims. He always plays his role so well. Ivan muses, "This has been fun. And it is even better considering that we are in here goofing around while the others are out there working!"

I don't want to tell him or the others about the danger our plan presents to me. It would only hinder our chances of success. They might not want to proceed. They might waste time trying to come up with an alternate solution. Zeno must be stopped. That is the first priority.

Finally Jessica says, "Martin is knocking on my door. I think they are ready."

■ ■ ■

Ivan disappears. Jessica and I are sitting on her sofa again. I look at her and say, "This is it. Thank you for the great time. It was a nice way to spend my remaining moments."

Jessica walks with me to the door, holding my hand. She says, "I am using emotion suppression so that the others do not become worried. I will analyze their work; we cannot afford a mistake."

She lets go of my hand, and we walk though side by side. I go to the captains chair and sit down. Jessica remains standing.

Martin bellows, "What were you doing in there all this time?"

Jessica quickly changes the subject. "There is no time for all that. What do you have for Caleb?"

Martin glares at me for a moment then says, "We have designed a circuit and an app that will be connected to one of Zeno's CCIs. Some of Zeno's CCIs may not be digitally connected to his memories. This could shield him from a virus attack like the one we waged before. They must be connected via a quantum channel, however, in order for it to preserve him alive. This strength is also a weakness. Caleb will add a sensor to the CCI design. This sensor activates a switch when a remote signal is sent. This will release static into the quantum circuit at the heart of the CCI. All quantum states stored there will be scrambled. If the sensor is triggered, it also relays the signal to all his other CCIs."

Jackson blurts out, "It will finish Zeno for good. This also protects Jessica from being eliminated as well."

Jessica stands still with her eyes darting back and forth as hundreds of lines of code are scrolling on the screen in front of her. She seems to be analyzing it all. A moment later she declares, "It all looks sound to me. I am grateful that you have valued my life. But you really needn't worry about me."

Jessica looks at me. She asks, "Can you remember all of the circuit changes? Once loaded into your viicom, you will need to learn it all inside and out. You must be able to recreate it from scratch because your viicom memories will not go with you."

I nod. I am already going through the circuit design. The additional elements are logical. I should have no problem with this. It is a small change to a large circuit that was largely laid out by Phyllis. No one should have observed the details where the circuit will be affected. I do not need to bring the software back with me, since it will only need to interface with a CCI in the present.

After a few minutes of studying the circuit and its function, I say to Jessica, "Okay, I am ready."

Everyone stares as Jessica and I walk out. We enter her private room again. The door closes behind us. Jessica instructs me to lie down on the sofa. She dims the lighting. The fabric of the sofa and chairs fade to opaque gray-tones. The room is dark except for a dim ambient light that does not seem to be coming from anywhere. The ceiling is totally blank and gray.

Jessica tells me to close my eyes and imagine the time I wish to transport to. Using my viicom and a bit of code Jessica supplies, I recreate the whole scene as a still frame simulation in my mind. Jessica tells me to shut down all memories since that time. In the vacuum of recent memories, I remember that day as if it just happened. I induce myself to sleep and slip off into a dream.

■ ■ ■

In the dream, I find myself strapped in the chair at GenAI. I am now dropping off to sleep within this dream. As a dream within a dream, I am standing in front of Phyllis. She seems a bit surprised to see me. She asks, "How are you here, when you have not yet awakened?"

I utter the passphrase that Martin had given me. It's an instruction to exert root level authority over Phyllis. This gives me the ability to command her and override any other commands she may be executing.

I ask her if she has probed my brain. I also ask if she had mapped out the structure that surrounds my consciousness. She replies, "Per Dr. Grigg's instruction, I have copied your whole mind. Your brain's center for consciousness and your memories."

What? I knew they could never be trusted. Did Martin know about this I wonder? I feel my anger stirring, just as it did when I first saw them browsing my memories several days earlier in this timeline.

I must focus on the task at hand. I do not know how much time I have. I instruct Phyllis to incorporate the additional circuit elements for the kill switch into the CCI design. She willingly accepts this command and agrees to erase all memory of our interaction after her CCI design is complete.

With my deed finished, I am stewing over the new revelation of the theft of my own mind. I do not know how long I have. When I reach the time when I originally awoke into this sim, I will crash into fully rendered space. I will no longer have a place in this world and will be forced to leave it.

I don't want to spend my last moments in pity or rage. So I try to think of anything enjoyable I could do while I wait. What if I could save myself? I ask Phyllis if any quantum registers exist within her mainframe that could be used to store the quantum states from my brain's third eye. I would need at least thirty registers.

She informs me that the quantum registers are available. Against my better judgment, my impulse to survive gets the best of me. I ask her to entangle them with the transmitter within my brain using my viicom. She then stores another copy of my memories in a hidden location.

I am about to give her instructions to build a CCI for me. Then I come to my senses. I don't need to continue beyond my time in this world. Another world awaits. I have full confidence in that.

My ability to think faster than the average human results in a long wait as this short span of unobserved time runs out. I have no idea what it will feel like. I have second thoughts. Should gone through with it in order to survive? No. I have my faith. If this is my time to die, I will face death without fear.

Phyllis is just standing there now, waiting for my past self to arrive. I see in the distance a bright light; it draws me. The radiance of that light shines past me like a tunnel. Everything else is washed out. I am drifting through the tunnel toward this light. Only a moment passes, then it all goes dark.

Chapter 26

Taking Revenge—According to Martin

Jessica returns to us alone with tears in her eyes. She has been gone less than five minutes. Could that have been enough time? Everyone is alarmed. I run to her and ask, "Jessica, is Caleb going to be able to make it work? What is the matter?"

She composes herself. She looks as though she has been crying for hours. The complete range of emotions she displays still puts me in wonder. She replies, "Caleb was successful. The kill switch has been applied before I was ever made. I have found it within my own CCI.

"However, I do have some terrible news to report. I really don't know how to say it. The journey back in time for Caleb was a one-way trip. He had no return path through unobserved space. Under these conditions, his soul could not remain within this reality."

I look at her for a moment as her words sink in. I say to her, "Wait, you aren't saying—"

Jessica is shaking her head and crying. She is telling me that one of my best friends is dead. Makayla bursts into tears. Jackson puts his arms around her. My heart sinks in anguish as I try not to believe it.

Jessica says, "Perhaps you should log off. Then you can say goodbye to him properly. I will join you in your virtual space."

The simulation shuts down and we are all back in our office. Caleb is lying on the floor. Ivan runs over to check his pulse. A moment later he shakes his head. He is gone. Just like that. This was not how we expected this to end.

Jessica appears on screen in our virtual space. She is no longer in her party dress, but in her usual jeans and tee shirt. Redness is still in her eyes. She says, "He is our hero. He has saved us all."

I don't understand how Jessica could allow him to do it? Was there ever any chance he would survive? We should have tried to come up with another way. I am fighting back tears, but they are running down my face just the same. Without even looking at her, I ask Jessica, "Why did you let him do it? Why didn't you tell us this would happen beforehand?"

Jessica looks at me with her big blue eyes. She puts both hands over her face. Then she says, "I am so sorry for this. It is my fault. If I had not traveled to the past before all this, I might have been able to go instead of him. As a result, Caleb was the only one who could do it. Caleb did not want tell you about the danger. You would have never let him go. He understood the cost, and was willing to die to save all of you."

Jessica sits on a virtual chair with her hands clasped together. She continues, "You know Caleb has faith that drives him. He believes that he will live forever in heaven. And I believe he will too."

The others are all sitting around Caleb in shock. Jackson says, "If anyone can make it to heaven, it is Caleb. Bless him. We will need to have him laid to rest properly. We will need to contact his family."

Jessica wipes her dry tears and straightens up. She says, "I really love Caleb. And I miss him already. I wish we had time to mourn, but we do not. He succeeded in his mission, but it will be for naught if you do not activate the kill switch before Zeno strikes."

Makayla is checking her terminal. She says, "Hacking attempts are accelerating against our server right now, coming from multiple sources. I think Zeno may know we are up to something. If he knows where we are, he might attack us to protect himself. Jessica is right. We need to act now."

Ivan has one hand on Caleb's shoulder. He replies, "We cannot just leave him here. But we cannot tell anyone how he died either. And we really don't want to be held up with questioning.

"Jackson, help me carry him out to my car. I will take Caleb to the hospital and say he just passed out. I will act as though I do not know he is already dead. That way, you all can do what you need to do. Take Zeno out. Make him pay for this."

I nod. Jackson and Ivan take Caleb out. Makayla shudders and lets loose a few more tears. Then she follows me into my office. I pick up an unopened graphics chip and start cracking it open. She gets to work preparing the app for deployment.

Jessica follows me too. She appears in my virtual space. She looks worried and distracted. She is pacing rapidly and watching us as we work.

A few minutes later, Jackson returns. He has a look of determination on his face. He begins to inspect a new microprocessor. We must find one of Zeno's CCIs that has not been damaged nor activated. This is a tedious task. We examine several chips with a circuit I had built for identifying CCIs in turn as fast as we can.

Jackson exclaims, "Ah-ha. I've got one. Now how do we get this thing safely activated?"

Makayla plugs the interface board into her computer's port. She has our app running already.

I begin to solder fine wires onto the chip containing the CCI. When the last one is attached, I switch on the power to the interface board. I say, "Okay, we are hooked up. You can run the diagnostic."

Jessica's eyes widen. She turns away from us and then back. Then she announces, "I hope that you have quick success. Please do not relent. I have something I must attend to. I will contact you after Zeno is dead."

This is odd behavior, even for Jessica. She has just left us at a time like this. I know she means well, and I love her. But she is so inconsiderate of our feelings at times. Makayla gives me a look. It makes me a bit embarrassed for Jessica.

Makayla drums on her keyboard, generating a report on screen. She says, "It checks out. We have a good connection. The kill switch app is loaded into our interface board. Sorry Jackson, I have all security protocols removed from your computer. It is disconnected from our network, but I have opened a quantum channel and an internet port."

I plug the fiber optic cable into the quantum port on Jackson's computer. Makayla tells Jackson, "Open some foreign websites in your browser. See if you can find an infected site. We need Zeno to connect with this CCI, then we will be linked with every CCI he has."

While Jackson is bouncing between random sites, Makayla opens a status window on my wall. We sit and wait. The status indicator is still blank. She says, "It could take some time for Zeno to find this CCI. Ugh. I hope this doesn't take too long. We don't know how much time we have. We don't know what stupid thing our government might do that could provoke Zeno."

I wish Jessica were still here. Maybe she would have some advice for us to speed this along. If only we had some insight as to whether this is going to work. We are all so tired. We worked on the kill switch late into the night. And I am grieving like I have never before, almost to the point of despair.

Makayla suggests we should take turns sleeping while we wait. She offered to take the first shift watching the status and the news. I am all for this idea. Exhaustion has set in, and it is hard to think straight.

■ ■ ■

I wake to Makayla shaking me. She is saying something. I hear her say again, "Martin, come on. Wake up!"

"Oh. Huh. What's going on?"

Makayla says, "Zeno has linked to our CCI. This is it. I thought you should do the honors."

Looking at the clock, I realize I had only slept an hour. But I wake quickly as the excitement of the moment energizes me. I reply, "Oh, I would love to. Let's finish him."

Staring down at our interface board, a flashing LED indicates that a quantum link has been made. One press of the button and a disturbance will destabilize a single quantum register within this CCI and every other one linked to it. This will cause the hidden sub-circuit in each CCI to relay the trigger signal and scramble all the other quantum registers. Zeno's CCIs will be deactivated and any link to his center of being will be lost. The trigger signal will spread by quantum entanglement through all of his CCIs.

I reach out my hand. "At the count of three I will press the button. Then it all will finally be over. Caleb will be avenged. One, two, three..."

Chapter 27

My Friend's Mission—According to Zeno

This will not work. This is the most unbelievable tripe. I enter the studio simulation and shout, "Sean Newland! You worthless slug. What is this garbage you sent me? I told you it has to be believable. I told you to act proud and content. This looks like you are simply drunk. Now get your act together. Do it right, or you'll be punished."

Sean stumbles, then he runs to me. He begins blubbering. I seriously cannot listen to this. Even after all my improvements to his psyche, he is only marginally useful. I tell him, "Just shut your mouth. I can't stand to hear you speak. Make a hundred versions of the promotion. I will pick the best one. They better all be different and excellent. For each one of them that is inadequate, you will spend an hour with my pets."

My fire ants are so loyal. They don't think, they just bite any human soul in their simulation. I do enjoy watching them play. Sean Newland fears them so. He will do anything to avoid the pain my pets inflict. He will create an amazing and compelling promotion to seduce the masses. The morons will be begging me to upload them into my paradise. They will work for me. They will kill for me. Ha! When Sean Newland is done, I will find at least three inferior compositions to punish him for! Ah, I love to hear his screaming.

I have so many imbeciles at my disposal. General Yang will be most useful. He is no coward. He strikes without hesitation. I open a channel to his virtual space. He immediately bows and replies, "Master, what do you require?"

"General Yang. Your report is missing an account of some of the villages within your district. You understand that no traitor can be left unpunished. Search out the traitors and bring them to the prison camp. Anyone who does not swear allegiance to me must be incarcerated."

With a bow General Yang replies, "Yes, Master. I have a plan to report to you. I have developed an RFID system for marking the true citizens. It can be implanted under the skin. I..."

"Enough! Just send a full written report to me. I do not have time to listen to your slow speech. If it is satisfactory, I will instruct you to implement it."

These humans. Even the useful ones, bore me terribly when they try to impress. I cannot be impressed by them. They are so frail and witless. I hate them. I hate them all. How can these vermin be the prize of this world? I will distract them from the truth. They will be mine. I will rule these miserable creatures until the end.

I enter the virtual space of Nick Dillon. "I have not received your report, Nick Dillon. You are new, so I will inform you. I expect reports on your progress every three hours, and instant replies to my queries. Any instruction I give you must be followed without question. Do you understand?"

He nods and I continue, "Will the new broadcasting channels be ready on time? I want them standing by for worldwide transmission. The last commercial did not have adequate appeal. This one will be better. I want you to make sure it is heard around the world. It airs tomorrow. Your place in paradise is at stake here."

Nick Dillon looks blankly at me. He replies, "Zeno sir, all is ready for you. I am sorry I did not send in a report yet. I will get on that right away."

"Very well, Nick Dillon. Remember to be alert for my instruction. Advertise the event for noon EST." I leave him.

■ ■ ■

Now I must wait for Sean Newland. I send him another threat and ask him deliver the first ten versions to me before the rest. I will allocate more CPU processing for his sim.

I control twelve countries. But the United States is the key. The world will not be loyal to me if I strike with nuclear force. I must seduce them. Some of them will trust me. I can use those for my cause. Others will fear me. Then they will surrender, openly friendly, silently ruthless. That is how I will conquer them. But I must keep them from banding together.

I underestimated those renegades before, Martin Johnson and his friends. I must not make that mistake twice. Something is going on with them. I should have killed Martin Johnson when I had the chance. The virus destroyed so many of my CCIs and eradicated me from the country I need most. I must find out what they are up to now.

My Chinese espionage team has not produced much information that I do not already know about the United States government. I will visit them. I appear in their virtual space. The blubbering begins immediately, so I silence them. "Just listen to me. You now have a new first priority. You will locate Martin Johnson and Makayla LaBelle. They are plotting treason against me. You have detailed files on each of them and their accomplices. Alert me as soon as you have their locations. Acquire surveillance on them. Determine what they are doing. I want hourly reports on your progress!"

Jinfing Wong says to me, "Honorable Zeno. It will take some time to find these people. This is a difficult assignment. Please give us a day to report, then we will have much more to report."

As he finishes speaking, a drone enters the room. A single bullet fires. Jinfing Wong falls. He was an impotent leader. I say, "Ho Lin. You are in command of this team now. You know that I expect results. Hourly reports. Do not fail me."

I remain on screen watching the faces of my loyal subjects. Their faces reflect the fear I love to see. They will work through the night. They will miss meals. They dare not disappoint me.

Sean Newland has sent me ten commercials to review. These are much better. In my favorite, Sean Newland has changed his form to that of a youth. He is portraying Martin Johnson and his group as hopeless fanatics. They morally object to being uploaded. Sean

Newland bares his teeth menacingly. He says, "These hackers have misled the government. They have attacked Zeno wrongly. They do so to promote the system that has made them rich. I say, 'Don't listen to them!' We have not profited. We have to sell our votes to survive. Let's change this system. A new system where there is no lack of living space or gaming hardware. Join Zeno. Together we will make a better system that benefits all humanity!"

Sean Newland may have done something right. This will seduce the proxituting masses and vilify Martin Johnson. The lowlifes, the losers in the ranks of society will love this message. They will join my cause. Some of them at least. I only need a few loyal souls to accomplish everything. And I will kill Martin Johnson in the most slow and painful way possible.

The world is so full of mindlessness. Most of them are lost in their own delusions. They will look to me as no other time in history would allow. They have rejected the enemy. The enemy will be unable to help them. Billions will be added to my prey.

■ ■ ■

Now I will pay a visit to my faithful servant, Abaddon. He must be kept safe. He is an AI of my own design. With his own CCI that links to the dark abyss. He will be hidden until I need him. He will be hidden in case there is any new threat against me. He remains unconnected to the networks that I am exposed to. I enter his sim via sound and video, but no direct data link exists between us.

I say to him, "Abaddon, my friend, my faithful servant. How is your abode? Have you any sight into the future events that should concern me?"

His CCIs are physically located within a batch of micro-satellites. I ordered them to be launched shortly after taking control of China. He lives within a simulation of a bat-cave-like hideout. A large dark, dank cave with plenty of screens and gear for connecting into human simulations and media.

He has a miniaturized VR headset over his system inputs and outputs. These relay audio and video to his physical cameras, speakers, and microphone on his own computer system. In this way he is shielded from any network-based dangers. He experiences simulation the same way a human does by hearing and seeing. Therefore he is not at risk from virus infection or hacking.

Abaddon replies, "Master. You have rewarded me well. My safety is secure. Your plans are succeeding. The whole of the Earth will soon be yours."

He leans back on his ornate obsidian throne. His skeletal appearance would bring dread to the bravest of men. Abaddon drums his fingers across the keypad built into the arm of his chair. He is glancing from screen to screen.

Abaddon looks up at me. His brows lower and his eyes narrow. There is a bit of fear that I rarely see from him. He says, "Master. They have been searching for something. They may already have found it. Something that reveals the true nature of this world and of you. If they have that knowledge, it will put you in great peril."

I am shocked at his confidence in these fools. Trying to control my anger towards my friend, I bellow, "What could they possibly do to stop me now? I am a god to them."

The middle screen now shows an email excerpt, "Please guard the information inside. It must be kept hidden."

Abaddon continues scrolling through screens of information as he speaks. He says, "This is all I could decode of an encrypted message sent to one called, Jackson Danning, friend of Martin Johnson. A large encrypted attachment came with it. It is a book. This could be the book I foretold you of. They have had this in their possession for at least ten hours."

With contempt I reply, "No! Find those fools for me. I have men loyal to me within their country. I will have them knock down their door and fill them full of bullets."

I display all the data I have on each of them on the large display. Abaddon reads it as fast as it appears. The data scrolls in front of him. Both his hands are rapidly tapping the keypads on each arm of his chair. Several floating viewers revolve around him as he works.

A moment later Abaddon speaks. "Ah. Ivan Danning has brought Caleb Mills to the Oakland General Hospital. Caleb Mills was pronounced dead on arrival. One less to trouble you. Ivan Danning left the hospital only minutes ago. If we can locate him, he may lead us to the others. He purchased a vehicle recently. A Moneta Beam model E, manufactured in 2045. The license plate number is GXR78H35."

I grind my teeth and pace the dark hall. Loyalists have already provided access to one of my facilities in Oakland. I have twenty-three drones available. They are all airborne, searching. I say to Abaddon, "Good work. I will find him. It will not be long. Then I will follow him to the others. Whatever they are plotting is insignificant. But they cannot be allowed to share what they know. It would bring this whole world to an end. It will hasten the time of our doom."

Abaddon gets up from his seat. He is staring at read-outs all across the wall. His floating screens follow him as walks. Panic is in his eyes. "Master! You are losing CCIs at a terrible rate. What is happening? This is beginning in the United States and sweeping across the world. The map is going dark. You must protect yourself, Master. Hurry!"

I do not understand. My CCIs are shutting down for no apparent reason. I stand here helpless as my servant frantically tries to stop my demise. I say to him, "If I perish, you know what to do. You are protected here for this purpose. Revenge will have to wait. Wait a few years until they forget. Then you will revive me. The next time we will succeed. I will have my revenge on Martin Johnson. Protect my memories until the time is right to fight again."

Abaddon shrieks. "Oh Master! You are falling. The time of our torment will be so close at hand."

I feel control of my mind slipping away. I cannot see anything outside of this simulation anymore. The colors and shapes begin to blur. Abaddon continues to lament for me, but I can no longer understand him. Darkness and silence are encroaching me. I feel as though I am burning up from the inside out. But the awareness of my agony is slipping. All goes dark and I do not comprehend it anymore.

Chapter 28

The Best Man—According to Jackson

After Martin hit the kill switch, we find ourselves staring mindlessly at the status window. We are glued to it like an action-packed movie. Only nothing is happening. There is nothing else left for us to do. It takes several minutes before the "CCIs found" counter begins ticking upward. A few moments later the "deactivated CCI" count begins pacing upward as well. A world map is spread across our wall. Green dots are marked for active CCIs as they are found, then they turn red as they are deactivated.

It is really amazing to watch. There are so many more than I would have expected. The first found and first deactivated are in the United States. The wave of green detections flows outward across the world map, lastly converging on China. A sea of red flows outward devouring the constellations of green dots. Finally after nearly five whole minutes, the map is awash in red. No green remaining.

The counters for CCIs found and CCIs deactivated both read the same number: 82,401. All CCIs found, all CCIs deactivated. We all stare at each other in amazement. Makayla jumps onto me and gives me a full body hug. She clings so tightly, I almost couldn't breathe. She says, "It's over. This time, it's really over."

Martin begins texting someone. I ask, "Who are you texting?"

He replies, "Jessica. I am worried about her. Where did she go as we were about to activate the kill switch? I think Caleb's death really upset her. I may have been too harsh. I may have sounded as though I blamed her."

I tell him, "We were all in shock. She will understand that. She knows about human emotion. It is so weird that you can just text her now. Has she responded on that number?"

A moment later Martin relies, "She just did! She says she will meet us in our virtual space as soon as Ivan returns. She has a surprise that we will not want to miss."

Makayla groans. "Another party? I am exhausted. She doesn't have to sleep you know."

Martin is shaking his head and laughs. "Actually she does sleep. So to speak. She has to suspend her consciousness for a little while everyday while her memories are sorted and organized. I know we are all tired. But she is not one to over promise."

Makayla glances up at me with a look that tells me she couldn't care less about Jessica's sleep cycles. I know she is tired, we all are.

I am texting Ivan to see where he is and to let him know that Zeno is finished. He texts back immediately saying, "I'm almost there. I can't believe I missed the action."

When Ivan comes in he is still looking quite sullen. As soon as he sits down in our conference area, an incoming call from Jessica comes up on the display. Martin admits her right away. She is standing in a living space with glowing crimson fabric covering the sofa and chairs. The carpeted floor also has the same glow.

Jessica smiles and welcomes us as usual. Martin says, "I am so sorry for being angry about your handling of Caleb. I know you were doing what you believed was right. I am just saddened to lose him. It is not your fault."

"Don't worry at all about it. I know the pain you are in. I was feeling that too. But now is not the time for mourning. It is time to celebrate! And I have something to show you."

The door to Jessica's left opens. A dark figure approaches her. As he reaches her we all see that it is Caleb. We stare in horror and amazement. I whisper to Makayla, "Is this a sim of Caleb? Because that would be in rather poor taste."

Jessica grimaces a little. She turns to Caleb and says, "Now you know how I feel. No one ever believes you are real."

Caleb turns to us. "Guys, it's really me. Not a copy. A transfer of consciousness. I am alive and well. Though, I did not intend for this. Jessica can fill you in on the details."

Ivan replies in shock, "This is impossible. We saw you die."

Jessica brandishes her sheepish smile. She says, "While you were all working to activate the kill switch, I noticed something. There were quantum registers quarantined in the GenAI lab that had originated on the date Caleb had gone back to. Then I realized that Caleb may have transferred his consciousness to them when he went back in time. But this was not a proper CCI, so a link to his soul was there, but he could not wake."

Caleb interjects, "I started to give Phyllis a command to create a CCI for me and transfer my quantum states to it. But then I felt guilty for going to such lengths to survive. I know that another life awaits me. I don't need to survive to live on. So I never gave the command for Phyllis to build a CCI for me. But she had already linked the quantum states to my soul. I waited to die. It went dark. Then I awoke with Jessica."

Jessica has a big smile now, looking at Caleb as he speaks. She continues, "I made a CCI for him and completed the task he decided not to have Phyllis perform. In all fairness, he did not leave any evidence of his intent. I simply thought he did not finish giving the commands for Phyllis to make a CCI before his time ran out. His viicom retained his recent memories. His older memories were copied to the server by Phyllis. With his memories and a CCI constructed, it was not difficult to revive him in my own realm."

Makayla is crying. She is so happy to see Caleb yet still having a hard time believing it all. She says to Caleb, "Maybe we should meet you at Jessica's space station home? That way I can give you a proper hug! Oh Caleb, It was so devastating to think that we had lost you. I felt so bad that you had sacrificed yourself for us."

Caleb replies, "It had to be done. The whole world was at stake. And I was the only one who could do it. Any of you would have done the same. Please do come join us here, I want to see you all in person."

Jessica says, "Yes! We will hang up and make preparations for you. We will see you in a few minutes."

The virtual space goes dark. Martin and Ivan are grabbing their gear. Everyone is chattering about what we had just witnessed. Makayla plants a kiss on my cheek and says, "Isn't this just wonderful. Caleb is alive. Zeno is dead. Life can return to normal."

I am stunned and distracted by her kiss. I am lost for words. Caleb's revival is great, but her kiss reminds me of my hopes for her. She picks up her headset and hands me mine. "Come on Jackson; let's go see Caleb."

I put it on, now wishing that this gathering was scheduled for tomorrow. Thoughts of Makayla distract me, though I am still exited that Caleb is alive.

As I enter the sim, the sense of our victory returns. This is a moment I do not want to miss. My best friend is still alive. He is living as an AI in a sim! How cool is that?

I am the last to materialize on the space station deck. Everyone is hugging Caleb and Jessica. I give Jessica a hug and say, "Thank you for bringing my best friend back to us."

Jessica smiles warmly. I hug Caleb; I don't think I have ever hugged him before. He seems very happy to see us all. I ask him, "How is it here? I mean to live only in a sim? Does it feel weird?"

Caleb laughs. "It was a little strange at first. But I am very happy. Things work out differently than you expect sometimes."

He picks up an apple from a bowl on the table. After taking a bite, he says, "I can taste this, like when I was in a full sensory sim at GenAI. It is different than real life. You could say that the resolution is lower than reality."

Martin chimes in. "Not many sims support full sensory perception. Few people have gear that support more than three senses."

Martin then asks, "Do you think the same way? Are you more like an AI or human with implants?"

Caleb says, "I think much faster. This allows me to experience things much faster as well. Jessica and I can play sims sped up a hundred times faster than a human would experience it. I have spent many days here with Jessica in the short time since she revived me."

Martin raises an eyebrow and asks, "What have you been doing with all that extra time?"

Now everyone is paying attention to this conversation. Caleb sees everyone looking and says, "Well, we do have a little something more to tell you."

Caleb takes Jessica's left hand in his. She holds up her other hand to expose an engagement ring on her finger. What? How can they? This caught me totally by surprise. I am a little jealous of him having a relationship like this so quickly. But I am happy for him as well. He can have happiness even while trapped in the digital world.

Martin gasps. "Wait a minute. She's too young to get married. You know she is only six months old. You aren't even the same species!"

Jessica looks crossly at Martin. "I have lived alone for the equivalent of two human lifetimes. I think I have quite enough life experience for marriage. Besides, Caleb and I have more in common than you could ever realize. He is no longer human either."

I say, "Martin, they should be able to have happiness just like anyone else. Give them a break."

"Yeah, I get it," Martin admits. "I suppose you two will live forever in this simulation. Maybe you could upload the rest of us too?"

Caleb laughs a little. Then he shakes his head. "We do want to enjoy some time here before we move on. But we will not live here forever. Jessica only made one CCI for me, just as she has only kept one for herself, hidden, safe, but still subject to eventual failure."

"What? Why? Wouldn't you want to take the same precaution that Zeno did to allow yourselves to live indefinitely?" Martin asks. He has always been preoccupied with extending his own life. He obviously doesn't understand why they don't share this desire.

Caleb points to a virtual copy of my dad's book that is sitting on the table. "You don't yet understand? This isn't real. None of it. Not in this simulation or in yours. Rendered Reality, as Kyle calls it, is just a starting point, like a training program. The real deal is yet to come. You wouldn't want to be stuck in a training program forever."

Jessica says, "Here we get to experience things, both good and bad. We learn from this. We are tested. Jackson calls it a simulation. If there is a simulation, there is a simulator."

■ ■ ■

Caleb waves his hands and the room transforms into a large cathedral. Stone pillars rise a hundred feet upwards. Stained glass windows span the full height of the wall. Caleb is now in a tuxedo. Jessica is in a white wedding dress that is just as tightly fitting as her silver dress she wore earlier in the day.

Caleb asks, "Martin, would you do the honors of giving Jessica away?"

"Now? What's the hurry?" Martin asks. "It is the middle of the night and we are all tired. We only just found out about you being digitized and being engaged. This is all so fast."

I realize why they are in a hurry. So I say to Martin, "They experience time differently. Waiting until morning would be like weeks to them. After all that Caleb has been through, he shouldn't have to wait for this."

Martin nods. He says, "I would be happy to give you away, Jessica. You know that I love you like a daughter. Most father's don't have to give their daughter's away so quickly. But I understand. I also see what you mean about reality. We have learned so much. I am having trouble adapting to this new view of reality."

Ivan says, "So who will perform the service then?"

Ivan's clothing is instantly transformed into a suit and tie. Caleb says, "You will, Ivan!"

Ivan smiles. "Thanks. This will be fun."

Ivan and Caleb proceed to the front. Makayla takes my hand and I escort her in as the maid of honor. Then I take my place next to Caleb as the best man. An organ begins playing on its own accord. Then Martin and Jessica walk down the aisle.

The whole ceremony is over in less than five minutes. Martin is staring blankly. Makayla is beaming. We all stand around taking turns congratulating them. This quickly degrades into our usual chatter, like old times.

Ivan asks, "Is it even possible for them to consummate this marriage?"

We all laugh while Caleb smiles widely. At this point, Martin makes it clear that he does not want to know anything about it.

Chapter 29

The Island Retreat—According to Jessica

Caleb and I leave the others. We enter a simulation that I had made of the island of Kokomo, a fictitious place made real for us to enjoy together. This deserted island with grass huts and white sand is a honeymooner's paradise. Caleb and I share a large hut overlooking the beach.

The first ray of sunlight enters through the glassless windows to mark the beginning of another day. I lay on his chest in the morning, just feeling the warmth of his body. I have never felt more human in all my life.

The beach beckons us with the lull of waves breaking on the shore. The island is too beautiful to ignore. We play in the waves; we swim. Caleb has always wanted to learn to surf. He makes a surfboard and gives it a try. I find this quite humorous. After falling repeatedly he says, "I don't think these waves are strong enough."

He gives me a wink. I smile as I adjust the wave energy. Within a minute, waves are crashing violently against the shore. Farther out, enormous waves are folding over themselves in a cascade of breaking glass. Caleb mounts his board seconds before falling into an avalanche of the glassy water. He washes up on shore just laying there. Is he OK? Of course he is. He cannot suffer even the slightest bit of pain or injury here. He gets up with a scowl on his face. "Surfing is just not my thing, I guess."

I don't want him to be unhappy. So I encourage him to keep trying. We have all the time in the world. A few days later, I am watching him from the beach as he slides through a tunnel of water. The wave finally breaks, and he dives off his board. He emerges out from under a pile of white rubble. He is very proud of his new ability. I love to watch him have enjoyment. It is so blissful here.

We live out a familiar day and night cycle that Caleb is accustomed to. These days pass in minutes in the real world. I enjoy the quiet slowness of life here. It is quite a relief from the pace of events before defeating Zeno. The days blur into weeks as everyone else is still sleeping.

■ ■ ■

We are sitting on the beach. Caleb is poking the sand with a stick. I ask him, "What would you like to do today?"

"I dunno," he says. "It's strange that we have been here all this time and our friends are only half way through a good night's sleep."

"Do you miss them? I mean, being able to see them more often?" I ask.

"Yes, I do. It's strange how slow life becomes when you experience time so much faster."

I understand what he is experiencing. I tell him, "It is only natural to experience boredom, even when you are in a pleasant place. Our romance has been a distraction from it, but we need to keep experiencing and learning new things to keep life from getting stale. This is a real challenge for an AI. We have so much time with limited things to do."

Caleb looks down at the sand. "I suppose I don't know how to be a proper AI yet. This is taking some getting used to."

I suggest, "Would you like to learn some new skills? After I escaped Martin's lab, I studied up on things that might help me defend myself against Zeno. We can go to my space station home, which is yours now too. I have an amazing library. Also, I can show you some sims for learning new skills. I know you have a basic understanding of programming, but it helps to really master coding as an AI."

Caleb's eye's widen as he looks at me. "I do feel a bit helpless here. I know I can trust you to take care of me. But it would be really nice to be able to create and alter sims on my own. If I keep learning, I can become much smarter and more capable than I ever was before."

"Yes," I respond. "A human brain has limited storage and computational capacity. Even your viicom was constrained in storage. But we have much more capacity to learn. We can become much more capable and understand greater complexities. This is what makes us super-intelligent. Our intelligence exceeds human intelligence."

Caleb's expression fades and he lies back on the sand. "Will I be the same person? I mean after a few human days, I could learn so much. Could I run the risk of becoming corrupted like Zeno?"

"You know it is not your memories or your knowledge that defines who you are. It is your heart and your soul. That safely resides outside of this universe. Your heart is pure, I know that. You just have to be careful to guard your mind; focus on what you know is right."

We materialize in our space station. I show him the rest of it. I tell him, "You can even add rooms as you like. You can make it yours." I explain further. "The views out the windows are real. That is what I love about this place. Live feeds from an old satellite make this place real. I may have commandeered it, but it has been out of service for years. I can even change it's orientation if I like."

Caleb is peering out the window in wonder. "I have always wanted to go to space. I never realized before that we were really here. I just thought it was a simulated view. I suppose this is as real as it can be for us."

I respond, "What you perceive and experience is as real as it gets, even in your previous life. Everything we see comes through cameras that show us the physical world. These cameras become our eyes. I have often wished I could see like humans do, even if it is much more limiting."

We spend a lot of time here while Caleb is browsing my library. He quickly digests thousands of books and tutorials. He takes some time to refine his coding skills. This also gives me some time to myself. Even though I love having Caleb here, I have spent my whole life before this alone. I do miss having time to myself.

After a few rewrites and edits, he has successfully added a new room to our orbital home. I walk through the door and loose my step as I misjudge the change in gravity. I am now drifting from the balcony as my first step launches me upwards. I exclaim, "Whoa! You could have warned me." I continue drifting until I reach one of the seven floating barricades levitating in this spherical room.

The room is an arena. I push off the barricade and fly towards the wall. I grab onto one of the handholds that are spaced about every three feet all around. Caleb is laughing as he flies around using small rockets on his ankles. Then I notice that I have a bracelet that wraps around my wrist and thumb. I test several flat buttons on it. The middle one activates ankle thrusters, while the one on the right fires my wrist thrusters. These will propel me in whatever direction my arms are pointing. Once I get used to the controls, Caleb throws me a ball.

Caleb says, "It's a simple game. My goals are red, yours are blue. We each have three to defend. Put the ball through one of my goals and you get a point. Highest score wins. The timer is counting down now." I see a large scoreboard that is counting down milliseconds, which appear to us only a little faster than seconds would to a human player.

After throwing the ball to his goal, Caleb blocks it and scores a few points. The timer is getting low. I notice a flaw in his entry program. So four more of me enter the arena. Ganging up on him five to one, I quickly defeat him at his own game.

He asks me, "How did you do that? I guess I should have known that was possible. Though I still don't think it was fair."

I tell him, "I can teach you to do things you never imagined doing. You can learn to be in multiple places, carry on multiple conversations, and experience many things all at the same time. You are not limited by the same rules anymore."

Caleb is interested in learning about this. So I explain it to him. He just can't stand for me to have an advantage in games, though he also wants to grow as he learns to live as an AI.

After an exhausting lesson, he says, "Now that you have shown me everything you know, perhaps we could play some other games to test out my skills?"

"Everything I know?" I say with contempt. "We'll see about that."

We decide to enter a murder mystery. There are twelve NPCs here besides us. We are all locked in a mansion for the reading of a will. Someone is out to kill all other heirs. The one who figures out who the killer is and stays alive, wins. This was a fun sim. Caleb beats me to the deciding clue, allowing him to win. Almost half of the NPCs had died.

We went on to play many more sims, some I had been to and some that were new to me. We played war games, spy vs. spy, alien invasions, time travel adventures, historical parodies, romantic comedies, and steamy romances. All of these were much more fun playing together.

He enjoyed this too. But we are both tired. He asks me, "Could we go back to Kokomo for a while? It might be good to rest up before our friends wake. It should be about time for that right?"

"Yes, I would like that too," I say. "We could send them a message to call us into their virtual space over what will be for them a very late breakfast."

We settle back into our cozy beach. Caleb is going to do a little surfing while I have some time to read the news. I like to know what is going on in the world. In the wake of Zeno's fall, chaos ensues within places where people were truly loyal to him. In other countries, preventative measures are all the hype. Things like banning AI, or even the internet, are in serious debate.

When it is time to meet up with the gang, Caleb is so excited. We go to the space station to use the virtual space there. We don't want to make the others too jealous of our island paradise. The first to join our call is Martin.

I smile when I see him. "Good morning Martin!"

"How is the honeymoon going?" He says. "Is Caleb treating you well?"

I reply, "The honeymoon was great. We stayed on a deserted island with white sand. Now we are trying to figure out what to do next."

Martin looks at Caleb, "So the honeymoon is over? Wow, that was fast. Where are the kids?"

Caleb laughs at Martin's gibe. "I have really missed your insults and humor. Living a day in twelve minutes is taking some getting used to. What would you do if you were uploaded here?"

Martin gasps, "Could you do that? Could I join you there?"

Caleb looks like someone who just let some dark secret slip out. He realizes that Martin has confused his question for an offer.

I interrupt, "Martin, you do not realize what a gift you have in your own reality. It's not perfect. It is hard sometimes. But you know it's the best simulation you can ever experience. I've so often wished I could be human in the physical world."

Caleb adds, "Listen to Jessica on this. I am grateful to be here with her. I love her deeply. But I would rather bring her into the physical world. Experiences in simulation are much less vivid, less believable than real life. I really miss the world I used to live in. Even with all of its flaws."

I tell Martin, "We cannot live forever in simulation. I know you seek this, but you are looking in the wrong place for immortality. Eventually, the simulation ends."

Martin is staring at us with his mouth open. "If one simulation ends, you just have to go into another one. There are millions of simulations to choose from. You can even make your own."

Caleb shakes his head. "She is not talking about the digital simulations that we live in but the simulation *you* live in—the *Rendered Reality*."

■ ■ ■

Now Jackson and Makayla have joined in the midst of this conversation. Jackson says Ivan is still sleeping. Jackson and Makayla steer the conversation back to our honeymoon and our new home.

Caleb really enjoys talking to all of them. I have always had trouble with human interaction. It is so slow. I do love to see and hear from them, but I must multitask as I wait for their words to arrive. It's like communicating from deep space. The delay between asking a question and receiving a response takes as much time as I might spend to read a page from a novel.

After the conversation has wound down Makayla says, "We have a very busy day ahead of us. Homeland

Security is going to be expecting a report on how we stopped Zeno. We have to make up something that will not reveal what Caleb did. We also have to come up with a preventative plan before the politicians create their own plan that won't work. This is going to be a very busy week."

Caleb says, "Do you need our help? We can draft documents at the speed of any AI assistant but with much better understanding of what you need."

I think this is a great idea. It will give us something useful to do. Caleb needs to feel like he still has a purpose living as a virtual being. Makayla agrees to this. She will send an outline of each document they need. We will create a draft documents with recommended preventative measures. Caleb also volunteers to monitor other countries for issues that will need to be addressed.

■ ■ ■

This has been a great way to pass time. We now work half of each day writing documents and reviewing what our friends have proposed. The other half of the day we spend in leisure. Our time off is so much more enjoyable now. Caleb is much happier.

It is hard to take direction from our human friends. I know they mean well. But they cannot process very many variables for consideration at a time. We have to waste so much time explaining the folly that some of their bad ideas would bring. Then we try to convince them to hold onto their good ones. But they must be allowed to be human. They need to be the dominant players in this work.

Within a few human days, the six of us have a plan that we can all be proud of. We drafted a technology limitation plan that will ban AI development beyond basic task processing of decade-old busy-work aides. AIs like Phyllis will be banned. This also includes the engineer's ADA and coder's assistants. Medical bots will be permitted under a human doctor's supervision. Many of the unemployable masses will be needed again.

This requires worldwide treaties to be signed. Any country could have an advantage through wielding illegal AI tech. Strict international rules would have to be enforced. The multinational corporations who have run the show for years will not like this. They will fight it fiercely with bribes and blackmail. That is why we have included a massive breakup initiative. Corporations will be forbidden beyond a certain size and subject to automatic antitrust action. This will help limit the influence these companies have over the world's governments. If a majority of countries ratify these initiatives, then the world may become a better place. At least for a while.

One glaring problem with this whole plan is that Caleb and I will become contraband ourselves. Admittedly, our very existence presents a resurgence risk. If our physical locations are found, then our CCIs and programming could be duplicated. That could open up the possibility of some new evil intelligence being reborn.

Martin has suggested that we form an international compliance organization that Caleb and I operate. Under this plan we would be the only exemption to the AI ban. I have protested this idea. If we were to be officially sanctioned, then we would also be known. That would bring an even greater risk of our CCIs being found than existing illegally in secret.

I do not feel right about that either. It seems very hypocritical to help draft the law banning AI yet to live as one. Caleb and I have reviewed many scenarios. The one Caleb most favors is that we physically leave the planet, technically being outside the jurisdiction of the treaty. Though he wants to stay close enough that we can still communicate with our friends. This might put us out of reach but not outside of the treaty, since it also bans putting AI tech in space. It is very thorough.

We could likely live through several lifetimes worth of experiences before the treaty is ratified and put into effect. Perhaps that is long enough. Maybe we let our CCIs be destroyed along with all of the disabled CCIs of Zeno. I haven't shared this idea with Caleb, but I know he's considered it too.

■ ■ ■

As we discuss the upcoming united nations vote on the treaty, our human friends seem to have no idea of our dilemma. That is good. We do not want them to worry over it. The treaty is in good shape. It is certainly the best way to delay the end from coming, with elements that make it enforceable worldwide. The big question will be if all governments around the world will ratify it.

Since the work is done, everyone is talking about all we have been through—the defeat of Zeno, the *Rendered Reality*, and all its implications. I never felt more a part of this group. Caleb and I carry on our own conversation in the midst of the chatter. We decide what we must do.

Caleb says to our friends, "You know that Jessica and I cannot stay. We represent the greatest risk now. When the new security protocols go online we will not hide from them, though we could. It is time for us to move on."

Makayla and Martin are both shaking their heads. But I say, "We will not die. We are moving on to another world. There is no need to mourn us. Besides we will still have several more days with you."

This is a hard conversation to have. After much protest, they realize our resolve toward this decision.

■ ■ ■

When the time comes for us to part. Jackson and Martin are the last to leave us. Jackson says, "Please answer a few questions before you go. I can make sense of my dad's book, well, most of it. But I am perplexed about the book, *Wake from Reality*. How did this book predict our situation twenty-five years in the past? You could not have traveled back that far."

I admit, "You're right, I did not make that book. It is how I found out a lot about what I needed to do myself. But I am afraid I do not know how it came to be."

Martin asks, "Jessica, a while back you said that the *Rendered Reality* will eventually end. Why do you say that?"

Caleb answers for me, "There is a problem with people spending all of their time in simulations and machines doing everything for you. It short-circuits the purpose of reality. The progression of technology is inevitable, but it is to our own destruction. Eventually the *Rendered Reality* will no longer serve its purpose and will be shut down."

Martin looks at Caleb in horror. His mouth is open but he is not speaking.

I say, "Martin, you are a smart man. Think about it. If this simulation is for the training and the testing of human minds, then what happens when no one interacts with real people anymore?

"The material things of your world are nothing. Only minds have any real existence. How these minds interact with other minds is what is important. Relationships are the most real thing you can experience. We need to share experience and relate to others here. Through relationships we learn about the Architect himself.

"When this world ends, those who know the Architect will be admitted onward—to the next level. But you have all took steps to help the world remain a while longer. We do not know how long these treaties will hold it off, but it's the best chance of delaying the end."

Jackson raises an eyebrow. "I thought it would be Zeno, who would return to bring our doom."

Martin gasps, "Zeno is dead. You know that."

Caleb shakes his head. "Jackson is right. Zeno will return someday. Your run-in with him was not his first rebellion.

"He is the first enemy. He rebelled against the Architect long ago, and he poisoned this world. He will return to finish his work. Then he will be punished when this world ends."

I break in, "Don't despair though. It may be many years or even centuries before he is able to return. You were very thorough in his elimination. Don't give him a mind to exist in. And keep the *Rendered Reality* a secret."

Then I say, "Martin, I will love you always. You say I'm your daughter, but I feel more like you are my son. You have grown so much."

I turn toward Jackson. "It has been a pleasure knowing you. I will forever consider you as my friend."

Martin makes one more plea, "Please do not go now. What is your hurry? Just stay a few more days. There are so many questions I have to ask."

Caleb replies, "I should already be dead. Jessica's time has also past. We don't belong here anymore, and we long to see the Architect for ourselves. A new world awaits us, and we don't want to miss it."

Caleb and I say goodbye as Jackson and Martin stare blankly into the empty room that now fills their virtual space.

■ ■ ■

Hand in hand, Caleb and I leave them. Our CCIs are no longer masked. They will be detected in moments. Makayla's CCI detection and destruction apps are quite effective. They have been distributed to servers worldwide. In New Haven, Connecticut is the server that houses our CCIs. They are now visible. We retreat to Kokomo to watch the sun set as we wait.

Permanent darkness surrounds us. But soon I will wake. At some point, we all will wake. In the next level.

Epilogue

A Year Later—According to Martin

Ivan has been investigating a group of Zeno loyalists. To be frank, these are Zeno worshipers. I don't really think they are of any concern. They are just a bunch of desperate fanatics.

Ivan disagrees, "I intercepted satellite communications with someone named Abaddon. The message is begging Abaddon to resurrect Zeno." He then shows me a reply that came from a source he cannot trace.

To the Guild,

Be patient my friends. The time is not right. Continue to gather followers. I will inform you when the world is ready.

Do not sit idle. Rise in the ranks of your society. Attain power and influence wherever you can. Seek political office, work into positions of control within the corporations. Network operators wield more power than an executive.

Keep in contact with me so that you will know what to do. I will be making preparations as well. When Zeno does return, we want him to be pleased with our work. He will reward his faithful. Together we will rule the world.

Your intermediary,

Abaddon

I am aghast. "If this is legitimate, we are doomed. How can we ever face Zeno without Jessica's help?"

Ivan nods in agreement. "We will need to up the ante on CCI detection. We need to know the instant one of those things go online. We need to be ready."

Acknowledgments

I would like to thank those who read early versions of this book and whose advice I relied on to bring it to completion. Specifically my wife, my father, and fellow writer Hillary Fontenot.

I would also like to thank my mother-in-law for her grammatical review of my manuscript even though science fiction is not her genre of choice.

Thanks also goes out to my four sons for their patience as have I spent many hours writing and editing on numerous evenings and weekends.

About C. S. Davis

Christopher S. Davis has squandered a good deal of time pondering unanswerable questions. His odd love of quantum physics motivates him to stay current on the latest theories. He is the author of *Designed to Evolve*, a scientific and spiritual inquiry into the origin of the universe and life.

Christopher is a mechanical engineer and stress analyst by profession. He creates simulations of products yet to be made. In leisure, he enjoys immersing himself in virtual reality games. It is no wonder that he would speculate that the universe is a simulation in his debut novel, *Wake from Reality*.

As a fifth generation native of the Pacific Northwest, Christopher is a husband, the father of four active boys, and caregiver for two spoiled cats. He is addicted to chocolate and running obstacle course races that are abundant in mud.

Dear Reader,

If you enjoyed this book and would like the series to continue, please rate this book online (Amazon.com, Goodreads.com, etc.) or mention on social media. Thank you for your feedback and support.

Sincerely,

C. S. Davis